Black Ice

by

Stephen Tesher

Dear Steve, Sarah
& Sam,
Enjoy the read & thanks
for being great neighbors.

Steph Tesher

The characters and events in this book are fictitious. Any similarity to real persons, living or dead, is coincidental and not intended by the author.

Part One

PROLOGUE

His hands throttled her throat. He squeezed tighter. Her breath came in coughs when it could come at all.

"Stop! You're choking her!"

"So what?" he shot back.

"You're gonna kill her!"

"So what?"

"Why… why are you doing this?"

His eyes went very cold. Inhumanly hollow. "Somebody needs to be the bad guy," he said.

At that moment I realized he would kill me next. If he could kill her, he could kill me without blinking. I needed to stop him! A tsunami of regret for everything wrong that I ever did to anyone and everyone in my life rose up along the turbulent shores of my conscience; it threatened to wipe it out. The kind of devastation that doesn't even allow for the thought of rebuilding. If this was it I needed to make it right. At least a shot at the chance of an apology.

Doesn't everyone deserve that?

At least once?

CHAPTER ONE

Three months earlier.

Lewis' Dad's private den was a mahogany warehouse of books. The décor was professorial good old boy. It screamed of success, the kind of money that allowed Lewis to be, well, Lewis. Lewis' party was raging throughout the house but I was eager to get Marcy, my girlfriend, alone. It was time for *the talk*. The restricted study of Lewis' power-lawyer father was perfect.

"Why are you taking me in here?" she asked. We were both pretty wasted.

"Shh," I whispered. I set the lights to dim, subduing the wood-paneling. I closed the door, muffling the laughter from outside. I tugged at Marcy's hand towards a leather sofa, placing my whiskey and ginger ale on an oak coffee table.

"Come on, David," Marcy whined. "Can't this wait?" I sat down on the plush leather. Marcy reluctantly sat down as well, keeping an odd distance. Maybe she sensed where this was going.

"Marcy," I said. Her eyes were a mesmerizing deep blue and always seemed to be smiling. They threw me off momentarily. But then I regained my focus, and my purpose. "I don't know how to say this. I love you." I blurted. Marcy sighed, irritated. "I really do. But, I mean, we've been going out for almost a year. And I just feel, like, we're just not progressing, you know?" I looked up for effect. Marcy looked shocked. Wow. I guess she didn't see this coming. Whiskey and weed danced up a fog in my head, but I tried to hold on. "I mean, it's like we're just holding each other's hand, and not really doing anything about it." She kept staring at me in disbelief. "So, I guess what I'm saying is, I think we should see other people. 'Cause maybe we're just holding each other back."

Marcy looked at me for a long time. Then her eyes began to well up. This was my moment. I put my arm around her, pulled myself a little closer. "Or... we could try... progressing?"

She pulled away. I'd gone too far. "Marcy... I'm sorry...."

Marcy laughed.

Correction. Marcy exploded with laughter. "Stop," she said. "Stop!" Hysterically beside herself.

"Marcy? You okay?"

"Stop. Seriously," she chortled. "You're an idiot."

"Marc – I know it sounds –," she cut me off.

"I broke up with *you*! Last week! At *your house*!" She laughed again. "You're right, David. It's over. Thank god, it's over!"

She rose off the plush leather couch which immediately re-inflated itself where her weight had been, erasing even the slightest impression of her. "David, I'm worried about you," she said. "You're wasted. You're wasted a lot." I couldn't look at her. I was lost, confused, and far too close to sober to deal. "I know what's happened to you hurts, but you're wasting your life. There's more to high school than getting drunk and high. When you figure that out… well, give me a call." I downed the rest of my whiskey, watching the lone ice cube slowly melt into the empty glass. Marcy let herself out. The den door clicked closed.

I was alone.

Below the television set was a liquor cabinet – one I was well-acquainted with. I set myself up with a refill and tried to remember when Marcy broke up with me. It took me two refills.

I finally stumbled out of the den and into my gracious host. Lewis' parents were away and he had the run of their huge house. People poured in. Booze flowed, drugs were everywhere. There was an available girl around every corner. Being formerly attached to Marcy, I never tried to hook up with any of the other girls. Now I felt like I had wasted my time.

"How'd it go with Marcy?" Lewis asked. "You finally lose that cherry? Won't be going into college a virgin!"

"Not so good," I said.

"C'mon…. What'd she say?" Lewis was so eager for me to lose my virginity it almost made it more painful.

"Did you know she broke up with me a week ago?" Lewis looked as perplexed as I was.

"Yeah. Didn't you?"

My silence gave me away.

"Wow, Dave! Ballsy move. But post break up sex usually works. Don't give up," he said, patting me on the back and moving on. "A guy with your looks and build should be able to get anyone."

Yeah, but what about my loser status and downer personality, I thought.

I retreated back to the den where I drank myself into a warm comfortable black out.

Mental cobwebs ripped from their moorings and jerked me out of a passed-out sleep. A thin rope of drool ran from my bottom lips to the pillow. I'd somehow found my way onto a bed in Lewis' house. A Japanese character print about the size of a prison window hung on an otherwise bare wall. I was still dressed, still alone. Birds chirped outside.

Lewis burst in with a glass of fresh squeezed orange juice. His blond hair was slicked back from fresh shampoo with a cologne splash that announced his arrival. A cigarette dangled from his lips. Lewis smoked about two packs a day. His whole family smoked so nobody noticed if the house reeked of cigarettes. He handed me one and I lit up.

"You're going out for the fashion show!" he said.

"What's a fashion show?" I asked.

"Marcy was a hiccup. You have to lose that cherry. In order to do that, you need to meet girls and the best place to meet girls is at the fashion show tryouts. Sharla Unger's the

Artistic director."

"Sharla Unger?"

"It's her show. She'll put in who she likes and there are never enough guys."

"She's totally out of my league."

"Fischer, give me a break. You're a half decent looking guy. You work out like crazy. Girls dig you. But *you* take yourself out of the game."

"Sharla's a total brain and a goody-goody and miss popularity..."

"...and stunningly beautiful, and you would totally die a young death if you could be with her."

"She'd never want anything to do with me."

"She's not such a goody-goody," Lewis said, smiling. Lewis would know. "Besides, there are a lot of hot babes at that audition. Pretty much every hot girl in school. And they're all there for the same reason."

"To show off how beautiful they are."

"No, stupid. They are there hoping to be *convinced* they're beautiful. Newsflash – most beautiful girls have incredibly low self esteem." He raised his eyebrow and pointed at me the way he did when he wanted me to get his point. Whether or not he was actually making a point was irrelevant. The finger and the eyebrow were indications that there was a point out there, and that I should be getting it. "Get showered. You can borrow some of my clothes so you don't reek."

"What – today?"

"Today."

Lewis and I drove up to the main entrance of Maple Hill High School where Jewish and Italian and Chinese kids revved their affluent parent's cars as they pulled in and out of the parking lot. Down the hill from the main entrance road was the 'other' entrance, known as 'Stoner's Corner' where kids hung out with loose joints, pills and other paraphernalia. There was always a low-hanging cloud over stoner's corner. We walked in the large double-door main entrance and took a left down the hall to the audition.

The Fashion Show team was using Mrs. Dove's History classroom. The desks were pushed to one side to make room in the middle. The walls were lined with girls. Lewis was right: some of the best looking girls in the school were there, dressed and lined up like it was a roped off night club with scrutinizing bouncers. Lewis and I found seats by the classroom windows, our backs to the streets of Toronto.

"See what I'm talking about?" Lewis said, nodding at the girls. "Each one of these girls is more beautiful than the next. If selected they get officially declared 'Most Beautiful' by the Popularatti."

The Popularatti were the school society of in-people: the rich and pampered. Lewis was one of them, only he didn't act it, so I didn't bug him about it too much.

Lewis was taller-than-average with droopy blue eyes. His blond hair was cut in a style girls called feathered because of the way it layered itself, like a blond duck's feathers, a tuft always hanging over one eye.

Other guys were auditioning, too. Guys who were also interested in hanging around beautiful, insecure girls. I suddenly viewed them as my competition.

Maple Hill High School was mostly rich. Kids who come from parents with money and influence are kids who have access: they get access to political figures; access to entertainers; access to industry; and access to the fringe benefits of all these arenas.

For us, at 17, access meant having the money to purchase a wide assortment of mind-altering substances, top shelf alcohol and the occasional weapon.

Lewis rolled a ten dollar bill into a straw-like funnel and brought it to his nose.

"Toot, toot," he said. "Hair of the dog."

"My dog was Johnny Walker Black," I said.

"Time to step up," he smiled. He unfolded the bill. There was still cocaine residue on the Queens face. He handed it to me and I gave it a taste. My tongue went momentarily numb and the buzz went to my eyes.

"Holy shit," Lewis said. "Pinch me, I'm in love." I followed Lewis's line of sight, not an easy endeavor since Lewis always had that shock of hair hanging over his eyes like a curtain. My efforts were worth it.

She wore white leather pants that looked like they were painted on, with a tight, white mini-t top. If a Barbie Doll could be recreated in human proportions, nature had done it with this girl: Tan skin, long flowing brown hair with blond streaks, and a perfect smile.

"Dude, how could I have never seen this… goddess before?" Lewis asked.

"'Cause you had your face in a pile of coke," I said. Lewis elbowed me in the ribs. It hurt and I flinched. Some of the girls across the room caught it. My embarrassment rose to my cheeks. To cover, I feigned laughter. I doubled myself over and rolled to the floor, fake laughing.

"Don't be an idiot," Lewis said. "Watch and learn."

Lewis pointed at the girl in the white pants. He pointed right at her, like he was picking her out for himself. She took the bait. Lewis' arm extended out with a confidence I could only admire. It was like he knew that he was in control, whether or not he was. He just believed he was and it made others believe it, too. Lewis didn't recognize rejection. One girl said no, he just moved on to another. No hard feelings, no self-doubt. It's the reason he lost his virginity at fourteen. It's the reason he would eventually be worth millions. He crooked his finger and the girl in the white pants crossed the room towards us.

"Is he *hokay?*" she asked Lewis referring to me, still on the floor and enjoying the view. The voice was a lilting honey soprano. The accent tasted of South America.

Lewis went straight for the kill. "I'm Lewis, and you are absolutely stunning."

"I'm Francesca," she sang. Lewis took her hand, and, ever so delicately, brought it to his lips.

"Enchante, Francesca," he said, kissing her fingers just below the knuckles where he once told me it was more sensitive.

"Enchante is French," I said. "She's Spanish."

"I am from Argentina," she said proudly.

"You are the most beautiful girl I have ever met," Lewis continued. "How come I've never seen you before?"

Coming from my mouth the same words would have elicited bored groans; maybe even a slap across the face. Francesca blushed.

He wrote down her phone number and sent her back into the line. He was fearless. He was fearless and I was on the floor.

"Get up," he said. I did.

There was a hush, followed by a buzz of excitement as Sharla Unger strolled into the room. She was cover-girl beautiful, like someone was air-brushing her as she moved through life. She walked with poise as if she knew she would rule the world someday. The room hushed again as Sharla took her rightful place at Mrs. Dove's desk, sitting on top of it and crossing her legs with authority.

Sharla was head Popularatti. She was also one of the brightest and most motivated students in Maple Hill. By grade nine she had already declared herself pre-law. She had already passed a preliminary L-SAT and was prepping her GPA and resume for Harvard Law. Hence Sharla was on every possible committee, edited the school newspaper, was president of the student council, captain of the tennis team, debate team, and was the only student representative to sit on the principal's advisory committee.

Sharla's sidekick, Miriam Levkowitz, plain looking and aware of it, was happy to be allowed the responsibility of pressing the play button on the portable stereo. Top-40 trash music came pouring out with extra bass and a Dolby mini-equalizer. What I would have given to listen to some Zeppelin or Rush – any decent music. But this was Fashion Show music, and if I wanted to be in the stupid fashion show, I'd have to figure out a way to move to it.

"This is a stupid idea," I said.

"David," Lewis began, folding Francesca's number into his pocket, "Look around you. All of these girls are here for one thing: self-confidence. They're vulnerable. And you, my friend, need to take that next step into being a man."

"What about that girl? Francesca – ?"

"You're not ready."

"Why not?"

"Same reason you don't take your first driving lesson in a Lamborghini. Besides, look at all the other girls you've got to choose from."

At three months shy of eighteen, I was still, technically, a virgin. By technically, I mean I had never actually experienced an orgasm in the presence of a sexual partner. Just alone. Lewis had a habit of reminding me of this. I resented it, despite the fact that it was true.

Marcy did give me something no other girl had. She had made me feel whole, at least for a while. When I didn't feel whole, I felt something else, something that was black and empty. The more I tried to ignore it, the bigger that black empty grew. It would get so big it felt like it would swallow me whole. Drinking helped me feel better. Beer worked a little. Hard liquor worked best. I didn't have any of either so I had to suffer it out dry with Lewis while the black empty grew inside me.

"My cousin Alan? He did this show like three years ago when he was a senior? He said the girls just fall over you. The cheerleaders, the brains. The fresh meat and sophomores, they will be eating out of your hand." By 'fresh meat' Lewis meant freshman girls, fourteen years old and curious, dying to make a mark on the social radar of high school. "It's like being a rock star. It is impossible not to score."

"Cool," I said. I tried being a rock star the old fashioned way – by playing in local garage bands. We rehearsed but never got anywhere. Probably because we never performed. We thought we were being mysterious artists. It worked. No one knew about us. So here I was, on my first try-out with the fashion show. From failed Rock Star to aspiring loser.

Sharla called out a name and a blonde girl I'd never seen before stepped up to the line. The music played and she started to move.

"Dude – check her out!" Lewis said, perking up.

She was pure sensuality on perfect legs. Her body moved as if she had choreographed it, every swerve of her hips calculated to arouse any onlooker – man or woman. Her torso pulsed rhythmically, and when she lifted her eyelashes, her ice-blue eyes revealed raw desire; and that desire was focused on one person – *me*.

The girl planted for a turn, looked up again – at *me*; she spun to reveal every curve of her flawless shape, smirking... at me. She ran her tongue across her top lip, spun and returned to her mysterious origins. She looked back once more, a last hair flip, an exclamation point at the end of a killer line, directed at... *moi*. Then, as quickly as she appeared, she vanished into the crowd.

"Dude! That chick totally wants you!" Lewis half screamed, squeezing my arm. Sharla shot us a disapproving look.

"Cut it out!" I said.

"If you don't do her, you're an asshole," he said.

"Thanks for the confidence," I said.

"If you don't do her I will," he said.

"Hey. She was checking me out."

"So, do something about it!"

I looked up for one last chance to match eyes with the mystery girl but she was gone. The excitement I felt from her attention suddenly abated. I was just Lewis's sidekick again.

When it was my turn to walk down the mock runway, I rolled up my short sleeves fifties-style to show off my arms. Then I pranced around like a guy who shows up to a black tie formal dinner in nothing but his underwear and acts like he meant to.

CHAPTER TWO

The Fashion Show roster went up on the bulletin board at the end of the week. Immediately a crowd of girls gathered to see who had made the final cut, and who was deemed unworthy. I stood off to the side with Zion, better known as Zee.

"Think you made it?" he asked. I shrugged like I didn't care. "Yeah. Right," Zee said.

Zion and I met in freshman year, both escapees of parochial Hebrew day schools, or "Jew Jail" as we called it. Somehow we both managed to avoid the Jew Jail high schools and landed in the clique-heavy, drug-laden, socially competitive world that was Maple Hill High School. Zion's parents were conservative, pro-Israeli Jews. They didn't go to synagogue all the time but they went to Israel a lot. They donated money to pro-Israeli causes and showed up at a lot of United Jewish Appeal fundraisers. When it came to their kids, they sent them to Hebrew day schools and Hebrew camps where they got taught tennis, swimming and archery – in Hebrew. They took them all to Israel at least once a year. Zion had his bar Mitzvah at the Wailing Wall in Jerusalem. He could speak Hebrew fluently on command. His parents named him after the holy land – the land of Milk and Honey.

Zion.

"I hate it," he said, when he first told me his name. We were riding our bikes home from school. We lived just three blocks from each other.

Zee steered us down a set of stairs that led to a running path behind the cover of thick brush.

"It's… intimidating," I said.

"Call me Zee," he said. He pulled out a package of rolling papers and a bag of weed. In the moment it takes most kids to dismount a bike, Zee had rolled a joint.

"Cool, Zee."

After that, Zee and I were rarely apart. We played baseball and rode our bikes through traffic, listened to Cheech and Chong records, and got wasted. We regularly met on weekend nights under a bridge, or by subway stations and abandoned construction sites. We would get high, and then walk it off through the city, discovering hidden back alleys, crashing strange people's parties and hanging out watching regular citizens go about their business. Zee had a little business going, selling weed or hash to whoever wanted, as long as they passed inspection. It brought him a little extra cash. Often we were able to get into bars and hang in a corner booth with some beers. We finished the evenings with pizza and soda drinks at our favorite by-the-slice dive.

Over the course of our high school years, Zee's parents went on more and more extended vacations; my parents divorced each other and left a mess where any stability used to be.

Now, in our senior year, the weed and hash had graduated to harder drugs. Coke, pills, and some opiates. For me the sodas had gone from main beverage to a weak mixer and Zee and I were two sides of a smoke-stained coin.

"You're full of shit," he said, smiling.

"What?"

"You want to be on that list so bad you can taste it. I can taste you tasting it."

"That's disgusting."

"Yeah," he said, smacking his lips with a foul-mouthed face. "It is."

Zee despised the social networking of high school. He hated groups or fads or anything that didn't come from original thought. He cut his own hair, a risky business in itself, wearing it like 'A Flock of Seagulls' lead singer, Mike Score, short on the sides, with a duck tail in the back rising high up on top with wings of hair standing like castle buttresses guarding the scalp from invasion. Zee was an aspiring musician with a crooning voice and a passion for the blues.

"Go," he urged, pushing me. I looked back at him, like a child checking for a parent's approval. "Look at all the girls, man. Go!"

One girl prettier than the next clambered over each other to get a look at the judge's final list; shapely bodies pressed against one another with a common hope. I wanted to be that hope. Some girls screamed with excitement while others sulked away, their lips pouting, eyes holding water.

"They need comfort," Zee said, watching a particularly pouty set of lips walk past us, books held tightly to a heaving chest. "Lots of comfort. Oh… possibly hours… days of comfort." He slapped my shoulder. "Man, if you don't do this for yourself, at least do it for me." I laughed. "Seriously, Fisch, think of all the guys who don't have the guts to get up and dance like a moron in stupid clothes you'd never wear. Girls love that shit. They will swarm, man."

"Don't be an asshole!"

He threw his arms around, something he did when he got excited. "Think of what you could do for your fellow man! Making an idiot of yourself so I can get laid! This is your life's calling!"

"I don't even know if I made the…"

"Oh, for god's sake, Fisch!" Zee pushed past me and through the pressing bodies of the girls dividing them like Moses' Red Sea until he could get a good look at the list. He stabbed his finger at a name, turned and threw his arms up in the air. His unique hair cut, huge blue eyes, his long, awkward neck and body, towering above a cluster of girls like they were his groupies.

"We're in!" he shouted.

Lewis got in, too, but he decided to drop out. He told me this while driving his mothers Mercedes aimlessly smoking cigarettes. I kept a beer between my legs and was taking sips.

"I can't afford the time. I mean my grades…" Lewis had an easy, unassuming charm that made him seem safe, even though he was always scheming. But school didn't come easily to him.

"I have to think about getting into college."

"Since when?" College was a problem Lewis's father could solve with one phone call. The thing I liked about Lewis, he didn't apologize for it. He just shrugged it off. "They're getting me a tutor," Lewis said, smiling.

"You dog!" I yelled and punched the ceiling of Mrs. Cohen's fifty thousand dollar car.

Lewis's last tutor was a twenty one year old college exchange student from Paris. She spoke French, Italian, Danish and German. She arrived at his home the first day in a business jacket and skirt and seemed, to his parents – his mother particularly – quite professional. In the privacy of Lewis' study area, the skirt hiked up as she crossed her legs, and the hair came down. She made a point to touch Lewis whenever she wanted to check his understanding. She'd touch his leg, his arm, his neck. And Lewis understood her perfectly. To hear him tell it, he taught the tutor a few things as well.

"The same one?"

"I wish," he said. "You're going to have to take care of those fashion show girls for the both of us."

Between Lewis and Zee I had a committee. It was their consensus that I take the responsibilities of negotiating with the opposite sex like a man. However, while my friends looked upon me with paternal-like faith, I had zero self-confidence. Less than zero – my confidence was into negative integers.

My parents separated my freshman year of high school. By my sophomore year they were divorced. It was quick and – as advertised to their surrounding society of friends and relatives - painless. But damage had been done.

What was once a Hallmark postcard family got shredded. Me and my sister Beth both felt duped. Like we were sold some idyllic vacation property in Florida only to find out it was a landfill, built on a foundation of garbage rotting in the tropical sun.

My sister, Beth, buried herself in eating disorders, my mother buried herself in a new career, my father buried himself in a new wife and I buried myself in mind and mood-altering substances. And, for a while, Marcy.

Now I was alone again and faced the world with anxiety, fear and a fresh sense of distrust.

Working out helped. I exercised a lot. It was a great way to get anger out. Rage fueled hand stand pushups, squats, bench presses, back squats, pull-ups; I ran and pushed and pumped my way towards relief. I played a lot of sports but never excelled in anything. I didn't care about winning and I didn't care about being part of a team. I just cared about me not hurting. So I pushed myself through hard workouts to stave off the darkness but it never lasted long.

The black empty was always on my heels, closing in, waiting for a moment of weakness when it could pounce.

Maybe the fashion show would help – another distraction; another crutch.

By being chosen to be in the Fashion Show I was officially voted popular. I could introduce Zee to some new girls, help him broaden his field of conquest. I shook my head. What was I thinking? Zee didn't need my help. I was the one who couldn't remember where the tongue rested for different vowel pronunciation when faced with the prospect of speaking to a beautiful girl. All thought generating capabilities shut down. I imagined a little engineer Scottie from the old Star Trek episodes living inside the engine room that was my brain, imparting to Captain Kirk the loss of power and their inevitable doom. Kirk would stare out of the two screens that were my eyes, curse the face of the beauty who had frozen my mental functions, furl his brow in determination, knowing he had to save his crew from this final, fatal end.

Just as my imagination was cutting to a commercial break I heard someone call my name. Sharla Unger looked up at me through blue eyes that sparkled against her perfect skin and thick, wavy, Farah Fawcett hair. Why she wasn't a model or playing a part on television I didn't know. Even her smile was a tooth paste commercial, and it was sparkling right at me.

"How does it feel?" Sharla asked. "I mean, to be in the show?"

"All right, I guess," I leaned against my locker, forgetting that it was open, and fell in, pulling my coat and several books down with me. People laughed. I was sure that Sharla would vote me off the show right then. But Sharla just giggled.

"You're funny. I know how you feel," she said. "I get giddy just thinking about it, too. Sometimes, when I'm home, my mind's so pre-occupied with details, I just walk right into a door, you know?" She smiled and bit her lower lip.

"Yeah. Sure," I lied. I was just trying not to look hypnotized by her beauty. That and the fact that I couldn't for the life of me calculate how this girl managed to do all the things that she did – and excel at them all! I felt completely inept in her presence. So I just kept nodding, way after it made sense to.

"We're going to be working closely, spending a lot of time in rehearsals and stuff…. There aren't many guys in the show, so you are really going to play an important role in the production. I think it would be good for us to get to know each other, don't you?"

"Uh huh," I said, nodding, nodding.

"I can tell we're going to have a lot of fun." She smiled her toothpaste smile, which seemed forced, like a calculated campaigning tactic. For some reason, she came across as anxious, like something was bothering her deep down beyond her cover girl image. "First rehearsal's this Thursday after school. Maybe we can talk after?"

"Sure."

"Or… later…?" Sharla twiddled my t-shirt with her fingers. I nearly fell back in my locker again.

"Okay," I said. "If I don't have to – "

"Have to what?"

Thursdays were Father-Son night. My Dad and I would get together for dinner and a movie. He wasn't particular about either the movie or the food and if I said I wanted to see a foreign art-house film and eat French food he was just as happy as if I'd suggested a drive-in and Mickey D's. Usually it was a slapstick comedy and Chinese. My Dad just wanted to make sure we stayed connected. I don't mean he was selfish. Actually, my father was the opposite of selfish. He was only concerned for me and my sister's well being. What I mean is, he was checking to make sure that we were okay, that our relationship was okay. It didn't matter what we watched or what we ate. What mattered to him was that we did it together and didn't hate each other by the end of the night. He worried a lot about what I thought about him, leaving the house, my sister and me and Mom. He was living with his new wife. My sister, Beth, she didn't want to have anything to do with him, so that made it harder and I felt like I had to make up for it. But Sharla Unger didn't need to know all this. So I just said…

"Nothing. Cool."

"Cool," she repeated. I watched her walk off in her loose fitting Levi's.

CHAPTER THREE

"It's some good hash," I said, inhaling.

"Shut up and pass it on!" Zee was impatient. Zee wasn't serious about much, but he was serious about drugs. It was business, after all; plus it allowed us some fringe benefits – we got to smoke his profits.

"*Don't bo-gart that joint, my friend,*" I sang. Zee stared off. "*Pass it o-o-over to me-e-e-e...*" I continued to sing as I passed the joint. Zee picked up the joint but not the Little Feat tune. Zee sucked in the smoke, held it and swallowed. It looked like he was eating it. In a lot of ways, weed smoke was Zee's main source of nutrition.

The autumn leaves, still hanging from the branches kept us hidden from the street. We stood a staircase down from street level, hunched on soft earth near the bike path. Every now and then we'd hear a car roll by on the wet pavement above.

"What's the deal?" Zee said.

"With...?"

"You and Sharla?"

"Nothing."

"Not what I hear," he said, inhaling deep off the joint.

"You gonna pass that back?" I asked.

"Maybe."

"Look, I don't go for this judgmental crap, all right?"

"Then don't go for it," he said.

"Huh?"

"Take off. You're half way doing it."

"I'm not getting you at all, man," I said.

"When's the last time we hung out together?" It had actually been only a few days but for Zee and I that was the equivalent to a year. "This show, this show, every time we talk, it's this stupid show and Sharla and the fucking show and finally I tell you I've got some really good dope and here you are. Like I'm just some schmuck with good smoke."

"Hey," I managed, "it's a commitment."

"And what's our friendship?"

"Zee – come on."

Zee snuffed out the roach on a wet rock and handed it to me. "Finish it," he said and walked away. I sat there on the rain-soaked rock. Match after match failed to re-ignite the moist roach.

Back at school the next day, the mystery fashion show girl was in the hallway walking towards me. I had slipped out of English for a break from the fifteenth century. She wore tight jeans over low heals, and a tank top underneath a man's dress shirt, tucked in and snug against her figure. Whether she meant to or not she looked sexy-as-hell. She leaned over a water fountain pretending to get a drink, bending at an angle that accentuated her physical assets clearly.

The bait was there. And I took it in my less than cool style, pretending not to notice. As I passed by her she backed away from the fountain, bumping into me.

"Oh," she said, feigning surprise.

"My fault," I said.

"My luck." She smiled and I felt my inner Scottie losing control of the ship as her magnetic beauty pulled me into her. "I remember you from the fashion show tryouts."

"Yeah," I said.

"Okay. I'm Kris," she said.

"I'm David."

"Nice to meet you, David."

We smiled awkwardly, extending hands, holding them rather than shaking. It wasn't exactly a business transaction we were making, although we were very much getting down to business. A trickle of water remained at the edge of her mouth, like an invitation. Her tongue drifted over to the drop by her lips and licked it away.

"I remember you, too," I said.

"I was hoping you did, David. You can really move – I was impressed."

"But you left…" I started, giving myself away.

"I don't like crowds."

"So… you got in?"

"To that popularity contest?" She laughed. "No. But it was fun to try out."

"But you were like one of the best there. I mean you know what you're doing, the way you move … you're beautiful…" The words slipped out. It took me a second before I realized what I had said. "I mean, not that – ."

"Thank you," she said. "I happen to think the same of you." She placed a hand on my chest. The same spot where Sharla twirled her finger. But where Sharla's was a shy gesture, Kris knew exactly what she was doing.

"Would you like to go out with me?" Kris asked.

"Me?"

"You don't have a problem with me asking you."

"What problem?"

"Some guys have a problem with a girl asking them out."

"No, it's cool, it's… no. I mean, yeah. Yeah." I said. She smiled. She inched closer. I could feel the heat of her body.

"Thursday night?" she said.

Thursday night. The night Sharla wanted to get together after rehearsal. Movie night with Dad.

"No problem," I said.

I had a problem. So, I consulted my advisor. I laid the situation out for Lewis. We were playing Nintendo basketball. Larry Bird versus Magic Johnson. Lewis was a master of button control. He said it helped him to manipulate girls' nipples toward orgasm. I studied his finger-work.

"Sharla says she just wants to talk," I said.

"So she says," he emphasized.

"Come on. She can have any guy she wants."

"That's your perception, Dave. Not hers. But that's not the point. The point – and I want you to pay attention here, because it's vital for your growth – the point is you have a burden of riches. You've got two babes who want you, right?"

"Allegedly."

"The blonde's a sure thing, right?" I shrugged. "Come on, Fisch! That body – what's her name?"

"Kris. But, there's something different about her. I mean, she's so forward it's scary."

"She'll spread for you in a heartbeat, man."

"If you say so."

"Take it from the mouth of experience."

"Could you rephrase that?"

"Sharla, on the other hand, requires special handling. Sharla's been told all her life that she's beautiful. Guys pay attention to her in a way they don't pay it to other girls. She knows she's smart, and she knows she's beautiful. But she's insecure as hell."

"Why?"

"Rule number one: The more beautiful a girl is, the more she needs to be re-assured that she is special as a person, not just as an object." He raised both eyebrows and pointed. "Are you listening to me, Fisch? I'm giving you gold here."

"So, I should go out with Sharla."

"Wrong."

"But Kris is the sure thing, right?"

"Right. First and foremost, to thine own self be true."

"Huh?"

"Look out for numero uno. Take care of yourself first." I stared at him blankly. "Lose that cherry, Fischer!!"

"Okay. And what about Sharla?"

"Guys don't blow off Sharla Unger. Most guys – normal guys – would give their right testicle just for the chance to hold her hand. You blow off Sharla Unger, she won't know what to do with herself. She'll probably have a fit – BUT! – she will respect you for it in the end."

I sat as if at the feet of a master lapping up every detail into the inner workings of the female mind. There was a glow about Lewis. Sitting there cross-legged on the couch, cigarette dangling from his lips, he seemed... wise.

On the monitor, Lewis's Bird slam-dunked over my Johnson for the game winner.

I rode my bicycle from Lewis's house back home. No cars in the driveway. Mom wasn't home from work. It was seven thirty which meant she was working late and I'd have anywhere from an hour to the rest of the night to myself.

I kicked off my shoes and hurried downstairs to the basement where I did my best thinking. I poured myself a nice blend of Chivas Regal and coke. The coke was mostly for color, so it didn't look like I was drinking a juice glass of scotch.

I put on Pink Floyd and lay down on the couch. The song 'Time' warmed over me like a summer night and I thought about my upcoming date with Kris. As I sipped my drink I imagined Kris with different layers of clothes missing.

When I woke up, my sister, Beth, was standing over me on her roller-skates, which she only wore inside the house. My back was arched and my hand was lying firm against the crotch of my pants.

"You're in trouble," Beth said.

"Why don't you knock before you come into a room?"

"You were masturbating!"

"I was not!"

"You were, too! Your hand's over your penis and when I came down you were smiling."

"Get out of here!"

"Make me."

"Just go!"

"You won't make me because you don't want to move your hand because that's where the sperm is." Beth held a silly grin on her face, her hair in ponytails; at twelve, and totally flat-chested she was still very much a little girl. I jumped up off the couch and screamed low and gravelly: "O-O-OUT!!" Beth's roller skates left deep marks on the basement tile, much like the discoloration on my jeans.

"What's on your mind?" my mother asked me. I told her I might have to change my plans with dad. I told her it was because of special commitments to extracurricular school activities. I wasn't much of a student so my parents were easily impressed when I mentioned school-type interests. But before my mother could relish her satisfaction, Beth piped in.

"He's in a fashion show."

"A fashion show? That doesn't sound like school activity."

"It's like a play with dancing and movement instead of words. Lots of people come to see it. Looks good on a college application."

"Won't it take away from your study time?"

"Mom, some of the brightest kids in school are in this show. I'm surrounded by good influence."

My mother looked at me closely, her nose wiggled and she sniffed audibly. "I smell scotch. Have you been drinking?"

"David was whacking off on the couch," Beth shouted. Her timing couldn't have been better.

"Well," my mother said, "I hope you washed your hands before dinner."

After dinner my mother washed dishes while I dried. I tried not to say much, which, with my mother, was difficult. We didn't spend much time together and most of it was strained. My mother was a big fan of catch-up parenting which involved asking me about every moment in my day that she didn't get to witness.

My mother passed me a dish. I noticed she was wearing her wedding ring. Weird.

"Is there anything you want to talk to me about, David?" she asked.

"Nope."

"School okay?"

"Yeah."

"Grades?"

"Yeah."

"Yeah? What does 'yeah' mean?"

"They're good."

"How good?"

"Good enough."

"For what? Pumping gas?"

"Come on, Mom."

"No, I won't 'come on, Mom.' You don't get a lot of chances in this world, David. You're only young once. You can't understand that now but –"

"Aw, JESUS MOM!!" I slammed the plate into the dry rack, hoping the lecture was over.

"Why can't we talk anymore?" she asked.

"Talking's fine. Lecturing's not."

"But I'm your mother. I've been there. All of it."

"Trust me, Mom, there are places I go you have never been. And if you DID I don't want to know about it, okay?"

"David, are you taking drugs?"

My eyes went wide but I kept them averted, focusing out the window where a chipmunk was busy collecting nuts for a long winter.

"I know it's been hard on you, being the oldest. Me and your father..." her voice began to tremble. It was a warning sign of more tears and trudging through the muck that was my mother's 'fair and non-judgmental' reasons for their divorce. It was a one-way car wreck of subjective 'poor me' rationale. With Dad out of the house I became the resident male, the emotional highway rest stop. Whatever my mother's expectations were of me, I was aiming way short of them.

"I don't give a shit!!" This time the plate cracked and I stormed out. My mother yelled something about good china and responsibility. It was the same yell whatever she said. I had my coat and shoes on and was out the door before she could finish what she really wanted to say: "Ungrateful...! Degenerate...! Spoiled...!"

As if these were qualities I had any control over.

CHAPTER FOUR

Stew's was a twenty-four-hour diner that was, as promised, always open. I was cold, but not hungry. I sat by a corner window looking out onto St. Clair Avenue, which also offered a good view of the bar. Raindrops began to fall at a light rate. A TTC bus pulled past, heading east towards St. Clair station. Faces looked out, like prisoners. An older woman looked down: thinking? Reading? Sleeping? Her expression reminded me of my mother, hunched over a sink of dishes, stranded in transition from a life she once had to the turmoil she now lived; a sink once filled with bubbles and the hope of lemony freshness, now just a basin of dirty dishwater.

Behind the woman sat a young girl, darkly tanned skinned – she looked Indian, or maybe Pakistani – gazing wide eyed at the concrete landscape as if for the first time. I wondered if she was in my school. Did her life in any way intersect with mine?

The waitress came and I ordered the blueberry pie and a beer.

"We don't sell beer."

"What're you talking about? There's a bar right there."

"If you're of age."

"I'm twenty two," I insisted.

"You're seventeen. You're a senior in high school." She waited. She was medium height with reddish-brown hair pulled

back with a felt clip. Her skin was freckled and dry and she looked
older than seventeen. Her nametag said Nancy. "We have Spanish
together, you idiot," she said finally. "Nancy Meyers. Not that
you'd know. You're not in class very often."

"Yeah. I dropped. Sort of. They just haven't figured it out
yet."

"It's amazing how thick they are when you don't tell
them," she said. "If you drop the course you can get an incomplete.
If not, they fail you. If you fail it goes on your GPA."

"I didn't come here to get lectured by my waitress."

"Then you should've stayed home."

"Can't think at home."

"You think?"

"Lay off."

"You want ice cream with the pie? We have vanilla,
chocolate and strawberry."

"Who orders strawberry ice cream with blueberry pie?"

"Vanilla, then," she decided and left. I watched the street.
I felt like the world was watching me. Nancy returned with the pie
and two coffees. She sat down across from me.

"My house, I've got three younger brothers and sisters
running around ever since my Mom died. And it's like my job to
be the mommy because my dad can't do it all himself. Not even
close. Half the time he's losing his shit, you know what I mean?" I
kind of looked at her sideways.

"You're not like... with your dad?"

"Get a life, Fischer."

"You know my name."

"Yeah. Probably from Mrs. Gonzalez repeating it every day waiting for someone to answer. Why don't you just put in the paperwork and drop the course?"

"If I drop Spanish I won't have a full time schedule. And I have to graduate this year. I'm a senior."

"So you took Spanish as a blow off credit course. And now you – you know, if you miss too many classes, they fail you anyway and you don't graduate. All you have to do is show up."

"I don't recall asking for your advice."

"Comes with the territory. It's my one perk on the job – between pouring coffee and laying down the check I get to tell people how to live their lives."

"You get tips for that?"

"You'd be surprised."

"I prefer to keep my problems to myself," I said.

"Hmm. A brooder. I should have known."

"What does that mean?"

"Nothing. How's the pie?"

"I'm done," I said and pushed it away.

Nancy picked up a fork and dug in.

"Help yourself."

"I hear you're in the fashion show," she said, with a mouthful of my dessert.

"Yup," I replied, coolly. "How did you know?"

"Everybody knows. Maple Hill is as superficial as it gets."

"You don't seem like the type to care," I said. Nancy shrugged and scraped the last of the pie from the plate, stuck the fork in her mouth and licked the tines clean.

"Aren't you nervous?" she asked, eventually. "All those people watching, the television cameras?"

"TV?"

"You think a Sharla Unger production doesn't get network coverage?"

"Tell me about it," I agreed and felt phony for saying it.

"There are some serious JAPs in our school."

"They've got the money," I said. *They.* Me.

"It's not their money, though, is it?" she said looking at me. I felt like I was being judged. "It's their parent's money." She paused to scratch her neck revealing a tattoo of an eye looking out of a snake's mouth. Her eyes rolled up to the ceiling on this next thought. "They don't know how easy they've got it." She didn't say a word for a moment and I just watched her think. She had a constellation of freckles along her nose and above her cheeks. She caught my look and she let a small laugh escape through her nose.

"So what're you doing out here by yourself on a school night?" Nancy asked.

"No one to spend it with," I said.

"Seriously? I thought you were one of those popular guys with girls chasing after you all the time."

"Yeah," I lied. "I just wanted to be alone, I guess." I could feel the black empty coming up from deep inside me. That black void that sucked everything into it and demanded love and attention at all cost. I reached across the table for Nancy's hand. "Listen, couldn't you just bring me a beer? I mean, who's gonna know?"

She pulled her hand away.

"No," her tone suddenly cool, guarded. "But good luck with everything." She put down the fork. "You're right. It's better with Vanilla." She got up to leave.

"Hey – ," I started. She looked, waited. "We should do lunch sometime." I smiled knowing how pathetic that phrase sounded.

"*Do lunch?*" she repeated, trying to get her head around it. "I'll see ya," she said in a way that made me certain I had hurt her feelings.

Kris had given me her phone number and her first name. Information wouldn't give out an address without a last name. I wanted to call but thought maybe it was too late. Maybe she had company. Maybe her parents were home and it wouldn't be cool, how would I explain myself: *Hi Mister and Misses Hot Blonde, I know it's a school night and I'm sorry to disturb you but I was wondering if I could have sex with your daughter. I promise I'll be quick. You have no idea how quick I can be. Unfortunately I have no idea how quick I can be, either, but I'm eager to find out.*

I didn't wear a watch but I guessed that it was around nine. I was good with guessing time. I always seemed to be aware of the fact that it was passing.

The diner boasted one of the last pay phones in the city, right outside the door. There was no booth but the phone was protected by the restaurants overhang. I plugged in the exact change and dialed the number in my pocket. The phone rang. It rang three times, five times, nine times. I hung up. Where was Kris at this hour? Maybe she was out with another guy. The way she approached me, that confidence, so different from the girls I knew. She probably asks guys out all the time. She suggested Thursday. Because her Tuesday and Wednesday were booked up with other dates! I couldn't believe it! She was cheating on me!

I slipped the change into the phone and dialed. This time it picked up after only a few rings.

"Hello?"

"Hi, Sharla. It's David."

"David who?"

"David Fischer."

"Oh. Hi, David," she sounded a little annoyed. "What's up?"

"I was just wondering," I said, my voice stammering. "I was wondering if I could see you."

"Sure," Sharla said, her voice turning sweet as honey. "When?"

"Tonight."

"Tonight? It's like... ten o'clock already."

"I know," I said, "I was just wondering... I have some things on my mind about the show."

"About the show? David, the show hasn't even started rehearsals and I've got a test to study for..." I should have hung up. I felt the edge coming. I'd taken a wrong turn but I wasn't about to slow down.

"You asked if we could get together and I was thinking of some things and it would be really useful to me – I mean, to you, I think – for us to discuss them as soon as possible while they're still fresh in my mind. I've got a lot of ideas, Sharla. I'm really excited we'll be working together, I really am."

I was going to drive this right off a cliff.

"I'm glad you're so enthusiastic, David. Frankly, I didn't think you'd be into it."

"Of course I am. Why wouldn't I be into it?" I asked.

"You're not exactly the fashion show type. More like the jock...." Just then another bus rolled by, its air breaks bringing it to a stop just feet away. "Are you outside? What are you doing outside?" Sharla asked.

"No," I lied. "My window's open and the bus is right outside." Just then a group of random citizens walked past me speaking loudly in various languages.

"It sounds like you're outside. Are you okay?" My opening.

"I just need to talk and I was hoping I could see you tonight."

"I can't see you, David. But I can talk for a little longer."

"I can come over if that's easier."

"That's not a good idea, David. I'm not ready to receive company." She said 'receive company' like a princess or something. I pictured her in satin on an enormous bed with a canopy and a eunuch fanning her with a giant leaf.

"Look, can I ask you something?"

"Sure."

"Why did you ask me out?"

"Ask you out?"

"Yeah."

"I didn't ask you out."

"You asked me if we could get together and get to know each other before the show."

"Right."

"So, you asked me to get together. So what was that about?"

"I said I wanted to talk about some things. About the show."

"And that's it?"

"Yes. What did you think?"

"Nothing, Sharla, I just got this distinct impression…"

"Well, you got the wrong impression and if that's what you're calling me about at ten o'clock on a school night then I'm going to have to end this conversation right now. I have a test..."

"No, no, no," I tried to hang on. "Look, I just really need someone to talk to right now."

"Don't you have a girlfriend," Sharla asked? "What's her name – Marcy Singer?"

"We broke up," I said. Pause. Sharla was one of those girls who was always up on the latest gossip. But my status was apparently news to her. It took her a moment to respond.

"I'm sorry to hear that. I'll see you in school tomorrow, okay?" I stood in the increasing rainfall, the dead end of a phone conversation in my hand. I hung up and dialed another number. Two rings, four rings ….. I was about to hang up when:

"Hello…?" I raised the receiver to my head to make sure. "Hello," she said.

"Kris…?"

"Who's this?"

"It's David Fischer. From school."

"Hello, David Fischer from school." Her voice was a silky warm fire in a storm.

"Am I disturbing you?"

"No," she said. "I just got in."

"Did I wake your parents?"

"I doubt it," she giggled, "I live alone."

CHAPTER FIVE

Our garage door still squeaked a little when you lifted it from the bottom. But if you put pressure on the outer edges of the handle it opened without a sound. Our driveway was on a hill. A little push was all my mother's Audi Quatro needed to roll back with the engine off in neutral. Our well-patrolled neighborhood was quiet. Taxes insured that.

In the past, cops stopped me several times walking home. I looked the part – hoodie, ripped jeans, work-boots unlaced. When they asked me where I lived I was happy to show them. Our Phillipino housekeeper, Gabriella, answered. I said 'Gabriella, tell him I live here'.

"I have pay-pers," she screamed, thinking they had come for her.

"Do you know this boy? Does he live here?" the cops asked.

"I have pay-pers! I have pay-pers!"

This time, I was the one in the car, checking out the cops as I drove by, getting their friendly reassuring nod. Did they actually think they were protecting anybody? My family had ruptured from the inside out. We were a broken mess. Night after night the cops sat in their cruiser while my home was invaded by misery.

I flipped them the bird pretending to scratch my nose, then I made a quick turn towards Kris' place.

Kris lived on a fourth floor walk-up in an old depression-era building on Queen Street West. The pre-war building was falling apart. The neighborhood was happening: tenement-chic. I buzzed the apartment number she gave me.

Kris' voice came on, sweet and gentle, in contrast with the bright fluorescent light ricocheting off the entranceway tiles. "I'll be right down," she said.

I stepped outside and lit up a cigarette, smoked half of it, then replaced it with a mint for my breath.

Kris stepped out in jeans and a turtleneck sweater, both of which hugged her figure. She wore a wool P-coat over that.

"Wow," I said. She smiled and looped her arm inside mine. I walked her to my mother's Audi.

"Nice wheels," she said. "Yours?"

"My mother's," I said.

"Couldn't get the Mercedes," she asked?

"Gimme a break, Kris. I'm not what you think." I opened her door first, then got in beside her. She slid into the leather seats. I turned the car on, the engine revved with German precision.

"I must come across as a real spoiled rich kid to you, huh."

"Pretty much," Kris said.

"I'm not. I'm just..." Kris put a hand on my thigh.

"Hey," she said. "Just be yourself." Her satin tone calmed me, while her hand on my thigh and her body sitting so close to mine made my insides do summersaults of desire. I settled into the leather car seat and pulled away from the curb.

We took in a movie – a romantic thriller where the woman discovers that the man she's fallen in love with is really the one who's been trying to kill her all along and she has to kill him in order to be free.

Dessert we found in an old café that doubled as an antique store. The chairs were old and high-backed. Some had velvet cushions. We cuddled into a couch and told each other a little bit about ourselves. She told me her father left when she was young and her mother worked two jobs full time. Kris had worked a long string of jobs in order to stay on her feet. She dropped out to work and to survive. She had done some modeling, a lot of waitressing, a bunch of retail jobs and she was a flight attendant for about a week. She was twenty years old. She decided to return to high school to get her degree and do something with her life. She'd be the first in her family to even finish high school. My story seemed like a cruise vacation compared to hers. She told me there was no point in comparing. It wasn't often she got to ride in an Audi or a Mercedes but then again, she didn't have anybody watching over her shoulder telling her what to do or when to do it. I told her maybe we could switch for a day.

"I wouldn't ever give up what I have," she said. "I love my freedom."

"It came at a high price," I said.

"You can't appreciate something if you don't have to earn it. Freedom, real freedom, isn't free. I paid my price. Now I own my life."

In that moment I thought Kris was the smartest person I had ever met. She possessed a worldliness I could barely fathom and instantly wanted.

"*Freedom's just another word for nothing left to lose...*" I sang. Kris smiled.

"Great song."

"I don't own anything," I said. "Except for a basketball and some clothes I bought myself with summer job money. And my music."

"Do you like Neil Young," she asked?

"Yeah."

"Good. He's on my stereo."

Kris lived in a tiny studio apartment with a bathroom attached and a walk-in closet. The walls were a warm, sponge-painted amber. There were dried roses on the windowsill inside petite smoky-rose colored glass bottles framed by sheer white curtains. Her floor was cushioned with thick white carpet. In the corner of the room, across from the window, bathed in moonlight, was her bed.

Neil Young's *Harvest* album was on the stereo and the song '*Old Man*' played over the speakers. We lay down on the carpet and looked through some photos.

"I model. I still do it when I need the money which is basically all the time," she said.

She was beautiful and exotic. I watched her fingers flip through the pages of her photo album as Neil Young sang '*Old Man take a look at my life/ I'm a lot like you…*'. I thought of my father.

"You have anything to drink?" I asked Kris.

"I have Pepsi, ginger ale, orange juice and water."

"No. I mean a real drink."

'*I need someone to love me the who-ole day through…*' Neil sang.

"I've got some vodka in the fridge." In the corner of her room was a small, half-fridge. Above it there was a hot plate.

"My kitchen," she said with a laugh.

She poured a tall glass of vodka and orange juice for me, and just orange juice for herself. "I feel something coming on," she explained.

I gulped down the drink. I flipped through the photos then turned my attention to the Neil Young album cover, studying the lyrics. I could feel her eyes on me. She leaned closer and I burned my concentration on the album lyrics, my terror of the moment rising, but the liquor gave me strength.

"Have you even thought about trying to kiss me," she asked. I tried to play it cool.

"Not really, but…" and I leaned in to her, "if you want to." Stupid. As I reached my mouth towards hers I felt like a jerk for what I had just said and felt also, somehow, that she knew I was a dumb kid with something to prove. Maybe she even knew what.

Our lips met. Our mouths opened. Her tongue met mine. I felt quivers down to the tiny hairs on my toes.

I considered myself an extremely good kisser. Girls had given me the compliment. I worked my magic technique on Kris, licking her lips with my tongue, lingering softly just above her mouth, making her reach for it, want it. There was some teeth knocking, but that is to be expected when encountering a new mouth.

Kris' hands wandered around my back and eventually down to my butt. I was lying on my left side, so I let my right hand travel down from her shoulder, brushing across her breast en route to her waist, then her hips, then, following the curve of her pelvis to her perfect derriere.

For a moment I thought about Marcy and the hole she left when she walked out. With the vodka inside me, and Kris in my arms, I felt the black empty abating.

Kris pulled away for some air. A long string of spit hung like a tight rope between our mouths. Before she could say anything a line popped from my romantically inexperienced brain. This one I'd been practicing for that special moment. And like most rehearsed lines, it came out wrong.

"You wanna make love?"

Kris rolled over onto her stomach, hiding her face. Her body began to shake.

"What's wrong?" I asked.

Kris continued to shake with a bad cough or maybe she was crying. It took me a while to realize she was convulsing with hysterical laughter. She finally rolled back over. Her eyes were tearing. She looked at me the way a woman regards a lost puppy. It was Marcy all over again.

"I'm sorry," she said. "It's just, the way you asked…." Laughter cut her off again.

"Well, how am I supposed to ask?" She said something about not having to ask. "But I don't want to presume…".

Finally, Kris turned to me, tear lines streaking her face. She leaned into me, pressed her lips against mine with soft aggression and said, "Just shut up and take off your clothes."

"I think there's something I should tell you," I said.

"You don't have to," she said. "I am honored to be your first." She kissed me long and sensually. Her body felt so right as she pressed against me. She climbed on top of me. "I promise you, this will be memorable," she said.

CHAPTER SIX

When I woke up, Kris was lying next to me, brushing her hands through my hair. I bolted upright. "Oh shit! I'm sorry!" I said.

"For what?" Kris asked.

"Falling asleep. Did I snore?"

"Like a baby. It was cute."

"What time is it?" I asked. She glanced at a clock by her bed.

"Late. You should go."

"I want to stay," I said.

"You can't," Kris said.

"Why not?"

"You have school tomorrow."

"Can I see you again?" I wanted to move in.

"Sure. Just don't expect anything."

"What do you mean?"

"No flowers or fancy dinners or surprises. I hate surprises. I'm not your girlfriend. And the last thing I want is a boyfriend. So don't hold out for what's not coming, okay? I just want to put it out there from the start. So there are no...false expectations."

I was crushed, but I figured this was her defense, keeping her guard up early. She'd probably been hurt before and expects it again. I got it. This was just a one-night stand. No promises. Most girls I knew wanted to call you their boyfriend, introduce you to their parents, and start picking names for your kids. Kris was the opposite and it made me want her even more.

She helped me pull my t-shirt over my head and torso. Her hands caressed my chest and ribs.

"You have an amazing body," she purred.

"Can I ask you something?" I said. She scrunched her face, like she knew what I was going to ask.

"Do you have to?" she asked.

"Well…? I mean… you know, considering…?"

Kris leaned in and kissed me wet and hot, sliding her tongue around my lips and inside my mouth. My whole body melted against hers. No one had ever affected me like this before.

"You were great," she said. "Now go home, young man." And with that, the black empty vanished.

CHAPTER SEVEN

I had a special technique for silently parking my mother's car in the garage when I came home real late. It was real late.

I would blow through the stop sign at the corner and cut the engine as I passed through the intersection. Momentum propelled the silent Audi up the small hill that was our driveway. The problem, of course, was the garage door. When my thinking is good I leave the garage door open from sneaking her car out. In my post-virginal coitus delirium I had no recollection if the door was open or shut or even attached.

Reaching the stop sign at fifty miles an hour, I cut the engine and the lights, coasted the car through the intersection, up the driveway and into the open garage where my mother was standing in her bathrobe, arms folded. I slammed on the brakes.

My mother's eyes were lasers aimed at me. I got out of the car and moved towards the garage door to close it. My system was blown. I needed an exit strategy.

"Don't walk away from me!" she ordered.

"Just closing the door!"

"I'm the adult here!" she screamed.

My mother was an intelligent, articulate, respected social worker. But not now; not at this moment. At this moment, she was furious and her fury short-circuited her intellect.

"Where the hell have you been?!"

"Out." I said.

"WHERE?!"

"None of your business!"

"It's my business when you use my car!"

"You're a thousand miles late for an oil change."

"And you're grounded. From now on, you're walking."

"Fine!"

So not fine. How could I take Kris out without a car? I pushed past my mom into the house and up the stairway to my room, a private apartment above the garage. I slammed the door behind me letting my sleeping sister know I was onto her for ratting me out. My mother pounded the door. When I wouldn't answer, she started to climb up. I took a stance at the top of the stairs. This time I was the one with my arms crossed and my face tense. After all, I had lost my virginity. I had graduated into manhood. And I had done it with a beautiful, mature, *non-Jewish* woman; I'd been christened by a former model, *shtupped* by a *Shiksa goddess*! Talk about a rite of passage, this was way bigger than a bar mitzvah. No way was my mother going to dampen this night. Not this night.

"Get out of my room."

"You ungrateful little shit!" she said.

I marched down the dark stairway, forcing her back. I grabbed the door from her hand and slammed it shut.

Stay out of my room, Mom! Stay out of my life! Keep your family-ruining little power trips elsewhere! I'm the man of the house now!

It was four in the morning but I called up Lewis anyway.

"What...?" he said, groggily, more asleep than awake.

"I did it," I cried. There was a silence on the other end. "Lewis!"

"Huh?"

"I had sex. For real. All the way. I'm not a virgin."

"Good," he said. Silence.

"I just wanted – "

"Huh?"

"Lewis, it's –

"Mmm," he moaned, "Sharla, is it time for my lesson?" I hung up. I stretched out on my bed and stared at the ceiling. All I could think about was Kris' naked body next to mine. I had to beat off in order to fall asleep.

I had to beat off twice.

CHAPTER EIGHT

Zee crashed his long, lanky frame against the neighboring lockers with a metal splash. A studious girl sitting close by sprang off shouting something about us being party-obsessed moronic degenerates. I resented the 'moron' part.

"So what's up?"

"Nothing," I said with a shrug, but my shit-eating grin gave me away. Zee handed me an envelope.

"Here."

It was a card. A cartoon elephant standing on its hind legs up against the backside of a camel. The camel had feminine eyelashes and a grin of pleasure. The elephant's trunk was raised in the air. The inside said 'Happy V-Day'. It was signed from Zee and Lewis.

"Since when are you and Lewis friends."

"We're not," he said. "He told me, and I went and got the card. So Mazel tov on dipping your little schmuck but go fuck yourself for not telling me first."

"It was four in the morning."

"I'm up. I'm always up. You know that."

"Doing what?"

"Same as you, actually. You remember that little pouty-lipped girl needed some consoling?"

"Man, you work fast."

"Hey, man," he shrugged, shifting his weight, "she likes to party."

Sharla walked by, her top tight, her jeans loose, her frosted brown hair swirling down as she swished her hips through the halls showing off her perfect salon-tanned mid-riff. Zee gave me a nudge. "Here comes your girlfriend," he said.

"Sharla," I said, stepping out in front of her. "I wanted to talk about that call – "

She stepped to the side and detoured right around me barely acknowledging my presence. I turned, bewildered, following her with my voice: "Sharla...." But she walked away.

"Great. Ass." Zee slapped his hand on my shoulder. "Lucky guy."

"Lucky? What're you talking about?" I asked, still watching the loose jeans and the glory obfuscated within them.

"'What am I -- ?' Fisch!... you don't remember who you did it –,"

" – with." My face was a dictionary expression of horror. I had called Lewis while he was dreaming of Sharla and his brain merged the stories together. "What an asshole!"

"Hey!"

"Where's Lewis?"

"You're starting to piss me off with this shit, Man. I know when I'm not wanted. I just like to be told that I smell when I do. Is that it, Fisch? Do I smell? Do I not bathe enough for you?"

"Do you think she knows?"

My question had interrupted Zee's rant. Ranting was a sport for Zee. More than just venting, ranting was, for Zee, a part of his belief system. Zee didn't like his belief system being interrupted. "That's it!! I'm sick of being treated like a second class friend!!"

"I'm sorry," I said. "I didn't do it with Sharla Unger."

"Awww CRAP!" Zee slammed his fist into a locker. "That sucks! That just -- ! Dammit!!" He slammed his fist again. People passing cut a wide detour. He kicked and elbowed the locker door into a dented car accident.

"Dude, that's somebody's locker."

"It's okay," Zee said. "I know the guy."

"Who?"

"I dunno," he said. He kicked it again.

"What's the big deal?"

"I just thought, you know, we'd get one for our side."

Our side was the guys who don't score sophisticated popular girls. Guys like us who don't ever experience nights with classy, articulate, intelligent, elegant, gorgeous Sharla Ungers. No, guys like us get the mysterious, sometimes odd outsiders like Kris. Maybe.

Once in a very long while. Which is why I felt so damn lucky.

"I did do it with someone else, though."

"Who?" Zee's eyes lit up.

"Kris."

"Kris who?"

"She's a transfer student. Blonde, about five eight."

"Is she wearing a green skirt with red stockings and a white top under a little sweater-thingy, looks like a bathing suit model who escaped from skid row?"

"I don't know. I haven't seen her today."

Zee punched me in the arm. "Well, I have!" Zee's smile grew slowly, "Dave, you scored!"

"You think?"

"A goddess." And he raised his eyebrow at me, the way he would at the end of a rant.

I smiled and kind of bounced on my feet. Kris turned the corner wearing the outfit Zee described. The sweater was mohair and the least flattering item on her body. But Kris could make a used garbage bag look sexy on her. I moved to intercept her. I couldn't wait to hold her again. I felt like the luckiest guy on the planet. Zee was staring and nodding obviously at Kris. He elbowed me as she came closer, nodding, nodding. It was a total giveaway that he knew. Except only Kris and I were supposed to know. At least, that's what I would find out.

"Kris," I called. She glanced at me, lowered her eyes and kept on. I watched her pass. I called her name again but she wouldn't respond. Zee was bouncing. When I saw the expression on his face – nodding, doing a silent 'uh-huh, uh-huh' I knew who the asshole really was. I slammed Zee into the locker.

"You just screwed me up!" I yelled.

"What – over her?" He tried to push me off but I held him against the locker easily. "Like you're the first?" His words hit me hard. They sunk beneath the chest and burned a route through my gut. "She's not exactly the girl next door. Why do you think I'm so happy for you?" I weakened and he slipped out of my grip. "You did it with an experienced woman, Dave. No prissy, school-girl-holding-hands-letter-winning-cheerleader-snob you're always bunching your pants over. And I hope you never do because I'd have to leave you for another best friend. But you didn't. You found the best woman to lead you down the path of righteousness and male deservedness. I'm proud of you, Fisch. I salute you and welcome you to the other side. We've been waiting."

I hated Zee then. Mostly because as much as I wanted to kill him, he made me laugh. "You're a dick," I said. He bowed graciously.

The kid whose locker we banged up came by to swap out books. He was a nerdy freshman, pimply faced, hair combed over, staring straight ahead to avoid eye contact. He stared at his locker – dented, bent, unusable. His face twisted with frustration and anger; then he saw Zee and me and he swallowed all that anger. He just squashed it down inside of him. I watched him do it and knew exactly how he felt.

I caught up with Kris before she entered a classroom. I was close enough to the door to glimpse that it was Mrs. Gonzalez, the Spanish teacher whose class I hadn't made in three weeks.

Gonzalez missed seeing me, but Nancy from the diner saw me and waved. I had to push Kris out of view from the doorway.

"Go away," Kris said.

"Just a minute?" I asked.

"I have class."

"Please."

"No!" She was attracting attention.

"Wait -- ! What'd I do?"

"I was looking forward to seeing you today. You seemed like a nice guy when we went out. Vulnerable and sweet, despite the ego. And I attribute that more to immaturity. But you just showed me you obviously don't know any better."

I stood there and I took it. I was my Dad taking it from my mother.

"Here, you're just another jerk trying to impress all the wrong people. Your friend – the tall one – he was practically eating me out of my clothes with his eyes."

"Zee. Yeah, I want to apologize - "

"He needs a leash."

"I'm sorry."

"Because you told him or because he acted the way he did?"

"Both. More because I told him. I just…" I didn't know how to say the rest. "I just wanted to tell him that…"

Just then a group of ninth grade girls rounded the corner from gym and heard me finish: "…I lost my virginity."

The group of ninth grade girls screamed with laughter, elevating the moment to the second most embarrassing experience of my life. Kris laughing at me when I asked her if she 'wanted to make love' was still in the lead. Kris was enjoying the whole scene. But she wasn't going to let me off easy.

"I am not somebody's prize!" She pushed past me into the classroom. I grabbed her by the arm. Nancy was still craning her neck to catch the scene.

"I need to see you again."

"Let go of my arm. Please."

"If I let go of you, will you go out with me?"

"If you don't let go I will scream so loud they'll have you dragged out in handcuffs." I let go.

Kris headed into the classroom. She turned around one last time. "And thanks for reminding me why I hated high school so much in the first place. You virgin asshole." Then she slammed the door in my face.

CHAPTER NINE

Sharla was giving a class lecture on the definition of '*Mens Rea*' in 'Intro to Law'. I sat in the back of the class, my books closed, watching her lips move and wishing I had never called her.

She looked my way and gave me a stern glance. That's when it occurred to me I must have been staring.

"David Fischer, do you have a question?" Sharla asked.

"What -- ?" I stammered, lifting my head from the desk. "Uh..."

Some kids turned to look my way. I wasn't a good student normally but I was really out of it today and Sharla was making it abundantly clear to the rest of my classmates.

"Do you..." she repeated, slowly, methodically, as if addressing a child, "...have... a... question...?"

It was the kind of tactic reserved for teachers to embarrass you into paying attention. It was an old but effective tool with me because I'm a wimp with embarrassment. Even though I'd laugh when it happened to someone else, because of the embarrassment game – someone gets embarrassed, you laugh because the next time it might be you. The logic is skewed, I admit.

For Sharla to use the embarrassment method... well, it was just too low a blow from student to student. Even for Sharla Unger. Now the whole class was watching what I would do. Yesterday I was the stud with two dates and a burden of riches.

Today I was flat broke. And a broke man, as the song goes, has nothing left to lose.

"Yes," I said. "Would you mind picking up the pace? You're boring the hell out of me."

The ensuing silence was deafening.

For her beauty, her brains, and her poise, Sharla was practically revered by every student in the school. Teachers asked her advice on the quality of their lessons. She was the one person who could elevate your social status from nerd to cool with the snap of her fingers. And she could take you down just as fast.

To publicly demean Sharla Unger was considered social suicide – if you cared about that stuff. I cared only about getting another chance with Kris.

"If you have constructive criticism, you may write it down on your case observation sheet," the teacher said, as if he concurred with me. "You won't get that courtesy in a real courtroom with a real judge. Carry on, Ms. Unger."

Sharla took the teacher's comments in stride but struggled to return to her lecture. She had left off with the intent to commit a crime being the burden of proof for the prosecution. Her voice trembled. Her eyes lost their steely focus and began searching the room for an ally. The class just stared back, watching the unraveling. Tears welled in Sharla's stunning green eyes.

Had I intended, just now, to hurt? To cause harm? When I thought about it, I'd have to say yes. I plead guilty, your honor. With a good reason.

And what reason is that, Mr. Fischer?

I got laid.

Congratulations, Mr. Fischer! You are free to go.

Sharla ran out of the room. The teacher looked at me with a bored expression. We both knew what it meant. I saw myself out of the class.

The news of my insulting remarks to Sharla spread through the school halls like airborne anthrax. Moments later an announcement came over the school intercom asking for Sharla Unger's closest friends to meet in the second floor girl's bathroom. One by one the most popular girls in the school left their respective classes and headed for the bathroom without a word of opposition from neither teacher nor student.

The fogged glass windows of the second floor bathroom opened at the back of the school. If you stood underneath, you could hear everything that was said and done in there. A crowd of boys were often lurking there, trying to catch some news. By the time I got there, there was a mob of about fifty kids, boys and girls listening intently. Some of them were taking notes.

"Blow your nose, Hon," Natalie Feinberg said, pulling tissue out of her purse as she entered. Natalie was the friend who had everything cosmetic on hand. "You need a little blush retouch, honey. Here."

"Valium," Jennifer Taub announced, rattling a bottle in her hand. "Oh, wait. Percodan. My mother must've switched doctors again."

Marion McManus stormed into the bathroom, shoved a pint of Jameson's Irish in Sharla's face, said, "Up the Irish, fuck the French," did a shot with Sharla, patted her on the shoulder. "He's got it comin'," Marion said. "You mark my words." She took another pull off the bottle and left. Sharla chased the pills with the whiskey.

One of them lit up a joint. The smoke rose out of the window from the bathroom out over our heads towards the back lawn of the school where Mister Hollorman, the custodian, sat with his lunch, sniffing, getting contact high, washing it down with the vodka-orange juice in his thermos. We cheered.

Another shot of Jameson's. Another pill. Another pull off the joint. The 'A' student, model of perfection, getting wasted in the shitter.

I re-entered the school as the bell sounded and the halls filled with students. As I walked through, people stared at me with what could have been awe or amazement, like I was either a hero or the stupidest jerk that had ever walked the planet. I had put Sharla Unger in her place. I had slammed my mother out of my room. I was a man.

I was an idiot.

Leonard, the nerdy science kid who Sharla sat next to only to share his notes, give him a chubby, and forget his existence as soon as the bell rang, shook my hand.

"I've always wanted to tell that free-loader where to go but never had the guts."

Girls approached. The '*other*' girls. The athletes, the band members, the stoners, the awkward quiet girls. They heard I made Sharla cry and they were thanking me.

"We hate that bitch...."

"...that snot..."

"...uppity you know what."

"Listen, don't feel bad, Fischer, you did us all a favor."

"Will you go out with me? You're like my hero now, oh my god!"

A young ninth grader approached me. Fourteen years old with a mouthful of metal.

"Congratulations," she said flashing her braces.

"Did Sharla pick on you, too?"

"No, I mean about losing your virginity."

That's when the announcement came over the school public address... "*David Fischer, report to the principal's office! David Fischer...principals office...Now!!*"

My friends weren't meeting me in the bathroom for drinks. My friends weren't even in school. Lewis was probably in bed with a girl, making phone calls to his stock-broker. Zee was probably at home with his new honey, cutting a block of Moroccan black hash into individual grams for sale. For us, school didn't matter. In the big picture of things, school was just an obstacle we had to navigate around on the road of real life.

CHAPTER TEN

I didn't mention the week-long suspension to my mother. Considering how little I attended class anyway it wasn't any different. In truth, it was a big relief. I didn't have to pretend to impress anybody in the stupid fashion show. Zee and I could get back to our usual routine of getting wasted and wandering the city.

As usual Zee's parents were away in Europe or Asia. His older sister and brother had moved out long ago. The pouty-lipped girl answered the door.

"You're David Fischer," she said.

"In the flesh," I said.

"I'm Allyson. Call me Ally."

"Back alley?"

"Cute. Not." I shrugged my apology. "How come I didn't get into the fashion show?"

"I wasn't a judge."

"Sharla Unger only picks her best friends anyway, everyone knows that. I don't know why I even bothered in the first place." She turned her pout down. It was sexy as hell somehow.

"I thought you were good."

"You weren't even in the room when I auditioned."

"I wasn't?"

"Nobody was. Sharla and her buddy Miriam barely even watched me. But thanks anyway."

"There's no reason why you couldn't be in it. It doesn't mean anything, really. It's just an obnoxious popularity contest."

"Finally talking some sense, eh?" Zee said, coming to the door still in his pajamas, lines of bed sheets were embedded into his face, his rock-star hair lay flattened out like the wall of china on one side, windswept on the other, like he was walking at an angle to the plane of the earth and might, at any moment, topple over.

Ally reached back and found Zee's hand without looking. It was instinctive; the kind of knowing that grows out of hours of intimacy. It was a knowing I hungered for, and wished I could have with Kris. It was an intimacy that had been gone from my household for years, long before separation, long before divorce. Something happens to you when you grow up in a cold, distant environment. You either become that same cold distant person, avoiding human contact from anyone, or you seek intimacy and love from someone else like a fix you can't get enough of. I got a big taste of it from Kris – more than I ever had from anyone; I wanted more so badly. Zee pulled a joint from his pajama bottoms pocket.

"You sleep with that?" I asked? He licked it and lit up, took a long drag, and passed it over.

"Wake 'n bake," he exhaled.

We went to the diner for breakfast, which was actually lunch for most people. Ally got up to excuse herself and I asked Zee "So, you two an item or something?"

"An item?" he said, pushing his lips together. "What's that – like a product?"

"Spending a lot of time together," I said.

"My life's philosophy doesn't put a limit on how much sex and fun I can have with someone I like. Ally happens to share the same belief system."

"I don't get it," I said. "You get laid all you want, nobody knows about it, the girls stick around. Me, I have sex once and it's a social misdemeanor. Kris won't talk to me. Sharla thinks I'm an ass...."

"So what?" he said scouring the menu.

"And now it's impossible to have another chance with Kris since you undressed her with your eyes telling her in no uncertain terms how much you'd like to have what I had. How do you think that makes her feel?"

"You care about her feelings?"

"Yes."

"The new David Fischer," Zee laughed.

"Shut up," I said. "You could pretend to give a shit!"

"Who called Lewis about getting laid?" he said. He still sounded sore about it. "Nobody knows about *my* sex life because I don't make it anybody's business to know. That's how I like it and that's how women prefer it."

"*Women?*"

"Your problem," he paused to sip his coffee, "stems from the fact that you need to live your life out loud. And *that* stems from your desperate need for attention."

"I don't need attention."

"Why did you call Lewis?"

"It was my first time."

"And it mattered."

"Yes."

"Exactly," Zee sipped his coffee. *"Otzma Enoshit."*

"Ain't no shit?"

Enoshit. Otzma enoshit. It's Hebrew. It means *Human Strength.* It's one of the motto's of the IDF." By looking at me Zee could tell I wasn't following his insider jargon. "The Israeli Defence Force? The Israeli army, dumbshit! That's what you need. Human strength. *Otzma enoshit.* You have outer strength. Christ, just look at you – you're built like a thoroughbred. But it takes inner strength to be a strong person. That comes from discipline. You have the potential. You just can't see it." Zee was right. He wore his hair like nobody else and he didn't care. He went to school when he felt like it and got good grades without blinking. And he knew me better than I did.

"I wanted you and Lewis to be…"

"Order something,' he said, channeling his inner Jewish mother. " Put something in your stomach, make you feel better."

Ally approached the table with Nancy, the waitress.

"Look who I found," Ally said.

Zee smiled politely. I held up my hand in a wave.

"Wow. So. Suspended, huh?"

Zee's eyes widened. "Suspended? This is something you don't need to tell me?"

I shrugged.

"I gotta tell you," Nancy said, "it wasn't the smartest move in the world, but I admire you for it. It's been a long time since anyone put Sharla Unger in her place."

"It was mean," I said.

"It was true, David. I'm in that class, too. Not that you would notice. She was boring the hell out of everyone! You just spoke what everyone else was feeling, that's all. She could use the constructive criticism. And if she can't take the heat..." And she pointed to the kitchen. "Get out." She and Ally slapped hands.

"Thanks for saying so," I said.

"So? What're we suspended from?" Zee asked.

"Everything," I said. "School, the fashion show."

"WHAT?!" Zee slammed his fist down on the table, silverware and glassware crying out in a single metallic rattle. Neighboring tables turned to scowl at the commotion. "UNACCEPTABLE!"

"It's Sharla's show," I said.

"That's what she wants you to think," Nancy said. "Actually, the show is a product of the school and the whole student body. Sharla doesn't know shit."

Zee gave Nancy the look of approval – he checked her out head to toe. He made no secret or excuse for what he was doing. Ally shifted in her seat. She raised the menu to her face. "Can we order, please?"

"I like the way you think," Zee said to Nancy. Nancy blushed.

"Zee?" Ally said. "Food?"

"I'm too pissed off to eat," Zee said. Ally ordered fruit salad and granola. All girls were on diets, I decided. I had the Denver omelet with sausage and home fries, bagel instead of toast, juice and coffee.

"Wow," Nancy said. "You always eat like this?"

"He always eats," Zee said. "Gimme a lox and bagel, extra capers, hold the onions."

"That doesn't make any sense," Nancy observed.

"You're a waitress or a critic?" Zee asked.

"She's both," I said.

Nancy left with our orders and me with a smile on my face.

"So, you're some kind of hero, now, eh? Took down the famous Sharla the Great?"

"Something like that."

"Ahh, she's just a cry baby with a hot body."

"She's incredibly beautiful," Ally said. And something about the way she said it, the way she looked out the window in a far-off way; there was sadness to it. "It's not fair, you know. The girl's so beautiful and it's all people can talk about with her. She can be the biggest tight-assed bitch on the planet and everyone forgives her for her looks. What a waste."

"What's the waste?" I asked.

"It's like, she can do no wrong because she's so perfect," Ally said.

"Oh, she can do wrong," Zee said. "She can kick my pal out of her fancy little show."

"I thought you hated that show," I said.

"But I loved that you were in it. You were my representative. I was in it with you. It's how I met Ally."

Zee put his arm around Ally and pulled her close. "Sharla's just a face," he said to Ally. "She doesn't have what you have: Soul, heart, sexiness." Ally collapsed with glee into Zee's body. You could tell she never got this kind of affirmation from a guy before. Zee could do that. He could make someone feel special and mean it, because he never lied about his feelings. It was an amazing thing, but it was true. Zee never lied about his feelings.

"Listen to me," Zee said, pointing. "You have to get back on that show. You gotta get yourself a girl. You gotta fill that hole Marcy left. Don't think I don't know what you're carrying inside you. You think your whole world falls on your shoulders, like it's your fault or something. You can't keep feeling sorry for yourself. Get back on that horse, man. Right, Ally?"

"Absolutely," Ally said, giggling into Zee's chest.

I spent the next two days and nights hanging with Ally and Zee, smoking joints, watching television and draining his parents' liquor cabinet. My Thursday night meeting with my father came and went. I was too wasted to notice.

CHAPTER ELEVEN

"NO BIG DEAL?!?!?" Lewis' eyes were wide marbles. We were standing in his heated, terracotta stone driveway. "What did I tell you? Like a rock star, baby. For both of us. Shit, you're such a dumb virgin."

"Not anymore."

"You still think like a virgin." He stormed off towards his house, then turned and stormed back towards me. "You can't let these people run over you, David. They're not your friends. They don't pay your rent! It's time you learn who in this world is worth taking shit from, and who you have to stand up to!"

My father had never spoken so directly to me. To boost me up when I was down, or scared, my Dad would tell me stories about the men who came before him – my ancestors, my heritage. There was my great grandfather Ruben – on my mother's side; they called him Ruby – who smuggled food and weapons in and out of a ghetto in Lithuania during the first world war; there was Hayim Krovetsky, my father's paternal grandfather, who killed three of the Czar's soldiers, escaped a Russian work camp and got his family out of the country. These men had guts. I never met them and they never gave me man-to-man talks. My Dad delivered their stories. He was the bearer of their legacy. My father was tender-hearted; he was a soft-spoken dentist who loved helping people. He had no real wars to fight - just a marriage.

Lewis Cohen – a lanky, carefree, seventeen year old chain-smoking playboy – was filling in where all the father figures in my life had vacated. He and Zee were my stand-in parents.

"At least do it for me.," Lewis begged. "Please. I can't be tutored forever."

I pulled away and looked at him. He closed his eyes, shook his head.

"That bad?"

"Big nose, long neck, she's an ostrich with tits."

"Good tits?"

"Perfect! Are you crazy? Gravity-resistant," Lewis said and grinned. "But what we need to concentrate on is you. You need to win your honor back."

"My honor?"

"You've been excommunicated from the Kingdom of Babe-a-licious! We have to get you reinstated."

"I kind of screwed it up with Kris."

"Who?"

"Kris. The one…. I called you."

"What are you talking about?"

"I called you after I was out with Kris to tell you I lost…" I remembered school, the ninth grade girls. I lowered my voice. "…lost my virginity."

Lewis stepped closer, "You got the card?"

"I didn't have sex with Sharla. Her name is Kris. You were dreaming about Sharla when I called…." Lewis listened. He looked confused.

"Why are we whispering?" he asked.

"I want to get back with Kris."

"Who?"

"From the show. The one dancing."

"Oh, yeah," Lewis said enthusiastically. "You should go out with her. She's into you, man."

When I reached home I saw my father's good-mood car in the driveway. He had two cars, a practical jeep sport utility wagon with lots of cargo space and a flashy 1972 Porsche 911. He kept it garaged, cleaning and polishing it in his spare time like a collector's item. *'Twenty five years, that's what defines a classic'* he always said. Later in his life he would claim that it was the only investment he ever did well in.

If it was the Porsche in the driveway, it meant he was in a good mood. Maybe his wife was with him. It wasn't beyond him to bring her around to the house, where my mother still lived a single mother life with two kids, one of whom, Beth, was always screaming for her and my father to get back together, the hope of it burning holes inside our hearts. The more we hoped, the deeper the holes grew.

Beth's hole was a well. With a well there is possibility. With a well you could dip your bucket down and miraculously pull up something wonderful, like water that tasted like a mountain stream; or a long lost toy; or healing.

My hole was a crater. With a crater you could see everything and see that everything is gone; with a crater there is no mystery and no hope. I took my crater inside to meet my father.

One day we were a happy family of four. We sang songs in the car on drives to the country. We had family pictures, everyone smiling. My Dad was proud, he worked hard, he could fix things, my mother took care of us, made sure we had nice things, good food, good teachers.

And then it was over.

My Dad sucked in his pride. My mother started barking orders. Everything was backwards.

I felt duped. Like I'd been tricked. Me and Beth, too – as far as I could tell. Anger doesn't explain itself, it just morphs from one form to another. We had safety. We had a promise of something good. We had a happy life.

And then somebody shut it off, as suddenly as if we hadn't paid the electric bill. Like a family TV show that got cancelled.

Over.

It sucked. It sucked so bad. And I had no idea how to handle any of it.

Then, one day, ninth grade, someone handed me a beer. I drank it. I felt better. Way better. I had found my solution.

My father stood in the kitchen talking with my mother. It was weird seeing the two of them together in the same house. They gave that up. I couldn't have them building a well where I had so painfully accepted my crater.

My mother scowled when she saw me and gave my father's arm a quick pat, her signal that he was now on duty. Then she left. My father looked troubled. He wasn't comfortable being the disciplinarian.

"You want to tell me what happened at school?"

"And hello to you," I said. I was going to give him a hug but I decided, upon the instant interrogation, to go up to my room instead.

"David…?"

"Same old stuff."

"You want to cut the crap, David? You got suspended."

"Oh, that."

"Oh, that," he repeated. "What happened?"

"Ah, it's stupid. This girl, she got upset about something I said and they made a big deal out of it."

"Principal Fowler told your mother that you tried emotional bribery with him."

"What?"

" 'You're not understood….'; 'Our divorce has affected you….' Crap like that."

"You think that's crap?"

"I think your feelings are perfectly valid. I think that using them to manipulate people – to get out of taking responsibility – "

"Taking responsibility. Are you kidding me?"

"David, if you want to talk about it…"

"I have homework to do so..."

"It can wait. What's this your mother tells me about the other night? You took her car without permission? You were out until three in the morning. On a school night?! Then I call to get together Thursday night. You're nowhere to be found. Where were you!?"

"Which time?" I said just to be difficult. What was I going to tell him? That I was getting laid one night, smoking a block of hash watching *Lost In Space* the next? I reached for my door and headed up the stairs. I didn't want to get into the twenty questions. I wasn't afraid of my dad. He wasn't a threat that way. I was afraid I'd see him crack. I'd feel responsible for doing that to him and I couldn't handle that.

"I'm asking you a question," he said.

"Hey! You've got your flashy new wife, your flashy car. Hey – go with it. But don't think you still have a foothold planted here."

I slammed the door behind me. I didn't care if he cried after all.

My father knocked on my door. It was never my father's style to barge in unannounced. The way I remember it, it was at my mother's hand that I suffered all indignation – eating a bar of soap when I cursed; spankings; screaming – that was entirely my mother's work. My Dad pretty much played good cop. I never considered that it was because he lacked the guts to be stronger. I always gave him the benefit of the doubt that he chose a kinder, softer way.

The way he tells it, my Dad came from a long line of really tough guys. Like his Dad, Hank Fischer, my Papa Hank, who found his business burned down and his money gone. Arson, he said. The cops didn't believe him. So he built his business back from nothing. And when it was all back and running, he went looking for the guys responsible for ruining him. He found one. He beat the crap out of him and left him for dead. He left him to tell the others what happened.

Nobody ever bothered my Papa Hank again.

I wanted to be like my Papa Hank. I wanted to be like my great grandfathers, Ruby and Hayim. I wanted to be that tough guy. I had no idea how.

"All right," he said after I let him in. He found the edge of the bed and sat on it. I covered the mattress with the duvet, pulling it over the stains from my nights alone.

"I'm sorry for busting your chops straight out," he said. "So. Let's hear it. What's going on? How's everything in your life? Man to man."

"Fine until you."

"Get over it, David. I apologized. Now talk to me."

"Fine."

"Where were you Thursday night?"

"Nowhere."

"David, your mother caught you driving home at three in the morning on a school night. You need to tell someone when you're going to be out late. You had her worried sick."

"What, do I need like an ankle bracelet – so you can monitor me? Is that it?"

He looked down, sighed again. I took the hidden meaning of that sigh and ran with it, the self analysis I could do on my own. I must have been the most helpful son two parents ever had when it came to reasoning with myself about what a jerk I was being. I just didn't do anything about it.

There was a part of me that wanted so badly to grow up from being a teenager and be accepted into the 'real world' that I was willing to let go of common teenage pride in order to get there sooner. I pulled out a book and pretended to read. I was just biding my time. My father raised his head. He squared his shoulders in decision. "David, are you doing drugs?"

"No," I lied.

"Are you having sex? Were you out with a girl?"

This is the moment when the big 'gross' and 'oh-my-gods' come gushing forth. Parents aren't supposed to know about their kid's sex lives. It ventures out of the safe zone of parent-child nurturing and into the red zone of 'none-of-your-business'.

"I'm not having this conversation with you," I said. It sounded so mature. I read the next page with a big proud grin.

"What conversation? You're not saying anything."

"That's right. Get used to it."

"Okay. You don't want to discuss it. Just let me tell you, if you are having sex, I hope you're using protection. You don't want to get any young girls pregnant who might want to keep the baby and make you a father before you're twenty."

"Did you do that?" I asked, curious.

"What? No! Come on, David. Get laid. Sew the oats. Enjoy. The girls at your age, they're all fresh and full of wonder. It's a great time to be sexually active."

The way he said it: 'Sexually active'. So clinical. So dry.

"Please, Dad..." Please lubricate your language. Please, if you're leaving leave. "I don't want to talk to you about this, all right...?" Now he pulls out the parental probe. You know, they cock the head at an angle, look at you up from under, getting in your face that way parents instinctively know how to...

"You really like this girl, don't you," he asked.

And just to mess with him I say:

"Who said it was a girl?"

His lips tighten. He tries to get the joke but his manhood, his ego – *His Son*!!! He stood up, brushed off his pants, then thought better of it, faced the door, turned.

"Call me when you feel you're capable of having a real conversation. Not this immature, childish... whatever it is you think you're accomplishing. And you better call. I don't like being stood up as much as the next guy – I mean girl. Just call me."

I felt like shit. I dropped a false bomb on the guy and it wasn't fair. He was the parent who had to leave. He didn't get to live with his kids anymore because he volunteered to abdicate. He was strong enough to move out and my mother wasn't. It was a shitty deal.

Now my father stood before me, a little hunched, heading out of this house again. It's almost three years and Beth won't take his calls, won't go over to his house, won't accept his new wife.

My sex life was less than a week old and already it was an issue. In my house everything became an issue. Nothing could just be allowed to happen, everything had to be probed. We had to consider the consequences. Of what? My dick in some girl's vagina? What were the possible consequences?

Death, said a voice in my head. It wasn't my voice. The voice belonged to an older Jewish man with an Eastern European accent. Ruby? Hayim?

'What?' I ask the voice.

Death, it says. The accent – Polish. Near the Russian border.

I have sex, the consequence is death?

Is she clean? You know where that vagina has been?

It's not like it's been dragged across the streets! It didn't come out of a bargain basement bin!

There could be disease. Gonorrhea. VD. Your thing just falls off! And then what?

She's clean!

You know this how? Has she been examined?

Examined?

By a Jewish doctor. Not one of those goyishe medical students finished last in their class.

Seriously, this is my life. I'm telling you.

Another voice: *You know, she's not Jewish.*

A *Shiksa*! (This is said with both horror and elation, an almost impossible combination except in the imagination of a seventeen year old Jewish boy.)

Yes, I tell the voice.

She's a Kraut? A Polack? Rusky?

No. She's a nice girl.

Sure, nice for shtupping. But for a wife? Feh!

These conversations really happen in my head. No kidding.

I listened at my window to the sound of my father's Porsche engine rev its classic parts up to a gravelly purr. I heard my father shift into reverse. I heard the high whine of the motor backing out of the driveway, the relaxed hum of neutral, shifting into first, a screeching of metal as my Dad mis-shifted, grinding the gear into second, then third, then purring off into the distance.

I told him I was having sex but not necessarily with a girl. My poor father who takes everything to heart. I could tell him the sky was green he'd think my eyesight was off, have me checked out, check the hearing too just in case, you never know.

In seventeen years I'd never heard my Dad mis-shift in that Porsche.

CHAPTER TWELVE

Lewis answered his door in an unbuttoned shirt and his belt loose. His hair was disheveled. Naturally, he was smoking. He looked at me as if I were a Jehovah's Witness who had interrupted his porno movie. He reached out, grabbed me by the shirt and pulled me inside.

"I'm being tutored," he said.

The alleged porno was actually 'A Midsummer Night's Dream' and all the fairies and nymphs and Bottom with his ass-head…

"The ostrich loves this stuff. You should see her, Man. The body on this girl!"

"I thought you said she was ugly."

"Nah – just a big nose. But the body – My god! And does she ever love sex!"

"But can she teach?"

"I can say 'I love you' in five different languages."

"So this isn't a good time."

"Nah, you're here. It's all right. She'll have to settle for only twice today. Keep her coming back for more."

Just then the Ostrich emerged, buttoning up a black blouse that hung out over Levi's. I could see both the bulge of her ample cleavage packed into a lace black bra and the soft ripples of her flat stomach muscles. She could have posed for the Sports Illustrated swimsuit issue.

Lewis pulled the Ostrich close to him. "David, this is Lara. My tutor. Lara, this is my very good friend, the one, the only, David Fischer."

Lara smiled. Her eyes were a light caramel color under shoulder length, dirty blonde hair. They looked at me from either side of an enormous Roman nose. "Hi," I said. Lara placed a hand on the small of Lewis's back, whispering in his ear something about the time. He leaned his face into hers. She dropped her hand to his butt. He turned her around and walked her towards the door.

I watched him take her coat from the closet and bring it around over her shoulders. He tugged at the coat lapels, pulling her into him. She wrapped her lips around his and kissed him long and hard, the kind of kiss designed to make you never forget and need to call in minutes.

Lewis walked me to the kitchen where he poured us both a glass of scotch and Perrier. He added a lime. It was a nice touch.

"I think I'm into a new genre: Ugly girls." He raised his glass.

"Lewis, she's not ugly! Not even close. She's got a great body, beautiful eyes…"

"Yeah, but that nose…. It just kind of messes up everything. Like a bad drawing, you know what I mean?" He left the kitchen. I followed down the hall. Lewis kept talking, excited about his new discovery. "That's the thing, though, Dave. Ugly girls, their body's get passed over because of their faces. I blame society for misguiding our tastes." We were in the den now, the same den where I tried to dump Marcy. We leaned back into the leather chairs. Beside the chair was his father's cigar box. He lifted the lid and pulled one out. "Want one?" I declined. Lewis plucked one of the cigars from the box. He pulled out a drawer from underneath the cigar box and extracted a stainless steel clipper; with surgical precision he snipped off the cigar tip like a mini circumcision. He replaced the clipper and brought a lighter to the fat end, puffed and puffed on it until the cigar's end glowed red. Finally, Lewis leaned back and continued his dissertation.

"The result is an abundance of girls considered unattractive by today's standards; girls walking around with amazing bodies, aching to be touched. They don't know what to do with them because they've never been given the chance. Beautiful girls, like Sharla Unger, for example...."

"Why is she always the example?" I interrupted.

"Pick a better one," he said. I thought of Kris, but didn't say anything.

"Beautiful girls grow up with all the attention, guys constantly hitting on them. Naturally, they learn to keep it away. Hiding the fruit. Follow?"

"Yeah." I lit up one of his cigarettes.

"What're you lighting a cigarette for when you can have a cigar?" Lewis sat up, he turned his head to look at the cigar box. "That's what I'm talking about, Fisch. You have Cuban cigars in front of you, hand rolled in Havana, yet you choose the machine rolled, factory-packaged cigarette. You have a Sharla in front of you – ."

"I don't," I said.

"She's teasing you, Fischer! Hiding the fruit."

"There is no fruit!" I yelled.

"No fruit? Are you stupid?" All I could do was sigh. Lewis persisted. "She's into you, man. She gave you high marks in the audition. She rates the looks, the attitude, body and sexiness."

"Seriously?"

"She's got a scoresheet. You had her in the palm of your hand. I mean, how did you ever get into that girls pants and then blow it with her?" He still didn't get it.

"Lewis, are you deaf? I never did it with Sharla." He stared at me. Lewis blinked a couple of times. I could see the realization was finally sinking in.

"Come on, Fischer. Don't do this to me."

"When I called to tell you I got laid, you were having a dream about Sharla and mixed her name in with the real girl. It wasn't Sharla. I never did it with Sharla." Lewis was quiet for a long time. Then his eyes watered up. "Lewis…?"

"Just give me a second," he said. "This is difficult to take in... so you didn't lose it?"

"Yes. I did."

"With who?"

"Someone else."

"What?! You can't lay that news out there and then not tell. Who's the girl?"

"The first time I told you, you immediately blabbed it all over school so Sharla thinks I told everyone I did it with her. I'm not telling you twice."

"I'm sorry. I was just so happy for you."

"The truth is I'm not even sure I'm interested in Sharla."

"Not interested?" I shrugged as if in apology. "Must've been some first time, eh?" he grinned like he knew my secret. "I've seen it before: The cherry-buster afterglow. You're on a pink cloud right now. Because you crossed into that other world. You got into the club. Enjoy it. Savor it. Because eventually, you're going to need to get more. The way vampires need to suck the blood of young nymphs. That's why you have to get back into that fashion show. It's a vital well-spring. Besides, she even rated your package.'

He puffed his cigar.

"How? She's never even seen it."

"And at the rate you're going, she never will." He pointed his finger at me. "I'm here for you, my friend."

"She rated my package?"

"High numbers, David. High numbers." I glanced down at my lap, wondering what type of fashion show director rates a guys package while feeling, I have to admit, a little proud.

CHAPTER THIRTEEN

The coffee at the diner was weak and hot. Still, night after night I found myself there, same corner booth, talking to Nancy.

"I think you're over thinking this thing," Nancy said. "I mean, did you ever consider the possibility that you can have a healthy, happy one night stand? No mess? No emotional hangover?"

I looked at her sideways. I never saw Nancy as the type for flings. "Don't get any stupid ideas Fischer. All I'm saying is, relationships are messy. I've got enough work between school and this job and my family. I don't need another guy's problems to deal with, on top of it. I'd like to just meet a guy who's confident enough to not worry about where he's going to fit into my life. But, since I haven't met that guy yet, I get my kicks listening to infantile boys whine about how they can't score the woman of their dreams."

I looked out the window and watched the buses with their multi-flavor of people roar by. Why did the problems of my little world matter so much?

"I'm not that guy," I said. "Maybe Lewis or Zee can see what they like and take it. Me, I don't work that way. I wish I could."

"Jesus, Fischer. Does it ever stop being about you?"

"What do you mean?"

"You know exactly what I mean," Nancy said. I did, too. Nancy was opening up to me about her life and all I could think about was getting mine. "How you hope to be with anybody is beyond me," she said and she walked away. That hurt, I gotta admit.

That's when I saw Kris on the bus. I couldn't believe it. I thought I had memorized every person who rode the late night bus on this route. The same people sat in the same seats in the same order on the same bus at the same time. Always.

Kris had a way of disrupting the order of things, she really did. The doors of the bus opened at the corner stop, and Kris walked off.

I was expected to go on to college, be a doctor or a lawyer or something. Anything. I could be a dog walker but I had to be the guy who turned dog-walking into a million dollar a year business. I'd be knee deep in dogshit and my parents would be oh so proud. But the only thing that I aspired to was convincing this girl that I was worthy of her love!

Kris glided into the diner. Where other girls were sexy, Kris was sensuality in motion. She was comfortable in her own body and knew how to show it off: high heels, short skirts, tight tops. My pecker was brainstorming escape routes beyond the zipper of my jeans.

I waved to her. She gave a blank glance my way and looked elsewhere for a seat. Something had to be done. My *schmuck* meter was running high with this girl. I was desperate to repair the damage.

So I stood up, erection and all.

"Hi."

"Hello yourself", she said, eyeballing my stature. "Something on your mind?" she added. I stood there, maintaining the embarrassment because she was worth the prize. An elderly woman nearby coughed into her chicken soup. Kris came over, lowered herself into the seat, slid along the Naugahyde and settled across from me, all in one easy motion. Even the way her head turned gave me the distinct humbling sense of being in the presence of a lady.

"I'm sorry."

"Why?" She might as well have asked 'what the hell's the matter with you?' We were so not on the same page.

"For the stuff I did. At school. You know." She looked at me like I was a Martian that had just farted. "You know, my friend Zee, slapping me on the back, yelling what a score I'd had." Her face went south.

"I didn't think you'd actually take me through it again."

"I'm sorry. I was a jerk. I admit it. Try the Reuben. It's the best thing on the menu for the money." She cocked her head to one side.

"You're a funny guy," she said, examining me.

"That's what people tell me."

"You hate being wrong, don't you?"

"What?"

"Yeah, you've got some ego on you." She said as she perused her menu.

"I'm confident."

She laughed. "No you're not."

"What're you talking about?"

"I see the way you are at school. You love people to watch you. You love being the center of attention."

"I don't tell people what to pay attention to."

"But you expect it. Because you need it. And that's pathetic."

"Right. Like I wake up in the morning wondering how much attention I'm going to get."

"What if people just didn't like you? Or, what if people didn't notice you at all? Would it matter?" I never thought about it. The idea seemed dismal.

She reviewed the menu more leaving me hanging on to her next word. When she looked up again, with those amazing eyes, she said "You've got more going on inside you than that, David. But you have no confidence in yourself. So you act like you think you should. You try too hard to be something you're not."

"You think you know me that well?"

"I'm an excellent judge of character. I don't just see who you are, David. I'd never have asked you out if that was all there was to you. But I see who you can be. I like what I see."

"Why'd you get off the bus just now?"

"I was hungry." She dropped the menu and casually looked for the waiter.

"You didn't see me sitting in the booth? In the window?" She gave me that look you get when you're wasting someone's time.

"It is amazing to me how you see the world revolving around only you, David." I liked the sound of my name on her lips. I forgave her everything that minute, forgetting that I was the one who had to earn her forgiveness.

"I'm glad you're here," I said. "I missed you. A lot."

"Stop trying so hard. Just be yourself."

"Really? Even after…?" She put her hand up in a 'stop' signal.

"Order some food," she said. People kept telling me to eat. I reached for her hand across the table. She pulled it away. Then I felt something else… a stocking foot climbing up my pant leg.

It was still raining when we left the diner. The first cab that we saw stopped. He wore a turban and his cab smelled like curry.

"Where to?"

"Downtown…" The curry cab driver rolled his window up and drove away. I stood in the rain shouting obscenities while Kris laughed.

Another cab pulled over. A balding driver with a round face and two-day old beard. I let Kris do the talking and soon we were being driven to her place, but neither of us could wait. She had her shoes off and her stocking feet running up the inside of my leg. I positioned myself to accommodate her desires. She liked to be in control. I had no problem with that. I caught the cabby's eyes in the rear view mirror watching us. Watery, lascivious eyes. Kris was unbuttoning my fly.

"Don't you want to wait?" I said.

"It's the rain," she said, "It makes me wet."

"Rain'll do that," I said. I heard Cabby say 'Jeezuz' to himself. Kris grabbed my hand and reached it up under her shirt to touch her breasts.

The cab bumped on a pothole. My forehead bounced off her shoulder. Kris had to brace her hand against the interior ceiling. I glanced at the rearview. The driver had a shitty smirk on his face.

"Buddy!" I said.

Kris shot me a look: "What're you doing?"

"Hey! Buddy!"

The driver looked me in the rearview eye to eye. "You talking to me?"

"You want to take it easy on those potholes?"

"No problem."

"Thanks."

"Just... you two seem to be in a hurry." Kris didn't like this comment. But she didn't say anything. I couldn't let it go.

"Nobody's asking your opinion, all right?" I said, sitting up taller.

"You taking a mouth with me, kid?"

"I'm your customer. I don't want your nose in my business." Was it Kris? This bravado, this confidence? This stupidity? The cabby pulled over. He stopped and turned around.

"How about I ask you to get out of my cab!" he said.

"What's your problem you can't fulfill the simple task of driving to where we asked you to?"

"Hey. Just leave it," Kris said.

"It's raining hard out there," the cabby said. "You want to stay in the cab you're going to have to do me a favor."

Kris' eyelids went half-mast with the senses of a survivor. I felt her body temperature rise and her muscles stiffen. It was automatic – a trained reaction to perceived threat. The cabbie leaned forward over his seat.

"That's a beautiful girl you got with you, Kid. Rich punk like you must've paid for it but that's none of my business is it?" Kris held it back but I could feel her boiling. "Tell you what I'm gonna do. I'll just sit here and you two can do what you want to do. No potholes. No bumps at all. Nice and easy." The cabby's grin spread on his face, tight lipped. "I'll just watch." He shifted his gum to the other cheek.

Kris stuck her foot back into her shoe. She drew her knee higher ready to run.

"You two make such a nice couple," he said. He smiled at Kris showing off smoke-stained teeth. He reached out to touch her stocking leg. I grabbed at his hand.

"Hey! Back off!" I yelled.

He snapped his fist back, backhanding me in the chin. He caught me on the downward movement, catching all of my open-faced weight. The impact threw me back against the cab door. The Cabby was reaching over for his next grab when Kris unleashed the corked weapon – her heel – and mule-kicked into his jaw. I heard the cracking of bone. His stubble-covered chin snapped up perpendicular to his neck so he looked, for a moment, like a cubist version of himself, his eyes wide in shock.

His head landed on the back head-rest of his driver's seat. He didn't move. His eyes stayed wide. They looked blank.

"Get out," Kris yelled.

"What – what's – is he...?"

"Just get out!" she screamed and pushed me out of the car before I could get the chance to ask her where she learned that move.

We ran down the street, shoes splashing through puddles, click-clacking away from the cab, windshield wipers beating squeaky time across the glass, thumping against the hood.

Squeak, thump, squeak, thump, squeak thump.

CHAPTER FOURTEEN

Squeak. Thump. Squeak. Thump.

We were at it with a hunger. The rush of the night's events pumping through us as we made animal love on Kris' bed.

Squeak thump.

The cabby's creepy threat, his fist in my face.

Squeak thump.

Kris' heel, his cracked jaw.

Squeak thump.

She might have killed him.

I didn't care. All I cared about was being with her in acrobatic glory; her on top, then me, climbing over and around each other, tasting and caressing every inch of each other. Pure ecstasy.

Candlelight flickered along the walls, across Kris' model photos and pictures of her family. All of them watching us now.

'*Yes, hi, I'm David. I'm with Kris. Lovely picnic this is. Is this an annual family thing... Oh? Just tonight? Well, I have to go back to making love with your daughter now. Save me some corn on the cob. Thanks.*'

Kris looked impossibly beautiful, her eyes almond shaped with pleasure and her mouth softly shaping a moan. I had been told that women have *that* face -- when you are in the midst of giving them real pleasure. Now, seeing it firsthand, it is a thing of beauty and it made me even more excited.

In contrast, *my* sex face took on a terrified and shocked appearance, as if I was facing my death.

Kris' back arched and her butt tightened. Every muscle in her body clenched and relaxed and tensed again. I held on and stayed with her, riding her wave. We clenched together, stiffened and moaned and climaxed together.

We slept beautiful, exhausted, love-worn sleep.

I woke to coffee. It was still dark out.

"Morning," she said, handing me the warm mug.

"Time to go?" I asked, and I reached for my shirt.

"Mmm," she said and touched my face delicately. "Maybe. Maybe not."

"Are you happy?" I asked – again, I didn't know why, the words just spilled out.

"Happy is irrelevant," Kris said. Her eyes flickered. It wasn't a blink. It was an inner camera shutter snapping open and closed in a millionth of a second, impossible to see unless you were looking for it. Something about the idea of *happiness* exposed a vulnerable side of Kris. She cracked and covered. It wasn't supposed to happen and I wasn't supposed to see it.

"Cream?"

I watched Kris' naked body move to the fridge, bend to retrieve the cream and return to the bed; and I never wanted to leave. I should have been content, savoring the moment, like Lewis had said. But something anxious moved within me and made the words come.

"What makes it irrelevant?" She poured the cream into my mug.

"Just what I said."

"You know what I think? I think you're afraid of committing to – ."

"Look!" she snapped, "I didn't grow up with your money and your cars and your judgmental attitudes. So back off!"

"Hey, I wasn't – ,"

"Judging? The hell you weren't. You're constantly judging. And not just me. Everyone. Yourself included. Just watching you is agonizing. The level of self-consciousness you operate on would tear most people in two. And then you turn it on me and I feel the burn of that critical brain inside that beautiful head of yours, wondering if you can bring a girl 'like me' home to meet the parents."

She let the comment hang out there like dirty laundry. I stammered to defend myself but nothing sensible came out. Kris read me better than anyone I'd ever known. And better than I knew how to lie. I reached out for her hand and she let me take it. I pulled her towards me. Holding her close felt better than breathing.

"I think you're a great guy, David, don't get me wrong. But you need to understand something. I come from a small town.

A poor working mother, a step-father.... I left home early. I had to. Our step-father...," she looked away, recovered.

"Kris...." She pulled away.

"And you expect me to feel for all of your problems – your parents didn't love you enough? The perfect family unit fantasy was a lie? Yeah, it is a lie. Because, you know what? It *is* a fantasy. I live reality every day of my life. My little sister's only twelve and she's braver than most people I know because she still lives at home and.... god, you don't know. You get upset, you grab a drink, drown it away, right? For me, forgetting is a luxury. Anybody can drink themselves into oblivion. I know. I've buried some of them. But I won't do that with my life. I can't. I'm twenty years old. I've worked since I could add numbers. I have a whole life ahead of me if I want it. But I can't afford to mess up. Not if I want to grow old. And I like the idea of growing old." She smiled briefly, considering the old lady she hoped to be and liking her already. "I'm not a fan of staying in one place for too long. I think we can have fun together, David, but that's all it's going to be. One day, I'll be gone. Don't try to get deeper into me or anything else because that's just not happening. If you can live with that, great. If not, there's the door. Just... don't push me, David. You probably won't like what you find."

"Okay." I lied. "I just... I really just want you to be happy. With me. You know?"

"I know," she said, cupping her hands around my face. "Just don't expect anything. Please. That's all I ask."

"Okay."

For the first time I realized how much I needed Kris' approval and her love. What I felt for her seemed like love. In my experience love was a combination of being completely safe and nakedly vulnerable. If Kris needed affirmation, it wasn't from me. Her independence frightened and intimidated me and made me want her approval all the more. Which is why, when she asked me what I was doing for the Christmas break, I invited her to my family's cottage.

CHAPTER FIFTEEN

"No fucking way!!" Zee yelled. The cottage was our sacred haven almost three hours North-East of the city in rural countryside surrounded by trees and lake and the stars at night. It was where we went to escape urban blight and parental scrutiny. Whatever happens there, stays there. For Zee and me, it was sacred. Until Kris.

"I've been looking forward to this since the summer and you're taking this *shiksa*!?"

"I like her!"

"She took your cherry, man. That's all."

"It's more than that. We've been hanging out together."

"Oh. Well. That *does* sound serious." He lit up a joint. I sipped my Jack and coke. "The point is it's a tradition – just the boys. No girls."

"Not this time."

"So let's make it a foursome. Me and Ally, you and Kris, just the four of us, kickin' back... a little mellow, sophisticated partying. Wine and weed." The truth is I didn't know if Kris would kick back with a drink and a joint. But I was pretty sure she wouldn't kick back with Zee. Not after the way he leered at her in school.

"It's just going to be me and Kris this time."

"It's a bad idea, Fisch. You're pushing for too much too soon."

"I'm going with Kris."

"Don't send a postcard," Zee said.

I picked Kris up in front of her apartment building in my father's Jeep Cherokee. He was away with his wife for a week and let me have the car. She wore another turtleneck sweater under a sheepskin coat. She looked like she walked right out of an Eddie Bauer catalogue.

"How do you do it," I asked taking her bag and placing it in the back.

"How do I do what?"

"Get more beautiful every time I see you."

"David…" She began with a tone of caution, then, blushing, deftly redirected the topic. "You have a stable of cars I should know about?"

"My Dad's on vacation with his wife. I have his car." I pulled her close and kissed her lips. She smelled like daisies basking in morning sunbeams. Her face lit up.

"Come on! Let's go! I haven't been on a road trip in ages." She bounced in her seat with excitement. "You know, I'm really a country girl at heart," she said. She popped a cassette into the car stereo and we headed north to Joni Mitchell singing about being free in Paris.

Two and a half hours, four coffees and six cigarettes later we arrived at the cottage. Snow was coming down in fat flakes, like we were in one of those glass-encased snowflake balls with the idyllic scenery.

The parking space off the road was blocked. Probably some jerk guest from the hotel down the road. Too drunk or too lazy to move it. Kris and I got our things out of the Cherokee and locked it up. I pulled out pen and paper and wrote a note, then slapped it on the intruder's windshield like a ticket.

"You can't write it any more considerately than that?"

"He's parked on private property, Kris. I mean, duh. There's a house right there."

"You don't know where they're coming from," she said, tearing up the note. "Maybe they wanted to take a moonlight walk and saw an opportunity to park. It'll be gone by the morning. Now, stop being a trouble maker and take me inside."

The cottage had a cabin feel but also the feel of a house: wooden structure with cathedral ceilings, a deck overlooking snow-capped evergreens and the frozen lake beyond; a fireplace commanded the main floor, opening into the carpeted living room which evolved into the terra-cotta tile-floored kitchen.

Off the other side of the living room space was the master bedroom, also boasting a cathedral ceiling and picture windows that ran the height of the tallest wall looking east to the lake.

Kris' eyes popped. A silent eruption of pure bottled joy escaped her lips. "Wow," was all she said. She walked down the stairs from the entrance landing. I stayed on the landing and watched. I did not feel above her or feel her below me. Kris had shined a spotlight on the differences between us, and the cottage was certainly one of them. Yet, for some reason, her coming here with me made me admire her even more.

Kris walked to the center of the living room. She looked at the fireplace, then went to the windows and looked out onto the lake, her thin neck craning to count the stars gathering in the night sky. She went to the sliding glass door that opened onto the deck and pressed her nose against it. Her hot breath left frost on the pane in the shape of her lips. Watching Kris take in the cottage was like introducing a non-believer to heaven, and watching their entire ideology accept the emotions of bliss for the first time.

Kris threw her hands in the air and twirled, her red scarf and hat spinning with her, the little girl inside her set free, unafraid and glorious.

I built a fire while Kris prepped dinner. It took a couple of hours to get some heat going but soon the air was filled with the smell of burning maple and ash logs and broiled sirloin steak. Kris made a salad of peppers, carrots and garlic.

"Good for the blood," she said, sucking on a clove. I pulled out a bottle of red wine.

"*Wine* is good for the blood." I pulled the cork and went to pour. Kris placed her hand over the glass.

"You need to let it breathe. Let the air mix with the wine and open the bouquet."

"What bouquet?" I asked.

"The wine needs the air to bring its flavor out. It's called letting the wine breathe. Wine should enhance the meal. Not just enhance the brain."

"It'll enhance more than that," I said, grabbing her around the waist and chewing on her neck.

"Watch it. I have a knife," she said waving it. "Now sit down." Kris perused the table she had prepared as if it were a Martha Stewart presentation. I poured us both a glass of the wine. She stopped me halfway. "Give it room to breathe," she instructed. She swirled the red liquid in her glass. The wine rose up its walls. "Now watch." She stopped swirling and set the wine on the table. The wine settled and made its way down the inside of the glass in lines. "Those are called legs," Kris explained. "They indicate what kind of texture and consistency the wine has. Is it a full bodied vintage or is it light and weak?" I swirled my glass, too. I watched the legs travel down the insides of the glass. We studied each other's glasses closely. "Looks good," I said. "Now," she continued, "stick your nose right in it." She showed me how, pushing all of her nose inside the wine glass and breathing in through her nostrils.

"My nose is bigger than yours."

"Just get it inside the glass as far as you can and smell the bouquet that emanates from the wine as it breathes. That means, as it gets exposed to oxygen in the air which helps the flavors bloom." I did. I smelled what I thought was asparagus and autumn rain. She explained that I was discovering the elements that went into making the grape. "All living things share the earth," she said. "Wine grapes share the soil with other vegetables and fruits and elements like iron or sulfur. They all go into the flavor of the fermented grape."

"You could give a wine tasting class," I said.

"Now, sip the wine and breathe in over it so that you kind of bubble or gurgle it inside your mouth. That's how you really taste the hidden flavors." She showed me and I copied her.

"Wow," I exclaimed. I tasted mint and apples with a hint of banana.

"Banana?"

"Maybe it was growing in some African soil," I suggested.

"Maybe you've got monkey brain."

"The guy who owned the house I grew up in before us had monkeys. He put their dung in the yard for fertilizer. We grew anything we wanted back there."

"So I was right. You do have monkey brain," she said.

"I've got monkey something. And you can't resist it."

"Gross. Now, let's toast to this wonderful meal. Raise your glass." I did. "To a fine young man, dashing, handsome and charming, thank you for opening your life to me. And thank the lord, Jesus, our savior for the food we are about to receive."

"Did you have to do that?" I asked.

"What?"

"The whole thanking god and Jesus and – it was a toast. You don't thank god or Jesus in a toast."

"Why not?" Kris asked, looking annoyed.

"You were thanking me for opening my life to you. That's a toast. Then you thank Jesus, like he has anything to do with it. I mean, seriously, we bought and cooked this food. You showed me the wine stuff. Let's just keep it between you and me."

"Don't tell me you're jealous of Jesus Christ, too."

She drew her knife across the meat, slicing into it like a surgeon. We ate in silence for a while. I cut into my steak voraciously and chewed and chewed.

"Did you know that red meat practically dissolves with red wine? The tannins and sulfates from the fermenting process work on the meat to break it down in your mouth."

She showed me, slicing a piece of steak and placing it delicately between her red lips. I watched her mouth work the meat. "Now the wine," she said and lifted the glass to her lips. She drank, chewed a little longer and swallowed. "Another small sip to wash it all down."

"Wash it down," I cheered and brought the glass to my mouth.

"Sips," she said, "with the meat."

I followed her instruction. With a small amount of red wine, the meat softened and went down with delicious ease.

"Wow," I exclaimed. "That's awesome."

"It's called culinary etiquette," Kris said.

"I keep learning from you."

"We learn from each other, don't we? I mean, isn't that what we are all in this life to do? Everyone we meet has something to teach us, even if they don't know what they're teaching and we don't know what we're learning, it still happens."

"So what do you think you're supposed to learn from me," I asked.

She leaned back in her chair, a cautious smile stretching reluctantly across her mouth. "I don't know.... Maybe I'm supposed to learn that not all spoiled rich boys are total assholes. Maybe I'm supposed to learn to trust my heart to a man again. Or maybe, after I get burned again I finally learn my lesson about dating younger men who don't have the same uphill battle to climb as I do and can't possibly understand how significant a thing it is that I learned how to appreciate the finer things in life... like wine, like good food. I don't come from a world of expensive cars and cottages. I don't even rent them. I only go if a friend invites me and I don't have friends who could invite me."

"I invited you."

"The last time I was in the country I was fourteen years old. I was at a camp for girls. I learned how to canoe and tie knots and rig a sailboat jib. I canoed down rapids with three other girls and we camped outside in the woods for four days and three nights. The first night we cooked steak, just like this one, but no piece of meat has ever tasted as good as that one, cooked over an open fire, under the stars, on a grill we loaded in.

"I haven't lived that long, David, but I have lived. And from what I've lived through, I have learned to enjoy life each and every day. I don't take it lightly or for granted. I know that I'm lucky to have my freedom. I feel lucky to be here with you, in this wonderful place. Do not, please, do not think for one second that I am interested in you for money or popularity. Those things mean nothing to me."

"I never thought that you – " she cut me off.

"Let me finish. This is important. I have seen that these things can be important to you – and I'm not judging you. I'm not."

"Feels like you are."

"I'm not. I just want you to know that… I care about you. I like you – I like who you are. The rest is icing. So, please, don't let this exterior stuff get in the way."

I smiled in agreement, but felt something powerfully sentimental coming up inside me. She could see the emotion on my face and paused, watching me with curiosity, giving me permission to unload.

"I spent my childhood summers here," I said. "My family. My friends. It was magical. And that's been gone for a long time.

But you're being here… it's like… it's like you're bringing new hope to my life."

Kris looked nervous. I was alluding to some kind of unity and her kneejerk reaction was up. It killed me.

"Look, you told me to just be me. This is me."

"I know. And all this stuff, this superficial, what's in your past stuff… I do like you for you. I'd be with you if you were living in a tent under a bridge."

"No, you wouldn't," I said.

"Okay, maybe not a tent under a bridge. But a cardboard box in a roofed shelter."

"Nuh uh."

"A studio apartment with a small fridge and a hotplate, going back to high school at age twenty…"

"That's why I love you."

I said it out loud. For a moment Kris stopped breathing. Imperceptibly, after she exhaled, she allowed her shy girlish smile to show.

"You don't have to say it," I said.

"David… let's not spoil a good time. Okay?"

"Right," I lied. I poured myself a very full glass of wine and drank it like water.

The fire roared orange and hot. We were entwined in each other, one body blending into the other, impossible to tell where she began or I ended. We made love with the flames licking their colors by our skin. The tickling heat sent shivers through both of us as we rose and fell, rose and fell through the passion.

Shivers rippled through me; she clenched and held me.

"Oh god..." I managed. A warning.

"Shh," she whispered. "Easy, boy."

I struggled to hold on. She slowed her breath. I slowed mine. She gazed up at me; blonde wisps lay across her face like the rays from an angel.

"David," she said.

"What?"

"I just want to say your name. I wanted to hear myself say it."

"Say it again," I said.

"David."

"I could listen to you say that forever," I confessed.

"Say mine," she said.

"Kris."

"Softer. Say it like I'm not here, like you're with someone else but you're thinking of me."

I closed my eyes. "Kris," I said. "Kris... Kris... Kris...."

"David," she said. "Yes, David." She pressed her lips to mine as her pelvis moved like waves lapping the shore. Kris moaned and I felt the shivers return. We convulsed together in ecstatic release. For that moment, we were as one. An old familiarity crept through me: a sense of home, a sense of safety. A home I had never been to, but a home I knew, the way eagles know they are meant to fly.

The fire dwindled while the cold air sifted through the cracks of the old wooden walls. We cuddled against the chill the way wolves sleep in tight packs. I thought of how wolves mate for life. I squeezed her tighter, holding her from behind. Being with Kris felt right. I didn't dare tell her that. She might laugh at me again, and I couldn't take that kind of rejection, not at the cottage where I had no place to hide my feelings.

"Too tight," she whispered and pushed my hands away. I let go of her and rolled away. "I'm cold," she said. I went into the bedroom and brought out old sweatshirts and a wool blanket. Kris pulled it on. Her hair hung messily over her face. It only made her look more desirable.

"Something to drink?" I asked.

"Tea," she said.

I lit a cigarette, put on the kettle for her and fished out a bottle of scotch from the liquor cabinet hidden in a bench.

"Do you have to," she said?

"It's a vacation."

"I want you with me."

"Where am I going?"

"Just… take it easy. Okay?"

"Hey," I said, "you don't know what this place is for me. This is my getaway. This is my sanctuary. Only the people who are closest to me can come."

"I'm honored," she said. "So, let's be together."

"You have no idea."

"You said that." She wrapped herself up in the sleeping bag and waddled over to the kitchen table. "I'm hungry."

"But it's important that you know that."

"I get it," she said.

"I just want to make sure you understand where I'm coming from. This isn't normal, me just bringing someone up here."

"What do you mean?"

"The way I feel. This is hard for me." I opened the bottle and poured myself a full sized glass of courage.

"What's so... David, don't. Please."

"Just to...." I took a sip. "I don't just invite *anybody* up here, you know."

"I understand that – "

"Can I finish?" I snapped.

"David, what's wrong?" If there's one thing I hate, it's when someone asks me what's wrong. Kris had no intention of pressing the button but the way she asked, there was something so condescending about it.

"Nothing's *wrong*!" I sipped my drink. The sip turned into a gulp. "Why can't you just listen to me? Why is that so hard?"

"I'm listening."

"I'm trying to *explain* to you!"

"Go ahead." The calmer she became the more patronizing it sounded.

"You know, Kris, it's not my fault that I have things. Or that my family has things."

"I'm not saying it is."

"Then why did you make a point of it earlier?"

"Oh, David, that's not what I meant. I thought you understood that."

"Yeah but, now...with the... with everything...!"

"David, slow down and just talk to me."

"I can't. You won't let me!"

"What are you talking about? I'm right here. I'm listening!"

"That's just what I mean!"

"What?"

"*That!!*"

I took another gulp and it was over. It clicked inside. I had so much to tell Kris, and such fragile words. I couldn't. I choked. I broke.

"*God...dammit!!*" I yelled. I poured another double shot into the glass. I was building up the defenses, my wall against pain. It looked good going in, watching the glass fill with the golden scotch. I couldn't wait to drink it. Kris backed away to the couch. "*What?*" I yelled again. When Kris spoke, she was very subdued. Almost monotone.

"I just want you to know, David, whatever's bothering you... I will listen. But I can't heal you."

"What's that? Some pop-psychologizing bullshit?"

"If you're going to be like this, I want to go home."

"You want to leave?"

"I want to enjoy this time with you. But we have an understanding. And if that's too hard... then maybe we should go back."

"You realize this understanding's just a little fucking confusing, right? I mean, one moment you're telling me you just want to be friends, then we're making love with more passion... then you tell me you want me to just be me, just be who I really am inside, as long as I don't mention the word love or anything about how I feel about you." I started to laugh, the whole scenario just seemed so absurd. "I mean, you basically encourage me to be as raw and real with you as possible and then you slam the door on it! It's fucked up, Kris!"

"I think you should calm down."

"I AM CALM!" I was chaos in flames. The black empty was taking over.

"Okay, David. You win."

"Whatever. Screw this, I'm going outside."

"You'll freeze."

I lifted the bottle in defiance. "Hey, I live for the cold. It's why I come here. It's probably why I'm here with you. I mean, I open up to you and you just leave me hanging there. Like an idiot. You're the fucking ice queen."

"We have an understanding."

"You say one thing but you show me another. I don't understand this understanding!"

"What do I show you? Affection? Is it my fault if I'm more..." she trailed off, thinking better of it.

"No. Say it." She shook her head. "Say it! You're more experienced! In everything! Go ahead! Remind me of how spoiled and immature I am! Tell me *again*!"

"You need to calm down."

"Yeah? You need to go fuck yourself!"

I chugged from the bottle, grabbed a coat and stormed out.

There's something about breathing ice-cold fresh air that brings your whole body to life. There's an infusion of alertness. My hands felt the cold first. I forgot gloves inside but wasn't going back. I tucked my hands into my coat pockets, stuffed the bottle in the inside pocket and zipped back up. Booze never gets really cold. If you keep it close to your body it can gather and regenerate the heat, adding warmth within the protecting layers.

The stone steps caught my feet as I climbed up to the road. Darkness. No street lights on a country road and the trees blocked much of the moonlight. I looked up at the trees and toasted them, looked up at the stars and drank to their health, may they light the way for weary wanderers today and tomorrow. I breathed in the cold air and breathed out my rage. It wasn't just Kris. There was something inside me that needed to come out. I didn't know what it was but I expected others to. Especially Kris. I had fallen in love with her, but I couldn't tell her, couldn't even mention it. It was killing me.

I reacted badly, I knew it. But I wasn't going back. When a man leaves a house, he leaves the house. He doesn't just turn right around and try and talk it out or apologize. I knew what I'd hear: *you shouldn't...you know better... you, you, you....*

I knew. I didn't care.

It was me and the black empty and we had drinking to do.

My feet crunched over the hard-packed snow. I slipped a couple of times. Took a run and jumped to a slide along an icy patch. I burst into a full run, arms and legs pumping. It felt good, letting it all out. I pushed it faster and faster, forgetting about the ice.

The oncoming lights that appeared from around the sharp turn were so blinding that I couldn't see where the road suddenly dipped. As the headlights bore down upon me I dipped forward with the road, head first. My arms went out instinctively and my left knee jutted forward to brace the impact. All I could see was brightness, brightness. When I saw the road again it was a millisecond before it met my face, before everything went black.

CHAPTER SIXTEEN

When you squeeze your eyelids shut you can recreate the stars. Popping lights, streaking lines. Blink, and it's gone.

When you come to you are reborn from the death that is black out. Black outs are moments without even subconscious awareness. Moments of your life that you can never get back. Never.

It's easy to do things to a person who has blacked out. You can reposition or relocate them by a variety of means. You can dress and undress them. You can write a story on a blacked out person. You can create an entire work of art with the body of a blacked out person. They wouldn't know until they came to.

When you come to from a black out you might find yourself in a different country. Or driving on the wrong side of the street. Or in a mid-air plummet to the earth from a tremendous height. You might find parts of your person removed. I once passed out on a floating mattress in Lewis' pool. I must have fallen off the mattress into the water. When I came to, I was underwater. The disorientation was frenzied, no up or down or sideways. I clawed frantically at the water, certain I was drowning. Water has scared me ever since.

This time, when I came to, I was on my back. Ontario December air was blasting against my face and teeth. I sensed someone standing near me.

"Took a good hit," the voice cut through the cold.

My eyes rolled to locate the source. Pain shot through what felt like every vein in my eye sockets. I tried to move my head. Lightning bolts ripped through the base of my skull and down my spine. I was certain my eyeballs were filling with the red cracked lines that form cartoon-like over the whites when we're tired or just been hit over the head with a sledge hammer, which is what I felt like. I couldn't stop the yell from coming out.

"Take it easy," said the voice. My limbs were almost numb. There was enough feeling in them to figure out that I was not hurtling through space, but that I was, instead, flat on my ass on the hard, cold gravel. Besides, not a lot of people talk you through your life-ending plummet through space. Not unless…

"Oh, god…."

"Not today, amigo," the voice chuckled.

I managed to move my arm against my left ribs. My hand touched a sticky, cold wetness. I brought the hand up to my eyes. Even in the darkness I could tell it was blood.

"Chivas Regal. Shame. That's why I go for the plastic bottles. 'Course I wouldn't waste my money on this overpriced shit."

"Who – ? Who – ?" I asked. I looked around. My head throbbed.

"Took a bad fall, amigo. Had to drag you out off the road. You just laid down there like fuckin' road kill. Drunken idiot."

My eyes caught it then, the deep-purple-ish truck accented with shiny chrome hubs and pipes. I could see a pair of jeans reflected in the mirror-shine of the chrome mud-splattered hubcaps; muddy work boots, dirty from the job, whatever the job was.

"Fell on the glass," the voice explained. "Wasted a whole bottle of scotch on your sweatshirt. My clothes are jealous." Laughter. Laughter into smoker's coughing.

"I need a doctor."

"Nah," said the voice. "Probably did more damage to the road. Not that anyone's gonna notice another pothole on this stretch. Not until there's a real accident. You know nothin's getting' done 'round here 'till it affects someone with money. You got any money?"

"No."

"All you cottagers have money."

"I'm not – not a cottager." Still couldn't see the guy.

"What's your name, kid," the voice asked.

"Where – where am I?" I avoided the question.

"Ah, I'll just read it off your driver's license here." He had my wallet. "David Fischer. That's a Jew-type name, ain't it, amigo?"

"Who are you?" I asked.

"I'm your friggin' guardian angel, Kid. That's who I am. You were running like a girl. I came over the hill just in time to watch you face plant. Slammed your head against the road like

you had a disagreement with it. Nasty. I dragged you off so you
wouldn't get run over. Been stayin' by you makin' sure you wake
up."

"Should I thank you?"

"Depends," he said.

"On...?"

"How you were raised." He had a high pitched laugh, like
a witch's cackle.

"Will you tell me who you are, so I can properly thank
you?"

"Not so sure you're gonna wanna do that, but....," He
reached a hand out to shake. I took it. "The name's Fred. Freddie
King. I'm known around these parts." It was hard to make out the
features of his face in the darkness. His face was narrow and he
had some kind of moustache, or so it seemed. He stood behind me,
so the steel toe of his boots was right next to my head. I could hear
the soles of his boots grinding gravel.

"Help me up," I said. He didn't.

"I know who you are," he said, leaning closer. His breath
was sour with beer and cigarettes. He was practically on top of me
with those steel toe work boots. Kick a head with those, you'd
kick it right in. "Think you can come up to my town and party your
ass off like you own the place. And I gotta find you passed out in
the middle of my fucking road like garbage the coons got to."

He squeezed my hand tighter, bent over me so I could see
his face. Light brown hair with peroxide blonde highlights sat high

on his head and then hung low in the back only. The kids from the suburbs and surrounding towns – some of them had their hair like that. Mullet. We called it hockey hair. Fred's hair framed a pock-marked face. The cheeks were hollowed. The eyes were bright and set a little wide.

"You can thank me later," he said, flashing a smile and squeezing my hand hard one more time before letting go.

He wore a Van Halen T-shirt underneath his jeans jacket and winter coat, both unzipped. Fred also sported what you could call a cops moustache, one of those rectangular jobs with no imagination to its shape. A patch of hair that serviced the skin above his upper lip like a patch of tar over a crack in the road.

"Where you livin'?"

"Toron – ," he cut me off sharp.

"I meant, which house are you partying in?" he asked. Which one? I must have looked confused because Fred suddenly lost patience. "Where the fuck're you staying?" His breath was so sour it stung. I started thinking about Kris. Was she okay? Was she still there?

Did she leave?

If he knew where I lived, he would find Kris. I didn't see how that would be a good thing. I tried to sit up.

"Forget it," he said. He pressed his boot down on my chest. I collapsed to the ground. "I know," he said. Then the smile. "She's a beauty."

Blood pumped so fast to my face I got a pounding headache. All I could see was this guys hand on Kris.

"What did you do?"

"I employed neighborhood watch. I asked around, see which house you belonged to? Mentioned that there was a drunk asshole lying in the middle of the road waiting for a car to run him over. The babe down the stairs here claimed you," he giggled, enjoying this. "Welcome home."

"You knew this was my home?" I asked. "Then why…?"

"No more questions."

"Is she….?"

"She's fine. And I mean, fine." A smile crept across below the moustache, "Tastes good, too."

I jerked up hard and got a reinforced steel toe to my chest. My head cracked against asphalt and ice. Sharp edges of little stones dug into my skull. It felt like a hundred little daggers slicing towards my brain. I brought my knees up, pushed off with my hands, somersaulted backwards, my neck rolling over the little stones until I was standing. I was bleeding, I stank of scotch, but I was squaring up against the guy, puffing like a bull. Fred laughed, that goddamn laugh.

"Man, you're one protective boyfriend, aren't you?" He stood relaxed. He was shorter than I thought. Small framed. But taut. "I'm just fucking with you, bro," he said. "We had a nice talk. Kris, right? I don't think she's too happy with you right now."

"If you even touched her…!"

"What if I did?" he challenged. He sucked his teeth and shifted his weight to the left leg, jutting his hip out like he was practicing a hockey check.

"I have to get back," I said. I moved stiffly towards the stairs to go back inside. Fred stuck his arm out. He was smaller than me and thin, but his arm was like steel. It was like running into a turnstile post that wouldn't budge.

"Hold on," he mumbled, chewing on something. "Let's get something out on the table."

Fred's eyes were dancing. There was a wild look behind the pupil. He took his time with his thinking, examining the ground.

"I'm not the kind of man does favors for someone who comes to my country – this is my country, see. This is my turf. You come up here and shit all over it. You think we're all a bunch of stupid hicks…"

"Hey, I never said – "

"Shut up. You're better off not talking right now, trust me," he said, poking me hard in the chest. "This is my town. This is my home. Your girlfriend understands that. You don't. That's why she's not out here checking up on you. She doesn't want to see what an embarrassing fuck-up you are, and you don't want her to see it."

He dropped his arm. The look in his eyes adjusted. He shifted his weight again, distributing it evenly between both legs, as if composing his body for battle. "I see you again, I'll have something more to say." He backed off. But I wasn't done with him.

"What did you do to her?"

"You and I are done for now."

"The hell we are!" I stepped to him. He froze like a building, rigid, ready. "If I find out you touched her, I swear to god I'll – "

Fred stepped forward, quick, his arm shot out lightning fast and his fist connected hard with my face. My balance was off and I stumbled backward. I went down hard. He was on me, hands squeezing my head, knocking my skull against the stones. Once. Twice. Tiny stones smashing into the back of my skull. Pain shot through me until I went loose. A second later, he was kneeling on me, pressing the air out of my lungs. I could feel the cool air against raw flesh, where the skin had ripped.

"What did you do?! Just tell me what happened!!" I coughed. Desperate, crying.

He laughed. "That's the problem with you weekend drunks. You pass out too easy. Now you'll never know the truth about any of this." He stood up. "But I will," he laughed again and walked away.

"Don't think I won't come back for you, asshole!"

"I'm counting on it, David Fischer," he smiled, tossing my wallet and ID onto my chest. "Believe me, I am counting on it."

I heard him get into his pick up, start the engine and peel out of the lot. The wheels spun on the gravel and sprayed it backward, stinging against my skin.

The rear lights of his truck disappeared over the hill. Then the night returned, dark and silent. Except for the amber lights that burned from inside the cottage.

And Kris.

Even in my drunk and angry state I wouldn't have left the cottage door open. But it was. I pushed it open further with the usual creak. "Kris..." I called. "Kris!" Nothing. *Shit*!

What did that bastard do to her? Fred beat me bad and I was feeling it in every step. The pain expressed itself in a brewing rage. I wanted to strangle him dead.

I found her in the bathroom, huddled on the toilet. She was holding herself and shaking. When I reached for her, she recoiled, like a tortured puppy, terrified of anyone's touch.

"Take me home," she whispered. "Please."

CHAPTER SEVENTEEN

I helped her to the couch and covered her in blankets. I made tea and built up the fire. I didn't want to take her home. I wanted to grow old with her here, with grandchildren running around us squirting water guns and throwing themselves into our laps screaming *'tell us that story about the bad guy and the road again, Grandpa!'*

"You have to tell me what happened!" Kris stared out the window. She played the catatonic real well. She didn't look wounded. "Did he touch you? Did he hurt you?" Nothing. "He said you talked."

She snorted.

"What?" Silence. "I'm sorry I left. I – I was mad."

"You were drunk."

"Yeah," I admitted. I was still woozy, feeling the effects of the scotch, which probably saved me from feeling the full effects of the pain. Small favors. "I was mad, too."

" 'Cause you were drunk. And stupid. And unbelievably selfish."

"Yeah," I nodded. "Okay." Could we move on? "So...."

"So...?!"

"What happened?"

Her sea-blue eyes turned cold. Her face hardened into stone and in a very distant, matter-of-fact voice she said, "He raped me."

Tears welled in her eyes before overflowing in streaks down her cheeks. She wiped them away like an annoying loose eyelash. Her expression never changed: hard. She was far away. She had left me.

She had been taken from me.

In that moment, in her victimization, I loved her more than ever. But I was disgusted with myself. Disgusted that I was passed out on the road while he was taking her. Disgusted that it took Kris to be raped for me to feel this much.

"I'm going to kill him," I said. She snorted, more to herself than out loud. "I will! I'm gonna kill that motherfucker!"

"All right," she said, dismissively, clearly implying that I was way too chicken shit to do anything like kill someone. She knew it and I knew that she knew it. Still, I never expected what she said next:

"It wasn't so bad."

NOT SO BAD?! Like she was talking about a movie. "What – You liked it," I said.

"I've had worse." She flicked on the television. A local news anchor came on and announced the birth of twin calves to John MacGreggor of Sunridge. The entire news team at Channel 9 was happy for John and his family. Kris smiled.

"Kris," I reached over to her.

"Take a shower," she said. "You stink."

That was it. She wanted a man who would take control, I thought. The stranger who takes her, holds her down, controls her – that's the kind of guy she wants.

She reached for a bowl of popcorn she must have made while I was gone. *She made popcorn while he was raping her*! Absently, as the television cut to an appliance store commercial for washers and dryers, Kris dropped her fingers into the bowl of popcorn and mechanically raised them to her mouth. She chewed quietly as if not to disturb the balance of things.

"Kris, you okay…?"

"Take a shower," she repeated. "Then take me home."

"I'm so sorry," I said. I tried to hug her. She stiffened.

"Why?"

"Because," I said. "I brought you up here – I invited you. And the first night I had to get all pissed off because things weren't going exactly the way I wanted them to go. So I had some drinks. I got stupid. I shouldn't've left you alone."

"Izzat it?" her face was harder than stone.

"I needed to win your trust and I blew it. I… All I wanted, for once in my life, was a real girlfriend I could let myself loose with and trust and… and I look up to you. I do. I don't think I could ever be the kind of guy who deserves a woman like you. You've taught me so much. Just about being a man and stuff like that. Not that I am because I know a man wouldn't run out like that. Men do, they get pissed off and storm off and get drunk. And that's what I did, I guess. But I don't want to be that kind of guy, Kris. I want to be the kind of guy you're proud to be with. I want to make you proud."

She looked dead at me. Dead. Steel eyes. She spoke slowly. "I…was…raped."

She let it lie there between us, like a pool of festering waste that nobody wanted to step in.

Kris stepped in it. She stomped in it.

"I…WAS…RAPED!!!" Kris exploded.

She swatted the popcorn bowl across the room. It smashed against the stones of the fireplace. "RAPED!!" She kicked over the television.

"Easy, Kris…!"

"AND ALL YOU CAN DO IS WHINE ABOUT HOW MUCH YOU DON'T HAVE?! YOU'VE GOT A HOUSE AND A COTTAGE AND CARS AND PARENTS… AND I GOT RAPED!! I GOT RAPED!!"

"It's my fault. I know."

"NO IT'S NOT!" Wasn't expecting that. "No. It's not!! It's not your fault that I got raped! It's your fault you got drunk! It's your fault that you left! It's your fault for letting him know there was a house with me alone in it! But! It's not your fault that I was raped! That was his fault! Not yours! He did this to me! Not you! You couldn't do this! You don't have the guts! Now take me home!"

"What? I don't have the guts?"

"TAKE ME HOME!!" She moved to the kitchen and grabbed a beer from the fridge. "God! Does it ever stop being about you?!"

"It's not about me," I said.

"I get raped, your feelings get hurt. How is that not about you?"

"I'm not supposed to care about you?"

"Oh fuck you, David! You don't care about anyone but yourself!!" She started to cry. "Oh, Christ. Oh, god!"

"Kris…" I moved to her. She swung out and caught me in the gut. She threw an elbow to my ribs. Then she slammed her fist on my kneecap, right where the blood was still wet.

"You're a moron when you drink," she said. "Take a goddam shower or something. The smell of you is making me sick!"

I would never leave her again.

We were half way back to Toronto, driving in silence, when it occurred to me to take Kris to the hospital.

"No."

"But, you don't know if…"

"No!" She screamed and turned on me so fast I weaved into oncoming traffic and had to swerve the car back over the yellow line.

"What if you're pregnant?!" I yelled. "I feel responsible."

"David, you're the furthest thing from responsible."

A couple of hours later I was dropping her in front of her apartment building. I offered to help her bring stuff up, get settled in her place. I got the cold shoulder.

"I'll call you later. Just to check in."

"Don't," she said. "Don't call me again. Ever."

I watched from the sidewalk as the light came on in her apartment window. She closed the curtains but I stayed there. Thinking. She wanted a tougher guy than me. Someone who could take charge; someone who could protect her.

The black emptiness manifested itself in a focused rage. What I had to do was clear. Nothing in my life had ever been clearer: With more than a week left in my winter break, I would go back to Laketon.

I would find Fred.

And I would kill him.

My great grandfather killed Russian soldiers. My grandfather beat a guy nearly to death with his bare hands.

I could do this.

And then I would finish high school, get good grades, go to a decent college and do something meaningful with my life.

CHAPTER EIGHTEEN

As soon as Lewis opened the door to us, the next morning, Zee was on him.

"You're a fucking schmuck!" Zee said, barging past Lewis.

"Hey," Lewis said, following Zee's movement. "You can't just come barging in here...." Zee's look stopped Lewis cold. It was clear he didn't want to say any more than he had to and he had already said too much.

Lewis was still in his robe with only boxers on underneath. There was a fresh hickey on his neck. The sound of movement came from above. Lewis looked to the ceiling, his thoughts on what was up there, something Lewis clearly wanted to keep hidden. "This better be important," Lewis warned. He ushered Zee and me in, disapproving of our appearance: Zee's clothes hung off him from over-extended wear. His tower of hair was listing to the left, as if he'd been leaning against a wall for several days.

Lewis looked at me and his face changed.

"Jesus Christ, Fischer. What happened to you?!" Lewis meant the numerous cuts and bruises on my face.

"He's fucked," Zee yelled from inside. "He's totally fucked. And it's your fault."

"My fault?!" Lewis half whispered, half yelled back.

"Yes. You and your big schmuck mouth."

"Look," Lewis said, still signaling Zee to be quiet, "how dare you barge into my house screaming insults." Zee studied Lewis' rumpled clothes and the softness of his face, despite his increasing anger. Zee opened his hands in a gesture of forgiveness.

"Sorry for interrupting your morning screw," Zee said. "But your friend here is talking crazy. And if you don't order us some breakfast so we can sit and discuss how to handle his newfound lunacy in a civilized manner, I am going to slice your fucking balls off. Where's the coffee?" Zee sat at the kitchen table waiting to be served.

"Make yourself at home," Lewis said sarcastically. "Breakfast is already on its way."

Zee took in the house in quick assessment, his eyes listing from paintings, sculptures, and photos. "Nice place," he blurted.

"You have something against good taste?" Lewis asked.

"Never said it was good." Zee said, quickly finding the cupboard with the coffee mugs. There was more movement upstairs. Lewis glanced towards the ceiling at the sound of running water. He passed his eyes by me and I knew what he was thinking – imagining some girls naked body in that shower, the water running over her hair, her shoulders, her breasts.... Zee watched Lewis. He slid into a seat in the sun-drenched alcove where a natural-stained maple table sat amongst a collection of Bonsai Trees. Zee reached for one of the Bonsai branches.

"Don't touch that," Lewis said, a little too tensely.

"Yours?" Zee asked.

"My father's. He's really into that Japanese stuff."

"Very Zen," Zee quipped.

"Thank you, Captain Obvious," Lewis said.

The doorbell rang. "That's breakfast," Lewis said. "I went to the trouble of ordering for you when you called before, at seven in the fucking morning."

"You're paying," Zee said.

"That what you tell your little frump when you take her out?"

Zee launched out of his seat and was instantly face to face with Lewis.

"You want me to rearrange your nose?" Zee threatened. Lewis brought his ever-present cigarette to his mouth and exhaled into Zee's face.

"Take it easy, guys," I said as calmly as possible. These days I was either depressed or furious. It was the black empty or red rage that ruled me, and it could swing in either direction at any moment.

Lewis backed away from Zee. He pulled out a credit card wallet from his bathrobe and marched to the door.

"Who keeps credit cards in their bathrobe?" Zee observed.

Lewis returned with a brown paper bag. He laid out plates on the table, a couple of placemats and began to dole out the food. Zee got his eggs and bacon. I got my western omelet, extra sausage. Lewis popped open a container with cottage cheese and fruit.

"Health nut?" Zee asked.

"I like to treat my body with respect," as he lit up a third cigarette.

"I see," Zee said. He cut into his eggs. The yoke ran out in dribbles. "This isn't over medium."

"So," Lewis asked me, "Has anyone asked you what happened to your face?"

"I fell."

"He took that girl up to the cottage with him," Zee said. "Now she's not talking to him and he's talking about killing some guy up there." He slammed his silverware down. "You got coffee or what?"

Lewis looked shocked. "You actually took her up there?" Lewis asked. I nodded. "Nice going, Fisch. How'd it go?"

"Are you deaf? He says he wants to kill some guy," Zee repeated. "How do you think it went?"

"What's going on, Fisch?"

"You know where I can get a gun?"

"Maybe. What for?"

"Maybe?!" Zee exclaimed.

"I'm handling this," Lewis said. Then to me, "What's the gun for, Dave?"

"Something I have to do," I said, trying to act nonchalant.

"Rambo here's gonna kill some guy," Zee said.

"Anyone I know?" Lewis asked, trying to calm the atmosphere with a little humor.

"How is this funny to you?"

"How isn't it? He got beat up, now he wants to kill the guy…? And you think he's actually going to go through with it?" Lewis chuckled. That burned me.

"HE RAPED MY GIRLFRIEND!" I yelled.

"Who did?" Lewis asked, startled.

"Fred!"

"Who's Fred?!" Now Zee was chuckling at Lewis' expense.

"The guy who gave me these," I pointed at my scabbing wounds.

"Wait – who got raped?"

"Kris!"

"Who's Kris?" Lewis said.

I glared at him while Zee explained it all to Lewis. Again.

"So… he's pissed because the blonde got raped by some redneck psycho?"

"I told you," Zee said, "He's fucked."

"How would you feel if it happened to you?" I said.

"Thing is, Fisch," Zee said, "It doesn't happen to me."

"Acting superior isn't going to help," Lewis said.

"Fuck you, Lewis. You give him shit advice."

"I advise him on girls. Right, Fisch? He needs to get laid."

"He needs a hospital. He needs a shrink." Zee stabbed at the yolk on his plate with a piece of toast. "And he needs to learn to fight."

"What're you kidding?" Lewis remarked. "The guy's an animal."

"Physically, not mentally. Fighting is mental. In the IDF they teach you how to turn off weakness and become a warrior."

"What the hell are you talking about?" Lewis said.

"He wants to join the Israeli army," I explained.

"Why?"

"I don't know." I turned to Zee. "Why *do* you want to join the Israeli army?"

"How the fuck is that even relevant right now?!" Zee said. "Fischer here wants to kill someone. Zero to sixty psychopath developing before your eyes and you want to know why I want to join the IDF?!"

"What makes you an authority on David?" Lewis said.

"Hey," I said. "I'm right here!" But it was like they barely noticed: My surrogate parents, arguing over me while I'm in the room.

"Telling him to go after girls above his head – phony, snob girls like Sharla Unger."

"She's a five star sophisticated beauty. He deserves it!"

"You're setting him up for failure!"

"He's finally having sex! How is that failure?!"

"'Cause he got the shit kicked out of him by a guy who raped his girlfriend! That's how!"

There was a stirring on the floor above, then someone descending the stairs. Lewis closed his robe a little tighter. "I have company," he said. Zee crossed his arms and leaned back. His impatience with Lewis was leaking out of his pores.

Lewis' tutor, Lara, the Ostrich, walked in. She wore a halter under an open work shirt. Her dynamic breasts pressed against the fabric of the halter. Her flat, worked out abdomen dropped into the darkness of the loose fitting faded jeans. None of us noticed that she was crying.

"Take me home," she said to Lewis.

"We're kind of in the middle of something. I can give you money for a cab, though."

"Don't be an asshole," Zee said.

"Take me home," Lara repeated, this time to any of us. "I don't care who. I can't stand to listen to you another second. A girl gets raped and all you can think about is whose fault it is."

The Ostrich was speaking for me, too. Zee and Lewis, fighting over responsibility, playing the blame game; just like my mother and father. They fought over my mess, one trying to get the other to own responsibility for them. They were my mistakes, why couldn't I own them?

"I'll take you," Zee said. The Ostrich smiled shyly. Zee pushed out of his seat. "I need to get out of here anyway."

"No," Lewis intervened, "I'll take her home. She's my guest."

"Excuse me? Your *guest*?"

"Okay. Tutor."

"Wow. You're an asshole," she said.

Lewis shrugged and lit up another cigarette.

"Let's go," she said to Zee.

"He doesn't even know where you live," Lewis commented.

"Neither do you," she said.

"I'll come, too," I said, offering to tag along. Lara glanced at me dismissively.

"Who are you?" she asked.

"David," I said. "I met you here the other - ."

"Let's go," she said to Zee, tuning me out completely.

"Get your coat," Zee said putting on his own.

"Sit down," Lewis ordered. "I'll take her home."

"No, thank you," Lara said.

"What about me? How am I supposed to get home?"

Zee gave me one of his famous looks that could kill. "Walk. You only live like ten blocks from here. Meanwhile, Lewis, why don't you take some responsibility for this mess you created."

"That *I* created?!"

"He's talking about buying a gun."

"So what am I supposed to do about it?"

"Change his mind!" Zee said. "Because if you let him go off to try to kill someone, you're going with him, you understand me?"

"Maybe I'll help him!" Lewis said.

"Whatever," Zee said, offering the tutor his hand. "Come on."

"Hey, Lara" Lewis addressed the ostrich. "You go home with him, you're fired!"

Lara stood her ground. "You're failing anyway," she said, "and I'm not just referring to your academics." Then Lara walked out ahead of Zee.

"Go home, Fischer. Cool your head. I'll pick you up later."

I pressed through the fiftieth push up of my fourth set of one hundred. I'd done four hundred sit-ups and one hundred squats. I would lift free-weights for the next forty five minutes and then go for a run.

I was training.

I didn't allow the knock at the door to interrupt my flow. I grunted out the push up and in the same voice said "What!?" and kept myself lifted off the ground, sweat dripping from my nose onto the carpet.

My mother walked in. She took a spot in the room near the door and positioned herself there. "It stinks like a gym in here!"

"Then get out!"

"I'll make the rules here young man and I'll decide who stays where and does what in my own house!"

"Dad pays for this house, too. So until he gets here you can get out of my room!"

"You listen to me, David Fischer – ," she stepped closer. I jumped to my feet acrobatically, chest swelled, heart pumping. I faced my mother square, not bothering to adjust my boxers.

"No. You listen to me. I've had it with your rules. You can't even run a family, what makes you think you have anything to add to my life!?"

"There's no need to be cruel," she said.

"Life's cruel. Now get out!"

"Did you get that piece of wisdom from a bottle cap? Yeah, the working world's really going to welcome you into their fold. You talk like a thug, you act like a derelict and you dress like a... like a...."

"Like a WHAT?!" My penis had shaken its way out of my boxers without my knowing and was now poking out like a flaccid exclamation mark.

Wiggling her index finger in the direction of my groin, she said, "You might want to... ummm... put that...." And then she giggled.

I'm sure she tried not to. But the embarrassment of the situation overcame any attempt at control. Despite her anger, despite me sweating my inexpressible rage onto her broadloom, my mother pointed at my exposed penis and laughed.

By the time she realized what she had done, it was too late. It was a moment's laugh. But it hung between us now, the laugh and the penis, like an emotional gorge between two land masses.

Shame was a daily waking state in my house. We had joined the club of a growing national statistic – the broken home. For so long we had lived outside the reaches of that numeric fad; then we splintered – the parents, the children, the dogs and the housekeepers – we all plummeted from our fragile innocence. Someone had named something: Unhappiness, discontent. Someone had named it and the walls came crashing down. The family dream – gone. Idyllic summer vacations on the lake – gone. The happy family at the four top in the Chinese restaurant Sunday nights – gone.

Anger made it feel worse.

Drinking made it worse.

And now, even sex made it worse.

I was in a spiraling state of loss that I could not escape from, with no end in sight and my mother was laughing at my penis. I was living my own Greek Tragedy.

I reached for the nearest object – a shot glass. "Please. Get out."

"I just came to tell you, you have a friend here," she said.

For a moment I thought she was talking about my penis, still hanging there, eavesdropping on our fractured relations.

"What would you like me to tell him?" she asked.

She could not realize the depth of the wound. I was ruptured, bleeding internally in a place where medicine cannot reach. But words still eluded me. And where there were no words there was rage. Rage begets violence. I threw the glass hard. It bounced off the wall, and fell to the carpet, unbroken.

Another failure.

I couldn't even rage properly.

I stood there breathing like a Neanderthal man who had just come back from hunting and caught a field mouse, his wife and children looking at him from their cave, hungry and ashamed while his Neanderthal neighbors were barbequing fresh Mammoth on their backyard grills.

My mother searched the carpet for holes or stains, or any possible flaw she could lose herself in as she backed out of the room.

"I don't know," she said softly, "what is happening to you. I do not know who you are. I don't know how to help you. And that makes me very, very sad. You have no idea how much this hurts me."

Then she was gone and I was alone in my little apartment above the garage, separated from the rest of the house, separated from the rest of the family.

My deserted island.

I placed my hands down in front of the wall, kicked myself up into a handstand, my back leaning against the wall. From this position I pressed down from the shoulders, through the arms, raising my body up the height of the wall. I counted off one...two...three...four...

"Dude!" Lewis stood before me, upside down, smiling in a mystified way. "No wonder you're so fucking strong. I should be taking lessons from you." Eighteen...nineteen...twenty... "What's up, with your Mom? She's totally uptight." Twenty two... twenty four... twenty six....

Lewis took a seat on the bed and lit a cigarette.

"You can't... smoke... in here...," I said. Lewis exhaled in my direction.

"Christ, Dave...you're turning purple. You trying to kill yourself?"

"Not me. Someone else."

"Right. The country rapist."

I dropped back to my feet after thirty five and collapsed to the floor, sucking air.

"You want to talk about it?"

"Talk about what?"

"Your stupid plan?"

"I'm going to kill him."

"Yeah. Good. Who needs details anyway?"

"What's your problem?" I asked.

"My problem?" He laughed. "*My* problem? Okay, *my* problem is, my friend Dave's lost his fucking mind. First he lost his cherry, then he lost his mind. You want to kill this guy somewhere in god's country because he beat you up in front of your fling?"

"She's not a one-time fling. And he didn't just beat me up. He raped her!"

"Let me ask you something, David. How do you know?"

"How do I know? How do I know?! I was there! He raped Kris and he rubbed my face in it!"

"You watched?"

"No! I was knocked out. Outside. And he – "

"If you were passed out…"

"I didn't say I was passed out. I said I was knocked out. By him."

"You sure you didn't manage to knock yourself out? Because you know, Dude, you're pretty good at that. The way you hit that bottle."

"I don't need this shit right now! Not now!"

"All right. Calm down. I've been making some calls… and I think Sharla might be ready to talk about the show again. And maybe take you back in."

"Forget it." I said, grabbing a towel from the closet and going into the bathroom. I turned the shower on and let it steam up the small bathroom.

"It could be good for you. Focus your energy, know what I mean?"

"I said 'no'," stepping in and letting the water relax me.

"Sharla's gotten softer on the subject. You haven't been around… absence makes the heart grow fonder. The way you turned her down, insulting her in class, it's all been adding up. She's into you."

I pulled back the shower curtain. "No, she's not."

"She can't get you out of her head."

"Not necessarily a good thing," lathering my hair.

"The most beautiful girl in the school – I mean classic, drop dead gorgeous cover girl beauty is interested in you and you're not sure that's a good thing. I dunno, Fisch. Someone must have dropped you on your head when you were a baby 'cause I've got no other explanation."

I shut the water off and toweled myself dry. I stepped back into my room to change.

I opened a small fridge. Inside were bottles of water, beer and rye. I grabbed a beer and tossed one to Lewis.

I opened the freezer. A bottle of Stolichnaya vodka lay frosted over, a frosted shot glass next to it. "The thing is, Dave. How do you know she's not lying?"

"Who?"

"The chick you're so nuts about. Whatssername."

"Lying about what?"

"The way it sounds to me, she might be the type."

"What type?" I asked as I dressed.

"You know. Lookin' for a little sugar daddy pity."

"Say that again, and I'm going to whip you with this towel." I wrung the towel into a tight rat's tail.

"You've got no evidence besides her say-so."

"He told me he did it!"

"The rapist? Who the hell is he?"

"Fred."

"Oh, I see. Fred. Well that explains it all. How do you know they don't already know each other? What if you were just set up?"

"Why would they do that?" I asked. The towel tight in my hands, waiting for an excuse.

"Only reason people do anything: money."

I saw red before I knew what I was doing. I heard the crack of bone before the lights in my head came back on. Lewis' scream switched them on. He was holding his arm and crying in pain.

"What the fuck, Dave?! Jesus!"

"Don't talk about her like that. Ever. You don't know her."

"Neither do you!" The way he said it, like driving a nail into a coffin. He winced. "Jesus, you're really fucked up over her, man."

"Let's go," I said. "We've got business."

I put Lewis in the passenger side of his own car and I drove north to a place we called 'The Jungle'. It's the low-income housing community, which is a politicians name for *projects*. This is where we came to score when we didn't have anything, or when I was with someone other than Zee and needed to get high. The kids in the jungle knew what we came for and why we came which is why they ran us around sometime, selling us oregano instead of weed. They knew we wouldn't come back to complain to the management. For them it was a built-in clientele. All someone had to do was drive up in front of a particular building. They came up to the car like street salesmen. You told them what you wanted, and they usually just opened their palm to reveal the goods. But sometimes, if you wanted something else, you had to go inside.

I recognized the kid who came to the car. I'd dealt with him before. "Yo, yo, s'up bro? Ten dollars a dime, two for eighteen."

"Two for eighteen? What kind of shit deal is that?"

"Two dollars off. Bargain sales, yo."

"What're you – K-Mart or something?" The kid laughed. What I liked about him. "What's up Travis?"

"Same ol' same ol'," he said.

"Listen, I need something bigger."

"Bigger?" The kid looked at me funny. "As in weight?"

"Something more powerful. Something that can do some real damage."

"Yo, I only deal with smoke," Travis said.

"Something else," I hinted. Travis started to get it. Lewis looked at me funny.

"Fisch, what the hell're you into these days?"

"Wait here," I said.

"What? No way!"

"Keep it running," I said and I got out of the car before Lewis could fully voice his protest. I shut the door behind me. Travis, was cool, sixteen at the most, but cool as hell. We shook hands like we would on the court.

"I'm looking for something real. I need protection. You know where I can get something like that?"

Travis caught my drift. He was used to talking in non-committal references. You never knew who was listening. "Yeah, I can get you something like that. How much you got?"

"Three hundred."

"T'ree hun-dred," Travis said in his Island accent. "That can buy you some options. Come. I introduce you to the man."

I looked back at Lewis watching from the passenger side, curious and a little scared. This wouldn't be the first time I did something really stupid on his watch. Like the time I jumped out of his car going forty five miles an hour because I thought I saw Marcy walking up the street. It wasn't Marcy, but the girl was impressed enough to give me her phone number. Lewis had to admit it was an effective pick-up move.

Lewis was shaking his head 'No!' but I was walking inside. If he was going to come with he would have to leave his car out front and there was no way Lewis would leave his car unattended in the Jungle.

Travis brought me inside one of the many three-storey, yellow-brick apartment buildings that made up the jungle. There were at least twenty of them. I counted once while I was waiting for a pick-up. Travis opened the re-enforced glass doors of the building and led me down a yellow-lit hallway. The place smelled of ammonia, oregano and cigarettes mixed with refreshing scents of Jamaican cooking. We walked downstairs to a darker hallway where failing fluorescent lights flickered eerily against cinder-brick basement halls.

We came to a metal green door. Travis knocked in a particular rhythm I later realized was a signal. A panel in the door slid across, a set of dark brown eyes peered out, spotted me then Travis. "Whatchoo wan'?"

"Customer here," Travis said.

"What's ee wan'?"

"You know. He's cool." I felt like I was being pampered in a store, taken care of like a regular customer. I gotta admit, it felt good. I was already thinking of reasons to come back.

"Come," the eyes said. The door opened. Standing behind it, square-shouldered, muscular, with enormous biceps and a tattoo of a chain around each one, was my salesman. I extended my hand to shake. He looked at me like I was weird. Then he nodded his head at one of his guys in the back, standing in a shadowy part of the room. An even larger man stepped forward. He placed his hands on me. My heart jumped. The guy patted me up and down. When he was done he nodded to the muscular host who nodded back and my frisker disappeared back into the darkness of the room.

"Yo, Travis say you cool, you cool. But you be cool or this shit don't go down, you understand me?" I nodded. "Ar'ight," he said. Nodding to my extended hand he added, "We shake after." His name was Chain and I was not going to argue with him.

Travis and I followed Chain into in adjacent room, behind another door. At this point, I was so far underground and behind so many doors, if they took me here I'd never be found. But I wanted what I wanted so I kept following my hosts and trusting that it would all turn out okay.

Chain reached into a closet and pulled out a small duffel bag. He unzipped the bag and began to lay out some options on a fold-out card table. I couldn't believe what I was seeing: semi-automatic rifles and handguns, six-shooters, nine millimeters. And the names – Colt, Smith and Wesson, Glock, Sig Sauer – stuff I had only read about or seen on television, but never up close, and my expression must have shown it.

"We got us a virgin, here," Travis said laughing. I laughed, too, trying to be a good sport, but I couldn't pull my eyes away from the selection of firearms. When Chain was finally done, there were about twelve guns lying in front of me. I reached for one and was immediately stopped by Chain's "Ah, ah, ah. You point, I hand it to you. That's the way. I don' wan' see you get hurt," he said, looking at me sideways.

"Are they loaded?" I asked.

Chain looked at me hard, then he laughed. "No, fool. They not loaded."

Seduction was a word I reserved for sex, but the options of power and force that lay before me redefined the term; .22's, .44 magnum – Dirty Harry's gun; .38 special. There was a sawed off-shotgun, an assault rifle, and an Uzi.

I pointed at the .44. Who wouldn't?

Chain shook his head. "So, you want to be the Dirty Harry, eh?" he said as he picked it up, released the chamber and spun it to show there were no bullets inside. He handed it to me like that, chamber hanging out. The thing weighed a ton. It was bigger than my hand. I needed something small, something I could conceal easily. I needed a gun I could take a man out with and get rid of easily, leaving no trace. I pointed to it. Chain's eyebrows raised and he handed me the Sig Sauer P230 single action with an empty 7-round clip. "Small," he said.

"Easy to use, easy to lose," I said. "How much?"

"T'ree fifty."

"For this little thing?" Chain nodded. "What about for the magnum?"

"Five hundred."

"The Uzi?"

"Seven hundred. Special price for you."

"I don't have it."

"You don't want it, you don't have to pay."

"No. I want it. The Sig. Will you take Three hundred?"

"T'ree fifty."

"I only have three. Take it or leave it."

Chain smiled. He extended his hand for the gun. I slapped the money in it. He counted it and, once he was satisfied, smiled. "Now we shake." He clasped my hand in his meaty palm. He could have crushed me whenever he wanted. "Travis is right," he said. "You cool enough."

"You think you could throw in a little nickel bag of some good stuff? Something for the way home?"

"Travis," Chain said, "take care my man, here." And he did.

When I returned to Lewis' car there was a small pile of cigarettes next to the driver's side window. I slid into the passenger seat.

"What the hell took you so long?" I reached into my coat pocket and pulled out a small bag of weed.

"Gotta wait for the good stuff. Otherwise they stiff you with that seedy homegrown crap." Lewis nodded; he'd been stiffed before.

"You're driving," Lewis said. "I don't feel well."

I settled into the driver's seat, trying to adjust to the weight of a concealed gun resting against my ribs.

I punched the gas and maneuvered traffic like an Indy 500 racer.

"Slow down!" Lewis asked.

"You afraid?"

Lewis turned in his seat. "You just passed a Volkswagon rabbit with two hot girls in it and you decide to punch the gas at the yellow light instead of pulling up next to them!!?" I didn't care and he caught it. "You wanna be a loser the rest of your life, that's your choice. I'm still in the game so please try not to mess it up for me."

"I'm just gonna drive to Kris'."

"Not in my car," Lewis insisted.

"What do you have against this girl?"

"She's just using you, man. Wake up!"

"I am in love with her!"

"No, you're not."

"How do you know?"

"Dave. When you've been around..."

"Oh, right. You can just wake up and tell because of your vast experience. You know, Lewis, you don't know the first thing about girls. They're just objects to you. And you sure as hell don't know Kris."

"Has she called you? Has she even checked up to see if you're okay after the beating you got? No. Why not? Because she's just playing you."

"Or maybe," I said, "it's because she was raped and she's possibly just a little upset about it."

"Has she called to ask you for comfort?"

"Why would she? Man, your tutor has you pegged. You are one insensitive asshole."

"Get out of my car!" Lewis said.

"What – did I strike a nerve?"

I pulled over and got out.

"You've met one girl – one girl – and you're changing for the worse," Lewis said. "You don't know what girls can do to a guy but this girl is doing it to you."

I waved Lewis off, swatting away his opinion. Lewis slid his lanky body over to the driver's side and put the car in gear.

"I may not be the kindest, most sensitive guy in the world, I admit. But when it comes to women, I do have some experience that could be useful to you. Maybe, just maybe, you might want to listen." He put the car in gear, checked the lane for merging. "Knowing you, you're going to have to take this one all the way to the bitter end before you figure it out. And honestly, Fischer, I don't like where it's going. You don't know what you're getting into."

Lewis drove off and I walked twenty blocks to Kris' building with an illegal handgun stuffed in my pants.

CHAPTER NINETEEN

"Come on, Kris, don't shut me out." She was on the other end of the intercom. I could hear her clicking on to listen. "Can we at least talk?"

"Talk," she said over the speaker.

People walked past me on the sidewalk. Some slowed to listen. This was Queen Street West where everybody watched everybody. There were store-fronts and bars and cafes everywhere in the neighborhood. People came down to this part of town to walk, shop, party and watch. It was a character feast. Punks, Mods, Emo's and hippie rockers mingling with tourists - rich kids slumming; middle-aged Eastern European businessmen hanging out of their run-down furniture stores; private school girls hoping to attract a brooding artist. Older, lascivious drunks and prowlers watched them all, licking their lips at the prospects, sexual preference not an issue.

One older, thin man with a dangling cigarette to match his dangling eyes, swayed in place studying me, undressing me with his mind.

I jabbed at the intercom. A guy with a gun shouldn't have to wait to be let in.

"I did a terrible thing." I waited. Silence. The street crackled with activity behind me. "I'm sorry. I'll do anything." The gun in my pants. *Anything.*

I slumped to the stoop step. School was going nowhere. The fashion show was a bust. Rumors had spread. I didn't care what people knew about Sharla but I was very protective of Kris. Her private life was precious to her. I understood that now.

The intercom crackled. Just for a second. Then came that high-pitched, mechanical buzz of the door being electrically opened.

Kris cracked opened the door quietly. She was wearing her usual jeans and t-shirt with her bare feet exposed. Her hair was a little wet and she smelled of floral scented shampoo. I breathed her in. She was so beautiful I wanted to cry. She stayed in the doorway, keeping the door closed a crack, looking as jaded and cynical as possible.

"Can I come in?" I asked. I had to clear my throat. I wanted to hold her close, protect her; I wanted to promise her that nobody would ever hurt her again. Not on my watch.

"What are you doing here?"

"I came to… I need to talk to you." My throat was tight. "I mean, I was hoping we could talk. Can I please come in?"

"No." And she closed the door a little bit so her face was barely visible. "Did anybody follow you?"

"Who would follow me?" The way she was behaving, it was as if it was me who raped her. "Listen, he can't hurt you anymore. I won't let him." Kris let out a tight laugh. "I'm going to make things right. I'm going to take care of it."

"What are you talking about, David?"

"What am I – ?" Was she in shock? Denial? "Kris, the cottage...?" She looked down at the floor. "Look, I don't want to talk about this in the hallway."

That's when I heard the cough from inside Kris' apartment. Kris shifted her eyes away, then back at me.

"You should go," she said.

"Who's in there? Who's with you?!"

"David!" She took a deep breath. "We had an understanding." The distance between us suddenly made sharp sense. But the sound of the fridge door squeaking open inside her apartment did not. Kris shrugged. "I only ever just wanted to have a good time."

"But...." I could hardly form the words. "I brought you into my family's home. I brought you into my life..."

"I'm grateful," she said. She dead-ended there. *We* dead-ended there. "I'm sorry," she said.

She tried to close the door. I jammed my foot in the doorway. Then I pushed my body in, knowing there was a guy behind the door. He probably had a weapon on him, also. Even if the guns came out, I was ready for it. I knew what I was doing was crazy. Yet, there was ancestral blood pumping through me sending the message that I could do whatever had to be done.

I was ready.

I pushed my way in.

I wasn't ready.

Zee sat on the edge of Kris' bed, sipping from a glass of orange juice. Kris looked away, shifted her weight on one hip. I felt like I had been punched in the stomach. I could barely breathe.

Zee stood up. "Hey, Fisch!" he said, excited. I was trapped in a bad movie: The best friend found with the girl of the hero... but it was actually happening. Kris began putting things away. Doing for the sake of something to do. "I came to plead your case," Zee explained matter-of-factly. Kris glanced over at Zee in a way that suggested something different.

"And she just let you into her apartment to do that. A total stranger," I said.

"You were a stranger when I invited you up here," Kris reminded me.

"And you let me make love to you!"

"It was sex, David. It's not like we got married."

Zee drew closer, trying, I could tell, to act the bigger man, the guy above it all. Shame had frozen me: My girlfriend gets raped in my own home, shuts me out, then sleeps with my best friend. If I were told that I would live out the rest of my life as a tequila worm, I wouldn't feel as badly as this.

Everything was hazy and vague. Zee was talking but I couldn't tell what he was saying. Then Kris placed her hand on his arm. The way she used to touch me. The red rage started leaking out.

"He's my friend. You're treating him like dogshit," Zee yelled at Kris.

"Yeah? And what are you doing?!"

I reached behind me. I could feel the cold steal of the gun in my clammy palms. I was about to pull the gun out and start firing when Kris said, "This threesome isn't working out for me."

"Fuck you!" Zee snapped at Kris. Then, out of nowhere, his hand rose up and slapped her face.

Before Zee's arm came back down, Kris had slapped him back twice, like a slapping ninja, she moved that fast.

"What the hell was that for?" he yelled.

"Get out!" Kris yelled back.

"You're nothing but a trailer trash bitch!" Zee yelled.

That's when I pulled it. I aimed the gun at Zee. Right at his head.

"Apologize!" I said, as calmly and as firmly as I possibly could.

"David… is that…? What are you doing with a gun?!" He paused, waiting for my reply. I kept pointing it at him.

"What the fuck are you doing with a gun?!"

"Get that thing out of my home!" Kris yelled.

"Apologize to her! You cannot hit her, understand? You don't. Ever!"

Suddenly, Kris realized she was bleeding from her lip and started screaming at both of us to get out. Doors were opening in the hallway.

"Let's go!" I said.

Zee and I barreled out the front door into sidewalk traffic, knocking into some guy selling wool hats and neck warmers. We ran and ran, legs pumping, arms flinging by our sides. Pedestrians and cab drivers barely glanced as we raced through crowds and hot dog stands; past the girls in short fur coats and fishnet stockings clipping the cold pavement in their high heels; past the leering eyes; past drug-bent minds dreaming of better times. Adrenaline was our speed. It wouldn't be the last time.

Out of breath and heaving, Zee leaned against a light post. He was trying to say something. I gave him time to rest.

"Da... Da... Dave..." he sputtered. "I'm... I – shit – I'm...." He cupped my shoulder in his palm and leaned on me as a friend leans on another friend.

I punched Zee in the stomach as hard as I could. Gasping for breath that would not come, Zee fell into a semi-frozen sidewalk puddle that was as likely human piss as melted snow. I pulled the gun and concealed it from public view with my coat. I pointed the barrel at Zee's head.

"Did you fuck her?"

Zee stared at the gun. "What – are you kidding ?!"

"Answer me!"

Zee shook his head 'No'. Turning it away from the gun barrel. I kept my grip on him.

"Look at me when you answer." From frozen reject to sidewalk hood, my transformation was so swift, like turning a page. Pointing a gun at Zee kneeling before me I felt like god. And I felt like shit at the same time.

"I didn't get that," I said. "Again?"

"No." His voice was feeble.

"Bullshit."

"I swear to god, Man. After I dropped Lara off, I drove to Kris' to talk to her. For you, Man. She set all that up in there. I was just trying to smooth it out but…"

"Who's Lara?"

"Lewis' tutor."

"Didja fuck her, too?"

"Seriously, Dave. I don't have that much free time."

He got up on one knee. I pressed the gun to his forehead. "Easy," I said.

He knocked it away.

"Are you kidding me?!"

"You've been salivating over her since you saw her. And ever since you knew I was getting into her you've wanted her more. You just love to prove you're one better than me, don't you?"

"I'm not the one holding a gun."

"How about I just plug two into your head right now?"

"Oh, sure, Fisch. Plug away. What're you Bugsy Segal now? Little Jewish Mafia re-enactment? Your Mom finds out you have a gun you're gonna be in deep feces my friend."

Kris put one through my heart. Somebody had to pay. He was in the room with her. It only made sense.

"Prove it," I said. The words came before the idea struck. But in a flash I recognized that it was brilliant.

"What?" Zee asked.

"What was that phrase you told me? That Hebrew… something *shit?* "

"Otzma enoshit."

"Human strength, right? So, prove that you were doing this for me. Prove your friendship!"

"Please tell me you're joking."

Zee was shivering and not from the cold. He was always the coolest guy in the group, carrying himself with a glide and a stride that elevated him from the norm. To see him begging confirmed my power. For the first time in my life I felt a sense of control.

"What do you want me to do?" Zee asked.

"I'll tell you at the diner. You're buying."

"Man, you are twisted over this chick."

"You have no idea," I said.

Inside Zee's 244 Volvo, Tom Waits bounced out of the stereo and off the beaten upholstery. I closed my eyes and thought about what was next. That's when Zee grabbed the gun. His hand fumbled around the gun trying to figure out how to hold it.

Zee blinked. The gun didn't look natural in his hand. He would have preferred a joint. He raised the gun awkwardly, and then he pointed it at me.

"You put this thing to my head, David. A Jew puts a gun to the head of another Jew! Like a concentration camp Capo, like a traitor you did this. Do you realize that?"

I stared down the barrel of the gun and laughed. "Go ahead," I said. "You'd be doing me a favor."

"Oh, please. Like your life's so terrible. This isn't wartime, David. We don't have militant anti-Semites firing at us from our borders. You're an upper middle class Jewish kid from the home of a dentist. Not some gang banger."

"It's not loaded," I said. I pulled out the clip to show him.

Zee pulled the barrel away from my head. Then he swung. The butt of the gun caught me above the temple. I went black for a second and saw stars. When I put my hand to my head, it came away with blood on it.

"You stupid schmuck," he said. The blood was trickling down my forehead. "Jesus, I'm sorry. Shit. Let's get you to the hospital."

"We're going to the diner."

"You need stitches. You look like a Halloween nightmare."

"I'll wash!" Zee shook his head. "I asked you a question on the street. I need you to follow through."

"You mean you want me to help you kill this guy, right?"

"Right."

"You're certain he raped her, certain to the point that you want to take his life."

"Yes."

"Jesus, you're really bleeding," he said. Something in him energized. "Okay. I'll help." I nodded to the gun in his hand. He shook his head. "You can't even handle an unloaded gun. What makes you think you can shoot a man?"

"I can do it."

"Guns make noise. We would have to get him somewhere where people aren't."

"We'll find him, get him somewhere secluded," I said.

"Just take him away?"

"I have his name, and a vehicle. People up there, if they don't know your name, they know what you drive. We'll find him."

"Great plan," Zee said with extreme sarcasm.

"I'm thinking it through now," I retorted.

"You want a friend to prove himself, Lewis should be doing some time on this one."

"He will. Believe me."

"Dave, Dave…. I know you really like this girl. And I know what it feels like to get the shit kicked out of you. But…

seriously. Killing a guy? I mean it's one thing to say it, but to actually make a plan and… take someone's life. Dave – you're talking about murder."

"Look…" I muttered, "I… I have to do it." My eyes filled with tears. "Look, I don't know if this is gonna make any sense, but if I can't tell you…. When my parents split up… it's like there's been this hole, and nothing fills it. I get wasted, it makes it worse. I can't escape it. Nothing works for me except Kris. She makes me feel… like I'm home." The black empty had spoken. My tears flowed. "And I know she's not reciprocating the love. I know that. But I truly believe that she can't. 'Cause of all the shit she's been through."

Zee placed a hand on my shoulder: The comforting hand of a true friend.

"Dave, you ever see my parents around? Anybody besides the housekeeper? Sure, I love the freedom, but I wouldn't mind some family. So I gotta fill the space, too, y'know. Believe me, I know how you feel."

"You think that's the same for Lewis?"

Zee nodded. "I think it's the same for everyone on this planet, Man." I looked up as if to ask why. "Because no one can possibly know how you need to be loved. Nobody really knows anybody. We just grope our way through and try to listen to the melody along the way."

"Were you groping with Kris?"

"David… Kris doesn't love you. I wish I could say it some other way."

"So you did do it with her?"

"No!"

"But you wanted to."

"I think of doing a lot of things. I've thought about grabbing girls in the middle of history class and fucking them on the teacher's desk while he continues lecturing. But I don't! Because that would be crazy! Your girl is hot, what can I say? But I did not go there to sleep with her. I went there for you. What we do and what we say: That's all the currency we have." Zee stared out the windshield at the cold road ahead. If he hadn't physically made it with Kris, he did mentally, and in a way that was the same. Because once the line had been crossed in the will, the deed was an afterthought. Zee handed me back the gun. His eyes were soft and wet.

"Look, let's return the thing and then," and here Zee lit up with that mischievous look, "let's you and I head up to the cottage and just party our asses off. Shipments recently unloaded up in Montreal and the St. Lawrence is flowing again. I've got over a pound of black brick and a couple kilo's of hydroponic. We can get high for days."

The city could be dry but Zee's Montreal connection was as solid as the hash bricks he delivered. Even when the ports were raided by a hundred RCMP on a tip, Zee's connect came through.

"Come on," he pressed me. "Just like old times."

Zee treated the act of getting high as an art. He had a closet in his bedroom painted midnight blue with glow-in-the-dark stars and planets and Pink Floyd or King Crimson or The Doors pumped in through Bose speakers. You'd get in the closet, the door would close and the trip would begin. Zee knew how to get you high and take you for a ride. He loved playing host to the intergalactic mind fuck.

"I'm bringing the gun," I said.

Zee's smile faded.

"And Lewis comes, too."

Part Two

CHAPTER TWENTY

Zee packed his guitar and a change of underwear. He would live in his black leather pants and black sweater for the next week. "Worked for Jim Morrison," he said. The rest of his knapsack was full of drugs: a quarter pound brick of hash, an ounce of hydroponic weed and the respirator – his favorite bong.

Lewis packed a hockey-equipment bag full of clothes. "In case we go out somewhere nice," he explained. Where we were going, we weren't going anywhere nice. But I didn't tell him that. I didn't want to give him an excuse to back out.

I brought a gallon of Chivas Regal, a litre of wine and a gun.

The usual two-hour trip took half an hour longer with Zee's cautious driving. "You want the cops to pull us over?" he reasoned. Good thinking since we were smoking joints and drinking the whole way up. Still, the further North we drove, the more barren the landscape became, and the more I felt the sense that I might not be coming back. By the time we drove into Laketon, we were all pretty toasted. We stocked up at the liquor store. I bought some red wines for meals, planning on steaks like last time. The guys bought a few cases of beer.

"That's all you're getting, Fischer?"

"I'm sticking to Chivas and wine," I said. It was what I drank last time, when Kris was raped. I wanted to remember how I felt then, so I could fuel how I felt now. I had my buddies with me, I had a gun and the bare bones of a plan. But I seriously doubted if I had the guts. I would need every bit of encouragement wherever I could get it, even from the smell of the scotch I was wearing when it happened.

Two hours later we were in the cottage, a fire going in the fireplace and Bruce Springstein's 'Born to Run' album on the stereo. Grocery bags lay on the kitchen table, food put away but anything drinkable was still out. In every way it looked like we were there just to party. And maybe that's what Zee and Lewis were thinking. But I couldn't shake the thoughts of Kris, and Fred, and the rage inside of me that needed satisfaction.

Zee got the respirator going. The respirator was a bong made from medical equipment. Instead of a long glass tube connected to the bowl there was hospital grade rubber tubing that connected to an oxygen mask. You strapped the mask over your head and breathed. Just like in the hospital, when they give you oxygen to survive. Surviving the respirator meant breathing straight weed smoke.

Zee put the mask on, lit the bowl and began. The smoke snaked through the tubing, then emerged swirling into the oxygen mask like Van Gogh's 'Starry Night' swirling stars. Zee inhaled.

The smoke disappeared into his mouth. His eyes watered and one single tear slid down the length of his narrow face.

He exhaled into the mask and inhaled again. In and out, in and out, Zee was literally breathing pot smoke; it was a love affair between a boy and his dope. Finally he rolled back, like he'd suddenly become very heavy, and lay still.

"Dude, that was insane!" Lewis shouted. Zee did not move. The oxygen mask remained strapped on his face. Lewis turned to me, smiling still, but showing concern. "Is he okay?"

I said, "It's like a trance. He's actually completely aware of his surroundings."

"But… he's not moving. I'm not even sure if he's breathing."

"He's smoking," I said. Zee lay flat, slowly emitting smoke straight up at the ceiling, like a human volcano that had erupted in only a slow, steady gaseous leak. Tears rolled down the sides of Zee's eyes.

"He's crying," Lewis said. "Is he okay? Zee! Zee, come on!"

Lewis reached over to pull the mask off Zee's face. Zee's hand shot up, like a corpse come back to life. He grabbed Lewis' wrist and squeezed.

"Oh, fuck!" Lewis yelled, jumping back. Zee had the mask off and was laughing so hard he could barely breathe. "Jesus Christ, how the hell can you just lay there breathing smoke like that?"

"Practice," Zee said.

"Give me that," Lewis said. He took the respirator and strapped the oxygen mask on. "Wait," he said. "You have any goggles?" I found Lewis a pair of ski goggles and he strapped them over his eyes. "Ready for take-off," Lewis said.

Zee lit the freshly packed bowl of Zee's KGB – Killer Green Bud. "Just breathe normal and relax. This will take you past the Milky Way, Man."

Lewis breathed in and out as the smoke swirled into the mask. Then his eyes rolled back and he fell backwards like a tree, his head bouncing off the carpet.

"No way," Zee said as he jumped to Lewis' side, checking his eyes. Suddenly Lewis coughed one giant volcanic cough.

"Again," Lewis said, starting to giggle. He and Zee burst into hysterical laughter.

That pretty much broke the ice.

Zee and Lewis weren't friends. They were just both friends with me. I was the glue that bound them together, which was weird and made me feel kind of responsible for whether or not they got along. As if their connectedness was necessary, which, in fact, it was. For me.

If I was actually going to pull off the plan of killing Fred, I would need both of them on board with me. I would need all the help I could get.

I drank my scotch on the rocks and watched the fire. There was something comforting about watching its flames devour the wood in the hearth. The more it destroyed, the brighter it burned, and the brighter it burned, the more it destroyed. I was willing to kill for Kris' love; the irony was not lost on me: I was willing to destroy a life in order to brighten my own.

Lewis was laughing so hard that he was actually not making any sound at all. His face was contorted into the shape of a man in immense pain but happy about it. And then the sound came back.

"You...." Lewis said. Zee shook his head, tears streaming down his face. "The way you... you..."

"What?" I asked, not getting the joke.

"You were staring into the fire like it was a strip show."

"Your mouth was open... ," Zee laughed, "like...," and he imitated me with an "*aaawwww,*" sound.

"You can see a lot in the fire," I said. "The flames can be very spiritual. Like reading tea leaves." It was something Kris had told me.

"You haven't had a spiritual moment since you were born! The only thing you saw in that fire was some chick's naked body." I forgot what a prick Lewis could be when he got wasted. He was going to remind me.

"What do you know about spiritual, asshole? All you care about is sex and looks."

"Watch it, Fisch. I told you chicks would fuck up your head if you let them. They want to rope you in and tie you down. Don't succumb, Dude. Resist!" As if on cue, a line from the title song 'Born to Run' blasted out of the stereo. Lewis sang along with it, his eyebrow raised and his finger pointing at me: *"It's a suicide rap, we gotta get out while we're young. 'Cause tramps like us, baby we were born to run!"*

"Quit it, Lew!" I said.

"Hey, man, loosen up. He's just messing with you," Zee added.

"Yeah, C'mon, Dave. Lighten up."

"I'm not in the mood. You know what happened last time I was here."

"Told you not to bring her up here," Zee said as he stood up and stumbled to the bathroom.

"I wanna be your friend, I wanna guard your dreams and visions!" Lewis sang

"You're with us now. The way it should be. Look – even my dick is smoking."

Zee left the door to the bathroom open. The air was still cold enough that steam rose off his urine stream, which did indeed make it appear as if his penis was smoking.

Lewis didn't eat much, but he had high nutritional standards. And he could cook. "It doesn't matter what you put into your body, as long as you eat right," he said chopping garlic for a salad. "This," he said holding up a clove, "this is the cure for all ailments. You eat this, nothing will harm you."

"Nobody will talk to you, either." Zee was busying himself rolling joints for when we left the cottage. "We *are* going out later, right?" he asked.

"Sure," I said, hesitantly.

"So I can get some real food."

"Funny," Lewis said. "And what exactly constitutes real food?"

"Pizza," Zee said.

Lewis prepared roasted breasts of chicken with a peppercorn-mushroom sauce and a side salad. The food was so good we all fell into silence.

"Good sign," Lewis said. Zee and I just looked at him. "When nobody's saying anything, it means the food's good."

"Or we're trying real hard to be polite," Zee returned.

"Fuck off," Lewis said. He was truly offended. That threw Zee off, and he did the right thing.

"No. Kidding. Seriously, this is really good. I'm not just saying that 'cause I'm stoned. This is good."

"But you're always stoned," I added.

"Which further supports my sincerity: I have never tasted anything quite this good cooked by somebody I actually know."

"Wow, that's the strangest compliment I ever received," Lewis said. It seemed to me their friendship was getting stronger. I got up and set the rest of the tone with some Miles Davis old school. When the meal was done, Zee lit up a joint. We passed it around. I was drinking red wine. More memories; more fuel.

"So, okay, out of anybody in our school, who would you want to have sex with?" Lewis asked. Zee fielded Lewis' question.

"Does that include recent graduates?"

"No, it does not," Lewis clarified. "They have to be in the school."

"Does that include girls we've already been with?"

"No, this is strictly fantasy."

"Well, couldn't it be a fantasy to be with them again?" Zee argued.

"Why are you making this so difficult?" Lewis said.

"The devil's in the details," Zee said. "Ask David."

"He asked you first," I said, stalling. There was only one person I wanted to be with and she currently hated me.

"All right," Zee said. "Mrs. Gonzalez."

"The Spanish teacher?!" Lewis exclaimed "Are you fucking kidding me?"

"She's an exceptionally sophisticated and sensual woman. Have you ever talked with her? I could watch her lips move all day."

"I have to admit," Lewis said. "She's a fine looking woman. And I notice you have a thing for full lips, eh? What's your girlfriend's name?"

"Fantasy only," Zee said. Lewis nodded his understanding. I felt like these guys were so much worldlier than me.

"What about you," I asked Lewis.

"Sharla Unger."

"Boo. Boring," Zee said.

"Yeah? Tell me you wouldn't want to have sex with her," Lewis challenged.

"Not my type," Zee answered.

"Bullshit," Lewis said. "The girl's a miracle of genetic inheritance. Think about it: the odds against her parents' chromosomes and genes lining up and matching in such perfect harmony to create her flawless features – perfect skin, hair, eye color, the shape of her face. Topped with Harvard Law School brain power. Forget it. She's like a basic test for testosterone: If you're a guy, and you're not a screaming faggot, you have to fantasize about her."

"What about that South American girl from the fashion show," I asked. "Francesca?"

"Fantasy only," Lewis smirked.

"No way," I said. "You slept with her?" Lewis shrugged and calmly lit a cigarette.

"Dave, you don't actually believe half the shit this guy says, do you?" Zee asked. I checked Lewis' expression again. I don't know what Zee could tell from it. Lewis seemed believable to me.

"Did you?" I asked Lewis again.

"One thing you should have learned by now, Fischer, you don't kiss and tell. Rumors spread. People get the info wrong. Bad PR."

"So. Sharla Unger, huh? I thought you wanted me to go out with her," I said.

"I do," Lewis said. "But that doesn't mean I don't want to have her to myself. Man, having sex with Sharla Unger would be like the ultimate."

"Why?" Zee asked.

"I don't know," Lewis said. "She just is."

"Having sex with someone… connecting with someone on a physical level… it almost doesn't matter what they look like. Beautiful or not, what matters is how your body chemistry works together. Sharla Unger: She's a beauty, but she could be boring in bed. She sure doesn't do it for me."

"Well, like I said, maybe you're gay," Lewis said.

"Why don't you bend over and find out," Zee said.

In certain areas, like the topic of sex, Lewis needed to feel superior. Zee wouldn't play along. So Lewis aimed at me.

"Who would you do it with, Fisch?" Lewis said. He glared at me with intense inquisitiveness. "Who's the lucky girl, Fisch? Must be a lot to choose from."

"Leave him alone," Zee said. "You know he's sensitive about it."

"We can't protect him forever," Lewis said. They sounded like my parents again, two more people I had tried to force together who didn't belong.

"I can handle it," I said. "I fantasize about a lot of girls. I'm not ashamed to admit it. I whack off like there's no tomorrow. I'm ruthless with my dick in my hand but I'm gutless with a girl right in front of me."

"Jesus, do you have to be *that* honest?" Lewis said.

"I'm not ashamed. This is good. This is good for me. I need to say this. You see I have this theory. I believe that if you beat off over a girl you know, you increase the chance of actually getting together with them. So…"

"I can get behind that theory," Zee said.

"Yeah, it's true," I said. "I mean, in theory."

"Are you seriously telling us this?" Lewis asked, horrified.

"What? Everybody masturbates. All we're doing is talking about the girls we would normally masturbate over."

"I don't masturbate over Mrs. Gonzalez," Zee said.

"Fine, whatever. The point is, I haven't been that honest with you guys. Or with myself."

"But sometimes I think about her when I'm having sex with someone else. Like substitution," Zee continued.

"That's not masturbating," Lewis clarified.

"More like… functional fantasy…?" Zee mused.

"Hmm. I like it," Lewis thought. "We should coin that phrase."

"I just did," Zee pointed out.

"Hello?! I was saying…?" Lewis and Zee suddenly seemed to remember I was there. "I was saying… I don't say the things I need to say. So I'm … coming out with it: Ever since I lost my… you know… with Kris… I haven't thought about any other girl in that way. The only girl I think about – ever – is Kris. It's an obsession, I admit, but… well, that's kind of why we're here."

"Okay," Lewis interjected, rolling his eyes "Top five. No thinking."

"Cheryl Brooks," I said.

"Did her," Lewis said.

"Everyone has," Zee added.

"Wild woman," Lewis said. "Claw marks, growling…forget it."

"Can I continue?" I asked. "I'd do the drama teacher. Great ass. And Melanie Hart."

"Supreme tits."

"What'sername – Tanya. Gymnast from…"

"Dancer! Hungary! Oh. My. God!"

"I can't even imagine what she could do with those legs."

"Insane."

"What about that new girl? Kristen something. She plays on some team, also."

"She's only like fifteen."

"So? That's just two years younger."

"I need a mature woman," Zee said. "Someone who knows herself, her turn-on's and her inhibitions, and is willing to explore them."

"Oh, please with the philosophy. We're talking about sex," Lewis said.

We kept on like that, around and around the table, naming girls we would like to sleep with, listing their perfections and flaws and debating the appeal of each. Eventually, even Lewis tired of the subject.

"Okay – new topic," Zee said, "Who would you love to beat the shit out of?"

"Jack Holt," I said.

"What – the quarterback?"

"He's so full of himself," I said. "He's such a dick. I nearly beat the crap out of him already. If he didn't have half the offensive line with him."

"How about you," Lewis asked Zee. "Who do you want to beat the shit out of?"

"Sharla Unger," Zee said. I laughed so hard I nearly fell off my chair.

"I would have you killed!" Lewis said in good humor, but he was serious, too. "I'd like to kick the shit out of Mr. Dwar," Lewis said. "I hate math."

"Would you kill him?" I asked. Zee stared hard at me.

"What?" Lewis asked.

"I'm asking you to take it one step further. Just hypothesizing. Would you kill him?"

"I don't know – what kind of question…?" Lewis asked. His hesitation was unsettling.

"Just answer it," Zee pressed, glancing at me.

"Fine. Sure," Lewis conceded.

"Wow. That's convincing," Zee said rolling his eyes.

"Okay," I said, "How would you kill him?"

"Just pretend? All right…. Hanging. I'd like to see Mr. Dwar hang."

"Harsh. How would pull it off?"

"Public viewing. From the flagpole. Right in front of the school where everybody coming and going – every teacher, every student, every parent, would have to pass by and watch him dangle."

"Wow. You really hate Math," Zee said.

"He does have a tutor," I reminded Zee.

"We met." Zee eyeballed Lewis on that. Lewis stared back. Another stand-off.

"How about you, Zee? If you had to kill somebody…." I asked. Zee glanced at me. He flicked at his Zippo lighter, watching the flame plume and vanish, plume and vanish. "I wouldn't kill anybody," Zee said. "But, if we are speaking hypothetically, I would have to take my direction from some of the Iroquois tribes. They killed because they had to, and they did it with honor and respect for their foe." Zee set his gaze on me now, his thumb working at the flint of the Zippo. "If I had to kill, I would use a knife. I would look my enemy in the eye, and I would cut his heart out while it was still beating. Then, as it was still pulsing in my hands, out of respect for my enemy, I would take a bite out of -- ."

"Gross!" Lewis yelled.

"They did not do that!" I yelled.

Lewis put his hand to his stomach. "Oh, god… that is just… nasty."

"And you, Dave?" Zee asked, still watching me closely. "Do you have a favorite plan for carrying out an execution of someone in particular?"

"As a matter of fact," I said, walking over to my bag, "I do."

"I think he should do in the blonde chick for messing with his head," Lewis laughed.

I pulled out an object carefully wrapped in a bandana. I un-wrapped it and set the Sig Sauer on the table. The silence that followed was palpable.

"Not exactly the Indian way," Zee said.

"What is that?" Lewis asked, jumping back.

"That is a Sig Sauer, P230 semi automatic, single action handgun."

"Why do you have a gun!?" Lewis asked.

"What have we been talking about?" I responded.

"Why – the fuck! – do you have that gun here?!" Lewis was about to lose it. I never knew he had such an aversion to firearms.

"You know what it's doing here," I said. "Same thing we're doing here."

"Fuck off." Lewis said. "Funny joke."

"It's no joke," I said. It was time to scout out the lay of the land. It was time to stop talking about it and put some footwork in. The more I sat around and talked about it, the less I'd be able to follow through. Zee and Lewis would try to talk me out of it and I would let them. I grabbed my keys and wallet and threw on my boots to let them know I meant business.

"Where are you going?" Lewis asked.

"To look for him."

Wait," Lewis said. He went to his bag, pulled out his toiletry case. Lewis' toiletry case was bigger than Zee's entire knapsack. Lewis unzipped the toiletry case and fished out a smaller leather case, something that might contain a man's manicure set, with scissors, nail file, tweezers, etc. With delicate precision, Lewis unzipped and folded back the small leather case. He smiled at what he saw: a small, thick envelope made from a folded magazine page tucked carefully into a pouch in the case, a piece of glass tubing, a small mirror and a razor blade.

"Anybody need a pick-me-up?"

"Lewis Cohen, I like your style," Zee said.

CHAPTER TWENTY ONE

Zee let me drive. I knew the roads, and Zee didn't want the responsibility. I was craving some smokes and chocolate milk. My stomach was feeling a little uneasy; chocolate milk always settled it. Cocaine dries you out, makes you thirsty. You can't drink enough. I pulled into Milk Mart, the local twenty-four hour convenience store of Laketon.

Laketon was one of those cottage-country towns that just never quite adapted to growth. Cottagers came up, mostly from Toronto, Mississauga and Barrie. And they brought commerce and tourism to the area. But Laketon was a small town, lived in year round by small-town people.

They didn't want big.

They didn't want new.

They wanted what *they* moved out there for – peace and quiet. Or at least they thought they did.

"I'll wait in the car," Zee said. He was acting very calm considering the circumstances. Maybe he didn't think I would really go through with it. I got the feeling neither of them did. Maybe they were right.

"So where exactly do you start looking for this guy you want to kill?" Lewis asked as we perused the aisles of drinks behind the glass doors of the coolers. The bright fluorescent lights of the store made me feel exposed.

"Why don't you say that a little louder? "

"Or you could just wave your gun around." I pushed Lewis into a corner of the store. We knocked a rack of Cheez-Its and Popcorn. The cashier – a pock-marked kid, barely sixteen – looked up, gave us a cold hard stare, and continued ringing up a customer.

"You're pissing off the locals," Lewis snapped.

"You got a problem with this?" I asked.

"Uh, yeah!"

"My girlfriend got raped by a psychopath. What part of that did you miss?"

"The part where she's your girlfriend," Lewis said.

"I'm going to do this," I said.

"That's great, Dave. But can we also have some fun while you hunt? Or is it a steadfast rule that we play humorless hit men who don't get to joke about anything? Just give me guidance 'cause I'm new to this killing people thing."

"Just keep your voice down, all right?" Lewis straightened his neon colored ski jacket. I headed for the chocolate milk.

"So, just what do people do for fun in this hick town anyway?" Lewis said, again too loud. This time the cashier looked up and stared. There was disdain on the kid's pock-marked face, but there was a sadness, too.

"You wanna keep it down?"

"Yeah, well they know what it is then. I mean, seriously, Dave," I cringed when he said my name, "it's not like we're bringing this news to their attention. It's a fuckin' cow town. That's why people live here. To be close to the cows." A woman passed us on her way towards the doors. Lewis turned to her. "Isn't that right, ma'am. Didn't you move here to be close to nature and livestock and all that?"

"I didn't move here. I was born here. And you're a very rude young man!" She left in a huff.

"You guys need any help?" the cashier asked in a pushy way.

"No thanks. My friend here's just being a dick," I said.

"Seriously, Fischer. Don't tell me you haven't been coming here as a holier-than-thou cottage owner since you were a kid. I mean, if you're so sensitive to the townspeople why is it you don't know a single person in this town except the guys that mow your lawn, fix your pipes and store your boat?" I felt eyes on me like I was a leper.

"I hate it when you get wasted because you do this. You start picking on people and think it's funny. It's not funny."

"Ah, come on, Davey, I'll buy you chocolate milk." He grabbed at the milk carton in my hand. I pulled it back. The carton slipped out, hit the hard tile floor and burst open. Chocolate milk exploded everywhere; it splattered Lewis' designer sweat pants.

"Aww, look at what you did, Fischer! Custodian...! Custodian...! Hey! Need a mop here! My friend here spilled."

"You grabbed at it," I said.

"Look at my sweats! They're stained."

"Look at my jeans," I said.

"Yeah, but these are my good sweats! And now they're ruined by a chocolate stain looks like I shit-sprayed my pants."

"Who wears sweat pants to a bar?!"

"Nobody dresses up in the country."

"What?"

"When have you ever seen someone in the country dress up? They don't have to. That's why they live here. So they don't have to wear nice clothes!"

"They don't go out in sweat pants!!"

"Then what's the point of living in the country?!" A small gathering of local customers was watching us. One of them, a heavy set woman, was wearing worn sweat pants and a large pillow-like down coat. Lewis pointed at her. "See?!" The pock-marked cashier marched over with a mop and a frown, tossing his long stringy hair out of his face with a huff. He slopped up the spilled milk into his bucket.

"I'm sorry," I began.

"Excuse me, are you the custodian, too?" It was as if Lewis was on a mission to piss off each and every citizen of Laketon.

"I'm the manager," the boy said. "Cashier, custodian, and bouncer. You need to leave."

"Wow. Good for you," Lewis said. "I mean, being so young and with that complexion, a job of this position and power must help you bag a lot of ass around here, eh?"

"Get out," he said. "We don't want your kind of business here."

"Jesus people are seriously uptight around here. Including Dave," Lewis complained back inside the Volvo. "You notice that, Zee? Dave seems a bit, I don't know, like a humorless drag?"

Zee noticed that we were empty handed and stained with chocolate milk. He laughed. "You guys change your mind?"

"Lewis got us kicked out," I said.

"How the hell do you get kicked out of a convenience store?!" Zee exclaimed.

"Who dropped the chocolate milk?" Lewis said. I wanted to drop *him*, right on his blond feathered head.

"You need me to go in there and get that chocolate milk for you?" Zee stepped out of the car. He stood tall in the cold of the night, breathing in the frigid air with enthusiasm.

"I wouldn't," Lewis said. "Those people are freaks. Seriously. The little cashier boy hates our guts." Something went off in Zee's head. He got that look of mischief.

"Gimme the gun," Zee demanded.

"What?" I asked. It's not that I didn't hear him. I suddenly realized that I had carried a gun into a store, and now Zee was

going to carry a semi-automatic weapon into a store. We were
high. We were almost drunk. We had snorted cocaine. And now
we were carrying a semi-automatic weapon into a convenience
store where people just want to buy milk. It suddenly dawned on
me that this was *not* our finest moment. We were de-evolving. We
were taking stupidity to a new level; and we were just getting
started.

Zee said to wait ten minutes, then pick him up and keep
moving. It was almost fifteen minutes now. The gas was low.
"We should have filled up," I said. Lewis was lighting another
cigarette. "You ever breathe air?"

"I've tasted it."

"Put it out. We have to pick him up and drive by."

"You realize, if he actually robs the place, we automatically
become accomplices. We've aided and abetted."

"So what should we do – just take off? Leave him?"

"We're driving the getaway car. We're implicated. First
offense, even, we're in for three to five, easy. Two, suspended, if
the judge likes me." Lewis' father had defended some major
criminals in his career. Got his name in the paper and a lot of
money, but it also earned Mr. Cohen a reputation for defending
scum. It was a reputation that had trickled down to Lewis. He was
always defending himself against it.

"Look, just because I know something about this doesn't make me paranoid. It makes me smarter. If you want to get out of this now, turn the car around and let's drive home."

"I'm not leaving Zee."

"Just drive the fucking car, and stop being such a whining piece of shit." I slammed my foot on the gas and threw Lewis flying towards the back seat. Then I jammed the break. Lewis slammed forward, banged his head and shoulder. He sat up, glaring at me. Then he raised the still perfectly burning cigarette to his mouth, inhaled and exhaled the smoke into my face.

Zee sauntered out of the store. Cool Hand Luke style. He slipped into the back and slid down in the seat, stretching what he could of his legs. I gave it gas and we sped out of the lot. Tires screeched. "Fisch. Take it easy."

"How much'd you get?" I yelled back at him.

"Papers. Pack of smokes for Mr. Cohen, here. And chocolate milk for the getaway driver." I pulled the car into a side road and stopped. Zee opened the bag and displayed the loot. Rolling papers, smokes and chocolate milk; no money.

"You didn't rob the place?" Lewis said.

"Why would I rob a convenience store? We have a cottage filled with booze and drugs. What movie do you think you're in?"

"So why did you take the gun?" I asked.

"To see what it felt like." He removed it from his pants and gave it to me. "I was thinking about sticking it in that cashier's pepperoni-face and demanding the dough. But then I thought, once we do this Fred guy, then we can go on a spree of robberies and pin it on him. He'll be dead. We'll be a memory."

Zee let it lie there, this rationale, like a crazed man lying in the gutter looking up at the stars and thinking himself perfectly aligned with the natural order of things.

Like I said, we were just getting started.

"You should listen to yourselves," Lewis said. "'*Do this guy*,' like you're in some gangster movie or something. I *know* something about criminals, how their minds work, and you guys are so *not* criminals."

Zee leaned forward in his seat. We both looked at Lewis. Zee started in: "We are not interested in a career in crime, despite the pay and benefits. But we – all of us – are here on a specific mission. And that mission is serious as shit."

Lewis started to laugh. "All right. All right. Quit kidding around. I get it. You have a gun and we're going to the dangerous saloon in town to stir up some trouble. So, we're playing tough cowboys, now. Okay, whatever."

"We're not playing," I said.

"You know, you pull that gun out on someone, you better be prepared to use it. What if they have a gun? Or a knife, or... or...." Lewis was trying to stretch a point. He wasn't naturally good at it. He was looking at the gun in my hand and he was stammering for another example for his point. "Or a bigger gun," he finished.

"You said gun twice," Zee pointed out. I just looked at Lewis in a way that told him I was not playing around.

"Forget it!" Lewis exploded and jumped out of the car into the sidewalk. He started pacing, puffing cold smoke breath. Zee and I followed him. Lewis was heated and liable to run off. Lewis running off into the dark Laketon night, in his stained designer sweat pants and his flashy ski jacket would probably make the local news.

"Get back in the car, Lew," I said.

"I thought it was a stunt!" he said, pointing to the gun in the front seat of the car. "To show this chick that you actually had some balls after she dumped you. Not killing someone for real," he shouted.

"*Would you stop yelling that all over the place?!?!*"

Lewis looked imploringly at Zee.

"You're actually helping him with this?" Zee nodded. "And you were going to tell me when? '*Oh, by the way, we're just going to kill this one guy and then get some pizza…?*' What the fuck?!"

"Keep it down," I cautioned.

"Fuck you, Dave," Lewis said.

"You want out?" I asked.

"I was never in! I came here 'cause you said you wanted the company. And I came – No chicks! No beach! No pool bar! – 'cause you've been having this psychotic episode lately over this girl but this, this shit is not on the program. I want no part of it.

Fuck, I can't believe I gave up Acapulco to hang with you two morons for this shit!"

Lewis got back in the car, crossed his arms and legs and sat there stiff as a nail. Zee looked over to me.

"It's your party, Dave. Whattaya want to do?"

The bus station was in the center of town. Lewis asked the teller for the next bus back to Toronto. The ticket teller said the last bus was leaving at eleven o'clock at night. It made stops in several towns along the way and it got in to Toronto at three in the morning. Lewis could call a cab and be home shortly after that.

Lewis bought the ticket. We returned to the car and waited. Lewis smoked. Zee mentioned how there were only a couple of times when a friend truly needs another friend. And those times of need go beyond one's own morality. Lewis smoked. I felt like an ass. I was forcing these guys into something they had no business doing. Lewis was making the right decision. Zee was rationalizing his to fit a moral argument. And he was only doing that because I caught him alone with Kris in a situation he couldn't justify his way out of.

It was ten thirty. Lewis had smoked his way through most of a fresh pack of cigarettes already. There was a small pile of ashes and butts outside his door of the car. We looked like a stakeout vehicle.

"You're doing the right thing," I told Lewis. I felt obligated to. "This is my thing and I don't have any right to drag you into it."

"As long as you keep your mouth shut," Zee added. I looked over at Zee. He had a very strong point. Lewis was not good at keeping his mouth shut. Case in point: Sharla Unger and the mistaken sexual conquest. Where did that lead? Suspension. Getting kicked off the show. A bunch of ninth grade girls knowing that I lost my virginity. Total embarrassment. Suddenly, Lewis' decision didn't seem to be such a good one. I turned the key in the ignition and put the car in gear.

"Where are you going?" Lewis asked. "My bus leaves in like twenty minutes."

"You're staying," I said. Zee watched me with obvious approval.

"But - ," Lewis tried to protest. I didn't give him a chance.

"But nothing. I can't trust you to keep quiet about what we're doing. It's like you said before – you're already an accessory."

"How?" He demanded.

"You didn't try to stop us." And with that I shifted into second gear and drove towards the edge of town, to a bar called The Weigh Station.

CHAPTER TWENTY TWO

Like a lonely highway outpost where trucks were weighed and inspected The Weigh Station bar was on the outskirts of town, far off the beaten path. I had gone there a couple of times before. It was the kind of bar where you could get as drunk as you wanted to and nobody cared. Fights were commonplace. If you got too out of hand, they'd throw you out into the parking lot and leave you to sober up there. I figured if Fred was going to hang out somewhere, it would be the Weigh Station Bar.

The wooden interior was covered in sawdust and smelled like stale beer and nicotine. I half expected to see Fred there, half expected to find out information about him. And wasn't sure if I really wanted either to happen, but I kept putting one foot in front of the other, right into the middle of the place.

The Weigh Station wasn't Lewis' kind of place – there were no lingerie models here, no hot single women looking for company. This was a great disappointment to Lewis, which he pointed out about a second after we walked in and were met with uncomfortable stares from everyone who looked our way.

"Wow. You ever feel like you're not wanted," Zee said. It didn't help matters that Zee was wearing his three-day old leather pants, a leather vest over a t-shirt and a long earring. And of course, there was always Zee's hair. Lewis was convinced the stares were directly due to the chocolate milk stains on his sweatpants. "These country people have no idea how to behave in public," he said.

I found a table in one of the corners, close to the men's bathroom. It was all that was left. "Remind me to tell you not to get a job as a Maitre D' at any restaurant in the world," Lewis said to me. We pulled out chairs at the small table. Its surface was big enough to hold a pitcher of beer, ten glasses and an ashtray. Zee took off his coat and rolled up his t-shirt sleeve revealing a couple of tattoos. Some of the locals showed their approval with a slight nod or grunt. Zee was good to have along. He seemed to fit in anywhere and nowhere at the same time.

"I'm buying the first round," I announced to the guys. Lewis was in a sour mood and needed to loosen up. I needed to re-stimulate my will with a decent buzz. Zee requested Labbat's Blue. A waitress blocked my path as I was heading for the bar. Her expression was even sourer than Lewis'.

"If you're going to sit at a table, ya hafta order your drinks from me. Otherwise, if ya order from the bar ya hafta give up the table." She had a husky, scratchy voice, probably from smoking too much, and the bedside manner of a drill sergeant. "What's it gonna be?"

"Two Labbat's Blue, one Brador and a round of Jack Daniels."

"We don't have Brador," she said coldly. "You boys must be from the city."

"Yeah, and if you can muster up an expression resembling anything other than cranky bitch, we just might tip you well," Lewis said. I smiled apologetically to her. "He has a gun," Lewis added, pointing at me. Zee kicked him under the table.

"So does he," the waitress indicated a fat man in a red and white plaid flannel shirt at a booth. "And that one," a trucker type, playing darts in the corner. "and that guy and that guy and that guy. And him," she pointed out a tall elderly man in a suit. "He's the town prosecutor. Not a lot of fans of his in here but nobody'll bother you if you just come to let off some steam. I wouldn't suggest showing off your gun, though, sweetheart. You'll get a few pointed right back at you." Then, for the first time, she smiled. "I'll be back with your drinks."

"What are you, stupid?" I said.

"Fuck you, Dave." Lewis had reached a state of defiance. In early child development, this is called the Willful stage. Lewis had regressed to the emotional state of a four-year old. That basically left me as the pissed-off parent.

Zee excused himself to the restroom. I took in the bar. It was full but not crowded. Tables were occupied and patrons stood around drinking, leaning against the bar, or standing by the pool table where there was a small crowd watching the action.

Men outnumbered the women in the Weigh Station about five to one. The women that were there were about as tough as the guys. And they proved it by drinking just as hard.

The waitress returned with our drinks. The total was fifteen dollars. I offered her a twenty. "There's another twenty in exchange for some information. I'm looking for someone."

"Aren't we all, Honey."

"Someone I need to find," I added.

She shifted her weight impatiently. She had a tray full of drinks to deliver, still.

"I'm kinda busy," she said.

"Twenty bucks," I said. She walked away.

"Smooth," Lewis said. He was scouring the room for an attractive enough girl to focus on. I left him and walked over to the bar. When I finally got the bartender's attention, he sauntered over, leaning across the bar at me with a bored 'why are you wasting my time?' expression. I laid down twenty dollars.

"I'm looking for someone," I said. "I need information."

The bartender kept a bored expression on me. He casually reached behind him to a shelf below the cash register, then slapped a phone book down in front of me. "There ya go."

"Will you help me if I order some drinks?" The bartender continued to offer his bored expression. "Fine. Gimme a pitcher of draft."

"Which draft you got in mind, the one in your head or the one coming in from the door?"

"Funny. You got any Brador?" I asked. He laughed and indicated the selection.

"Nothing that fancy, friend. Canadian, Export, Labbatts Blue and Bud in a bottle."

"Pitcher of Blue," I said.

"That's six bucks," the bartender said reaching for the money. I stopped his hand.

"There's an extra twenty in it for you. But it's conditional."

"On what?"

"Information," I said.

"Can I have my hand back?" The bartender said. He turned to the register, made change of the twenty. When he returned I flashed him the other twenty.

"You know a guy named Fred?"

"I know about six guys named Fred."

"Brown hair. About five seven. Drives a pick-up. Kind of purple, I think." The bartender thought and then began to nod.

"Yeah, yeah. It's the hair color that stands out. Don't get a lot of guys with brown hair in here." I looked around. When I turned back he was busting a gut and moving down the bar to fill another order. My twenty was gone.

"Hey...!" He signaled one minute to me. I brought the pitcher back to the table. Lewis slugged at his pretty fast. "This place blows," he said. "You see these women? They look like they should be pulling sleds in Alaska."

"What about the 'ugly girls' theory," I reminded him.

"The 'ugly girls' theory assumes a nice body. This here – this is just all-over-ugly. You want to just get drunk here, that's fine, but let's not waste any time keeping our eyesight good." He downed the rest of his bottle. "I've got the next round. How much are these beers anyways?"

"Six bucks for three."

"Hell, I'll pay the rest of the evening. Christ, this place is dirt cheap." Again, Lewis, too loud, brought ugly looks his way. Zee popped out of the men's room.

"There's some serious poetry on those walls," he said. "And I quote: '*we come to drink, we come to forget, we come together and share the bed wet*'. And who can forget the classic '*Will you still love me if I puke on your shoes?*'"

"The bartender took my money."

"Yeah, that's typically how it works. You ask them for drinks, they give you drinks, they take your money. It's called paying."

"You're supposed to ask Chuckles the Waitress for drinks," Lewis said. "Or we'll have to abandon our preferential seating by the toilet."

"I asked him for information," I said

"What?" Zee said.

"I offered him twenty bucks for information on Fred – ."

Zee suddenly grabbed me by the jacket and steered me backwards out the door. I was too surprised to resist. I heard the laughter from inside as Zee slammed through the exit door and out into the snowy parking lot.

"You *putz!*" Zee said. "Are you an idiot?"

"What?" I said, like I *was* an idiot.

"Why do you ask for the guy by name? Now the bartender's gonna know."

"I was hoping he would."

"Why would he tell you if he did?"

"Twenty bucks."

"Like he's never seen twenty dollars before?"

Zee sat down next to me. It was cold out. Our breath came out in clouds. Zee pulled out a rolled joint. Zee was perpetually producing pre-rolled joints. I rarely saw him roll them, they just appeared.

He was a magician who could only perform one trick: making joints appear out of thin air.

"Lewis is still inside," I pointed out.

"Good. He needs some bonding time with the locals." Zee lit up and immediately shifted tone. Smoking was Zee's primary method of segueing from one mood to another. The result, however, was random. What emerged this time was sincere curiosity. "What did this guy do to you that was so bad? And don't tell me he beat you up, because that's nothing to kill someone over unless you're some kind of psycho loser. You may be a gutless pussy sometimes, but you're not a psycho. So, what happened?"

"He beat the shit out of me when I was already down and he raped Kris – why am I repeating this...?"

"So what?" The abruptness of the question took me by surprise. I didn't have an answer. I never asked the question of myself, and immediately wondered why.

"So what?! Whattaya mean so – he raped her!"

"How do you know?"

"I told you."

"Because *she* told you."

"That's right." I took Kris' statement as truth. Never doubted it. Zee had all the ammunition he needed to embarrass me into a corner.

"How badly do you not want to question this thing, David? Or is it that you just don't want to question her?" He had me, and I knew it, but I didn't care. "Did you see it?"

"Nobody ever sees someone getting raped. Which is why it's always so hard for the girl to even say anything because most people – people like you– don't want to believe them."

"Oh. Okay, I get it now. You're a social justice vigilante."

"Yeah, that's it," I scoffed sarcastically.

"And now you go hunting down sexual offenders based on hearsay...."

I looked away and tuned him out. I had nothing. Zee knew I had nothing.

The night framed the Weigh Station's lit exterior with darkness. Maybe that was how our lives were: moments of light framed by darkness.

And then something came to me.

"Zee. What if your sister told you she was raped? Would you need proof?" Zee glared at me.

"Don't be an asshole." He looked over at the Weigh Station the same way I did. I wondered if he saw the same juxtaposition.

"Would you need to have been there?" Zee smoked quietly. "Or would her beaten, bloodied face, her bruises, her scared-to-death expression, her shaking bones – would that be enough for you?"

Zee studied my expression.

"I'm not making this up," I said.

He nodded.

"We should get Lewis." I said. I got up to head back in. Zee was still in deep thought.

"You coming?" I asked.

"You ever think… you ever think maybe he knew her?"

"Who?"

"You know who. Him. The guy."

"How would he know her?"

"I dunno. You know where she's from?"

I shook my head.

"She could be from anywhere," Zee said. "She could've known him."

"I dunno," I said, because not knowing was easier than trying to know. So I ignored it the way I ignored anything that hurt to think about. Like Marcy; like my parents; like Kris.

The way I saw it, I was owed some pleasure. I had paid my dues for stuff I did some time back when, I don't know. Whatever it was it was dark and angry enough to send my parents running from each other, severing our family, leaving my sister and me wondering what the hell happened. All I wanted was some peace.

I finally found it with Kris – or so I thought.

Then it was ripped away by Fred.

That was all the justification I needed to go back into the bar and continue my search. Until I spotted something in the parking lot that stopped me cold: a purple-toned pickup truck.

Fred was here.

Lewis had found a cute blonde girl and two friends. She was petite with a button nose, pale complexion, and red lips. Her hair was carefully blown and set into place in giant waves of yellow: big hair. Lewis was standing by their table, rocking slightly from intoxication and licking his lips a lot, a sign he'd been doing more blow. I glanced at our table. There were several more empty bottles and shot glasses. Lewis had been doing mood-maintenance drinking. I was only too familiar with the technique.

My eyes darted around the room, scouring for Fred. He was here, he was here, and he was probably watching me. As I drew closer to Lewis, I passed the pool table enveloped by onlookers. There was a gap in the small crowd surrounding the table, and as it is our nature to rubber neck, I peered right into that gap.

Some guy was bending over the opposite end of the table, taking careful aim at the two ball for a corner shot; his face was frozen in a familiar confident smirk. At the exact moment I passed by, the player looked up from his cue ball. His steely, cold eyes shot directly into mine, like he knew exactly where I was and that I was looking at him.

Fred.

We locked eyes for a split second, then he refocused on the shot in front of him, pumped his arm twice and slammed the two ball home. It sank with a loud crack.

A shiver ran trough me. Pure fear.

"Let's go," I said grabbing Lewis by his arm.

"Wait. This is Donna," Lewis said, introducing the blonde. She was young, maybe fifteen. Not much younger than us. But she looked it. She smiled awkwardly at me. "And these are her friends, Sally, and Thelma," he said.

"Helen," the girl corrected him. She was bigger than Donna and looked several years older. I quickly guessed they were taking their younger friend or sister out to get her good and drunk, like an initiation.

"Nice to meet you," I said. "Sorry we have to go."

"What's the rush? Donna was just telling me about how she made it onto the cheerleading squad at her school. It took her a lot of practice. Isn't that great?! To Donna!" Lewis downed a shot.

"He's here," I said. "We need to go."

"Look," Lewis slurred. He spoke in that loud drunken whisper that everyone around can hear. "These are the best looking girls I've seen since we entered this leper colony. And she's into me. Don't – !"

"Fred is here!" I interrupted. "We have to – ." Lewis ripped his arm from my grip and sat down next to Donna who looked more than a little uncomfortable.

I looked around for Zee, my backup. Zee was walking back into the bar with a direct bee-line for me. I turned back to Lewis. Suddenly, Fred was standing next to him, holding his pool cue like a staff.

Fred and Lewis were face to face in front of Donna, the cheerleader. Next to Lewis, who was tall, Fred looked particularly short and thin, but with rat-like poise. He made small look dangerous.

"Who's that guy?" Zee asked.

"That's him," I said. "That's Fred."

"That's the guy that beat the shit out of you?" Zee was pointing his long arm at Fred. I pushed it down. "That little guy?."

"You want him to see you? I tried to get Lewis out of there, but he's trying to score with the girl."

"Uh oh," Zee said.

Lewis was basically asking Fred what his problem was. Fred was smiling his rat-smile, only too happy to be engaged in conflict. You could see the joy in it for him – the taste of a fight – it was all over his face in a sickening grin. The pool crowd gathered around Fred and Lewis. Donna and the girls moved away.

I moved in. Zee hung back, surveying the situation more, recon mode.

"I don't see your name on her," Lewis was saying.

"She's not available. Move on," Fred said. He glanced my way as I approached, the wry smile frozen on his face, like he was expecting us.

"Look, little man," Lewis began, but Fred moved quickly. Nobody saw it coming unless you'd seen it before and knew the stance. Fred flipped his hand to grip the pool cue with the palm in, the back of the hand facing out to Lewis. When Lewis stepped forward to shove Fred back, Fred snapped his wrist upward, in one fast jerking motion. The thick, butt end of the pool cue snapped up… right between Lewis' legs. The blow was precise. If Lewis had been wearing anything thicker than his designer sweat pants, they might have absorbed some of the impact. Instead Lewis felt all of it. There was an audible *Ooooh* from the crowd, as if they felt the pain themselves and several other guys instinctively covered their own genitals in sympathetic reaction.

Lewis let out air but no sound. His eyes bugged and he dropped to his knees at Fred's feet. His face began to turn red.

"Who's little now?" Fred said.

Zee stepped forward, but not before Fred snapped the pool cue again up into Lewis' jaw. Lewis' neck snapped back like the cab driver, when Kris kicked him in the jaw. Lewis dropped to the floor in a fetal position.

"Lew!" I yelled. I knelt down on the floor next to him, lifting his head up. His eyes were rolling back in his head, semi-conscious. He looked purple.

"You fuck!" I yelled at Fred.

"How come every time we meet, you're on the ground?" Fred asked me. I leaped up and swung. Fred ducked the swing and slammed me in the stomach. I tensed my core in time to sustain the impact. I kept coming at him.

Other guys quickly descended on me. Zee was swinging wildly. His wingspan punch caught a few chins and jaws. Somebody slammed into me from behind. Fred stepped out of the way. I crashed onto a small table. When I turned, a thick-shouldered guy in a brown flannel shirt was coming down on me. I rolled away from a flying fist. Zee grabbed the brown flannel shirt and started pounding. An arm wrapped around Zee's neck and pulled him back and down. As soon as it started it was over.

Lewis finally sucked in air, his complexion lightened. He was groaning on the floor.

"Somebody get some ice!" I yelled, holding Lewis' head. Nobody moved.

"Get the kid some ice," Fred said. Several guys jumped at the order. Soon there were buckets of ice and a used dish rag. I placed the ice in the dish rag and held it to Lewis' jaw.

"Show them to their table," Fred ordered. I felt a grip on my shoulder and in a second I was dragged to my feet and sat down. Zee was placed next to me and Lewis was helped into the chair next to Zee. Zee struggled against the grip.

"Get off, asshole," Zee said.

Fred turned a chair around so it's back faced us. He lowered himself into it, folding his arms on the back rest, watching us.

"You guys met Gord?" Fred asked politely.

Gord was standing behind us with his arms crossed. He was tall and muscular with narrow eyes and a small mouth. "Gord drives the snow cats in the winter times, combs the hill for the snow bunnies the next day. Tell 'em what you like to do with that cat, Gord."

"Chew 'em up," Gord said.

"Whattaya like to chew up, Gordo?" Fred asked.

"Bunnies."

"He means the snow bunnies. Coming down the hill in some stupid puffed out neon day-glow like your friend's coat here. Right into the blades of Gord's snow cat." Fred smiled up at Gord. "Eh, Gord?"

Gord nodded. He seemed to be smiling, but it was hard to tell with his small mouth. Fred focused his sick grin on me. "How's your girlfriend? She miss me?"

Zee pushed away from the table, ready to move. Gord tossed the table aside like a box of tissue, eager to fight all three of us at once.

"Settle down, boys," Fred said. "You don't want to make Gord angry. He hasn't been fed today."

"What do you want?" I asked.

"I – we," he indicated the population of the Weigh Station behind him, "we want you gone," Fred said.

"We've all got every right to be here --," I said.

"No! You don't!" Fred barked. The bartender was talking to the girls and the waitress, eyeing the broken chairs and glass on his floor, looking pissed as hell.

Fred jabbed his finger at my face.

"You got no rights here. This is my town. Keep asking questions and you'll see." The bartender pushed his way towards us.

"You! You! And You!" he said, pointing at me, Zee and Lewis. "Out!" He turned to Fred. "You make sure they get out, or you're out, too!"

"No problem," Fred said. He jumped off the seat and took a performer's stance, holding the pool cue like a microphone on a stand. He started talking in a radio commercial voice:

"Enjoy your vacation, boys. And thank you for bringing your tourist dollars to Laketon, Ontario, where you can ski, relax by the pool at one of our motels, eat at the diner, drink our beers, screw our women, piss all over our town. We're just so pleased that you have graced our little hamlet with your city sophistication. How could us rednecks ever survive without you?"

He smiled, proud of himself, and continued. "And when you're heading back to whatever fuckhole you came from, remember the good times you had here, because they will be your last." He flashed a shit-eating grin.

"This is *our* town. You come up to your cottage, you *stay* there. You don't come out until you leave, understand? Or me and my friend Gord here will fuck you up. And next time, you won't walk away. Now get your Richie Rich asses out of here!"

"We'll call the police," Lewis threatened, as we were being escorted to the door.

"And tell them what?" Fred asked. "Somebody threatened you? In this bar?" Fred laughed. The waitress laughed. The bartender smirked. Gord almost smiled. "We'll be checking up on you from time to time. Remember," and here Fred leaned in close, "I know where you live."

Fred smiled as he and Gord pushed us out the door and into the parking lot. "Hey, say hello to that girlfriend of yours – what was her name? I had trouble understanding what she was saying with my cock in her mouth!"

Fred's cackling laughter echoed across the sky long after he closed the door.

CHAPTER TWENTY THREE

Lewis finished puking the last of his vomit onto the gravel-stained snow bank of the parking lot. When he was done we walked him into the back seat to sleep it off. Lew had a bad combination of too much booze, hash and coke in him. He was a playboy smoker, not a heavy hitter like Zee or me. We propped his head on a towel and cushioned it on each side with clothing so his neck wouldn't move.

"I hope he doesn't puke in my car," Zee said.

"We should get him to a hospital," I said when Zee and I were finally inside the car, waiting for the heat to come on.

"You're right," Zee said, I assumed about Lewis. "That asshole deserves to die." As if in agreement, Lewis moaned from the back seat. Zee left the car running for a long time, just staring at the Weigh Station, like he was trying to stare through the walls and find Fred inside, stare him down, let him know we weren't going to just go away.

The door to the Weigh Station opened. Gord came out first, looking both ways. Fred followed, with Donna, the young blonde, holding his hand. He was holding her close, but she seemed resistant. Fred walked the young cheerleader across the parking lot to his purple truck. He opened the door for her like a gentleman, went around to the driver's side and got in.

The engine of the truck roared and the lights came on. It stayed there, parked. Then the interior lights dimmed out. Soon, the windows of the truck were steaming up. Then the cab started to rock. A small, fifteen year old hand pressed hard against the inside of the driver's side window. When she pulled it away, the hand print was complete, no gaps of air to highlight the lines in her palm. When someone presses that hard, they're trying to push off or push out.

Donna's girlfriends showed up at the front door, calling Donna's name, but Gord ushered them back inside. Nobody else came out.

Fred's purple truck stopped rocking. A rag appeared against the inside of the windshield and wiped the inside fog away. The two faces that appeared with each wipe were Fred's and Donna's. Fred's face held a frozen smile of contentment, of victory; the girl looked upset. She hastily reapplied her lipstick.

"He raped her," Zee whispered to himself. "That cocksucker just raped that girl."

"But she got in there with him," I said.

"Look at her," Zee said. "Look at her face!" Lewis rose in his seat at the sound of our conversation and peered between us up at Fred's truck.

"Shit," he said.

Fred pulled the truck up to the Weigh Station, picked up Gord and drove off. The girl was still inside. Zee threw the car into gear and we followed them. "What're you gonna do?" I asked Zee.

"I don't know," he said.

"Follow them," I said.

"Good idea," Zee said.

So *not* a good idea.

We followed Fred's purple truck as it pulled into the McDonalds. Fred parked and so did we, a good distance away. The girl got out of the truck and hurried into the McDonalds. Fred drove off. After a while, Zee opened the door and walked towards the restaurant. A few moments later he was standing in the doorway waving us in.

Lewis spoke carefully. "Donna...? Donna...? You want to call your friends? They're probably wondering where you are." Donna shook her head. We were sitting in the McDonalds, towards the other end of Main Street. Donna didn't want to call her friends. They had warned her not to talk to Fred but she fell for his tough-guy magnetism. She soaked it all up when he asked her to dance, then to sit and talk with him, then drink and drink some more. She fell for his touch when he hiked his hand up her back, massaging her neck, then on her legs, massaging her thighs, climbing higher.

"They'll just yell at me," she cried. "I feel so stupid."

"It's all right," Lewis said. Lewis was being very charming and sensitive to her. He could barely keep his eyes open. "It doesn't say anything less about you. You're still on the cheerleading squad." Lewis was trying his best to cheer her up. She kept reapplying her lipstick, trying to cover what had happened. I thought of Kris after Fred got to her, rocking on the couch, eating popcorn like nothing happened, shutting down.

"I was wrong, the way I was acting before," Lewis said in a confessional tone. "I was drunk and being an ass and...."

"That didn't give him any right to hurt you the way he did," Donna said to Lewis. Lewis smiled and touched his neck. He winced in pain. "Does it hurt," Donna asked. She reached towards him. It was the gesture of one wounded animal commiserating with another.

"Not too bad," Lewis said. He reached out to take her hand. Zee saw the ploy – Lewis working his wounded puppy act to woo the cheerleader – and he saw red.

"Can I talk to you a second?" Zee said, grabbing Lewis by the arm and pulling him outside the McDonalds. Lewis still had trouble standing straight up from the blow he took from Fred's pool cue. He walked slightly bent, like Zee's personal pet being taken outside to be disciplined. As soon as they were outside, Lewis tried to tug his arm out of Zee's grasp, but Zee wasn't letting go. Lewis was too worn out and beat up to break free. Donna and I watched as Zee lectured Lewis, and Lewis waving his

free arm around like a kid telling his parents he didn't do anything.
But Zee kept at him until Lewis was only looking at the ground.

"You know him?" She asked me.

"These guys? Sure. They're my closest friends."

"No, I mean... you know."

"Fred?"

She winced. "Don't... say his name." She took a moment,
breathing harder then regaining her composure. "He told me I was
too young to be in a bar like that. He said it was for my own good.
That if it weren't him, it'd be somebody else, somebody worse."

"He said that?" I asked.

"Like he was teaching me a lesson or something," she said
it just like that, plain and direct, staring at the surface of the
Formica table and the remaining wrappings and boxes of our
McMeals. "I thought... I don't know why I just told you that. The
whole thing makes me sick. You seem like the kind of person who
would listen." She started to breathe faster. "That was the first
time," she said. "That... was it." Tears rolled down her cheeks.
Her body shook in silence as her fear, terror and sorrow rippled
through it. She suddenly cupped her mouth.

"I think I'm going to throw up," she mumbled. She got up
and shot back to the bathrooms. I waited at the table, adding up the
damage that Fred had done to others I knew. How many others had
he messed with? It was dawning on me: Fred was a force of evil.

Donna came back, slid into her seat quietly. She was chewing gum. I didn't know what to say so I just reached for a French fry.

"I had my first time just recently, too," I said. "She was older. And... I was pretty much a dork about the whole thing." Donna raised her eyebrows in curiosity, as if to say 'go on'. "We were making out on the floor of her place and I said 'do you want to make love?'" exaggerating my voice to bring out the full corny effect of the moment.

"No way," Donna giggled. I nodded. "What did she say?"

"She laughed. Hard." Donna laughed out loud at that. "It was embarrassing as hell."

"I bet," she said, and she bit into her hamburger, enjoying the taste. Comfort food was an easy thing to fall back on when your world is caving in all around you. "What happened after?"

"I lost my virginity to her. And now she won't talk to me. And I think I love her." Donna let a small grunt escape. I watched her soft features as she chewed; innocent and sweet. What kind of person would destroy that? Fred was more dangerous than I thought. I ate more fries.

"Do you? Love her?" Donna asked.

"Yeah."

"So, what're you doing about it?"

"Trying to prove it to her," I said.

"Don't give up," Donna smiled and chewed.

Zee got the phone number out of Donna and we dropped her home. Donna walked up to her parent's house, her shame hanging off her like a dark cloak. In a moment I saw Kris in Donna. I saw the shame she must have felt for herself, and I saw the blame she felt towards me. Donna's front door opened. Her father stood in the doorway. Donna walked into his arms. Her body shook with sobs. Her father wrapped his arms around her. It was beautiful and painful to watch – that father was about to find out his little girl was raped after getting wasted in a bar.

Nobody was there to hold Kris when she returned home. Nobody was there to comfort her and make her feel safe. Kris was alone in the world.

Kris called it freedom. I wasn't so sure.

We drove in silence back to the cottage, each one of us adrift in our own interpretations of what we were really up against. Fred was now as real for them as he was for me.

We stayed in the car long after we parked at the cottage. You could see the lake beyond through the bare trees. Moonlight reflected in the few spots of water that were not frozen. Lewis was smoking out the open window.

"You're talking about killing a man, Fisch," Zee said.

"Not just any man. This guy's an animal."

"He's just a guy."

"'*The last good time you'll ever have.*' ' *I will fuck you up for good.*' What do you think that means?"

"I don't know," Zee said heatedly. "How should I know what some psycho thinks? It doesn't matter. What matters is that we decide what we are going to do."

"You guys are scared, aren't you? You saw what he's like and now you want out."

"We're only saying we have to think about it," Zee said. He glanced back at Lewis. "What do you think, Lewis?"

"Call the police," Lewis said.

"They can't do anything. Besides, if we call the police, our mission's busted. We'd never be able to kill him and get away with it. Not if he's on the cops' radar."

"Oh, yeah," Lewis said sarcastically, "As if killing this guy was ever a realistic option. You should listen to yourself. You're ridiculous."

"Yeah? Like getting your jaw smashed in 'caused you talked to some girl? *That* kind of ridiculous?"

"We all knew what kind of people we were going to meet at The Weigh Station. Didn't surprise me," Lewis said.

"You sure looked surprised lying there on the floor holding your nuts," I barked.

"Shut up, Dave!" Zee yelled.

I didn't care, I didn't care, I didn't care. Fred was a dead man. He had to be made a dead man. Fred had ruined everything

that was good for me. I wanted my revenge. The black empty
demanded it.

"You both saw what he's like!" I said.

Lewis flicked the lit butt of his cigarette into the snow,
watched as it snuffed out with a hiss and burrowed a tiny crater
around it from its heat. Even a cigarette butt knew how to defend
itself.

"Dave's right," Lewis said, "The guy's a menace. I'm
calling the cops."

"No!"

"Yes, David! We are calling the cops!"

"The Weigh Station," Lewis repeated into the phone. It
was closing in on 1am. I had poured myself my second tall glass
of scotch, staring Lewis down the whole time he was on the
telephone. "The bar, yes." He paused, then grimaced at what he
heard and balled his fist tight. "Once again... we were at the bar –
The Weigh Station. We were physically attacked by a man named
Fred.... No, I don't know his last name. Just Fred. This man, he
raped a young girl named Donna.... A young blonde girl. She's a
cheerleader at the high school..... Okay, no, I don't have her here.
But we saw it...! I don't know... I can ask. So, what can you
do?" He waited for the phone voice explanation. "Uh huh. So,
basically we have to wait for him to do something really awful
before you can help in any way. So what the fuck good are you

people? My friend lives here, he pays taxes here, which means he pays your fucking salary and this is the best.... Hello? Hello?!" He hung up. "Lazy goddam fuckers," Lewis said. "I hate cops."

"Have a drink," I offered. He reached for it without looking and drank it down. The rest of the night took off from there.

CHAPTER TWENTY FOUR

The next day, I shuffled into the kitchen, past Lewis, who was already up and making breakfast, and made a bee-line for the freshly brewed pot of coffee. I took my mug of java to a seat by the window and let my mind slowly wander out into the grey afternoon. Lewis said something.

"Huh?" I asked.

"Morning," Lewis repeated. It was nearly three in the afternoon. Time had lost meaning. It was just the day after the night before. And another night would follow. "Man, we got so wasted last night," Lewis said.

"Yeah," I said, zoning.

"You were seriously wasted," Lewis said. "You drank that Scotch like it was water."

"Yeah," I said robotically. My head pounded. I sipped the coffee. Fred said he'd be watching us. Was he watching us last night? Was he watching now?

Zee was up about an hour later. By then Lewis and I had gone through a pot of coffee, two omelets and we were considering evening plans. Zee went straight for the fridge and extracted a coke.

"I forgot about your gourmet taste," Lewis said. Zee answered with one of his trademark burps, a cross between a fog horn and a tractor engine on steroids. "Nice. Eggs?"

"I like them scrambled."

"Like your brains," Lewis shot back, taking unfair advantage of having been conscious more than an hour already. Zee countered with a full-on ignore pattern, downing another coke and rolling joints until Lewis served up the eggs.

Zee smothered his scrambled eggs in ketchup. "I'm never cooking anything for you again," Lewis said. He took a newspaper into the bathroom with his coffee. It was closing on five and already dark.

"Crazy night," Zee said. "You were really wasted."

"You, too," I said. "There was a point you were just leaking smoke." Zee nodded. My head hurt. I added a little Bailey's Irish Cream to my coffee. It helped.

"Lake looks good," he said. "Silent." He lit up a mystery joint, slightly bent. I gazed out at the frozen silence of the lake, envisioning the act – us out there, finishing the job. I inhaled deep off my cigarette. It tasted good, the smoke filling my lungs with a warmth and purpose. "Could hide a body good in that water, eh?"

Lewis emerged from the bathroom going on about how he was swearing off drugs and alcohol forever. He only needed women. Women and cigarettes. Then he found some cocaine left over in his jacket pocket and he adjusted his pledge: women, cigarettes and coke.

"I couldn't sleep last night," Lewis said. "Too much pain." He scratched himself down there.

"Still hurt?" Zee asked.

"You have no idea. What was that Kung Fu shit with the pool stick?"

"Our opponent is a worthy adversary," Zee joked, speaking over random, mismatched movement of his mouth, imitating an English-dubbed martial arts movie scene. "We must use our intelligence as weapons."

"Seriously. If we're not going to the police, then we should get everything we can on this guy," Lewis suggested. "He drives a purple truck, right? What make was it?"

"How many Purple trucks can there be?" I said.

"Ford? Chevy? Toyota? Dodge?"

"It was dark," I said.

"Donna would know," Lewis said. "The cheerleader girl? She was in there, probably saw the insignia's on the steering wheel – you know?"

"I think she was probably more occupied with the fact that she was being raped," Zee said.

"Look, we've been here like two days already and I haven't had any sex. If this keeps up, I'm going to have a problem," Lewis said. "So, if we're going to find this guy, let's do it fast and go home."

We surmised that the only reason someone would have a purple pick-up truck was if they worked for a company or business that had a purple theme. And from that we surmised that a sports store that sold summer and winter ski equipment was the best option. The only place in town that did that was The Dock.

By the time we arrived at The Dock sporting goods store they were getting ready to close. Lewis got the salesman's attention by asking questions about snowboards.

"These new Barfoot's are awesome, man. The edges are pre-beveled and the turning arc is just too rad for words. You're carving on this puppy like slalom skiing. Powder spray," the salesman said.

"What about speed?" Lewis asked.

"Oh, this baby's the real deal, eh," the salesman said throwing in his thick Canadian country lilt and stereotypical 'eh'. I jumped in.

"Is Freddie here?" I asked. "He helped me out with some ski-do stuff and I really need to get some more advice. I mean, I don't want to ask anyone else. The guy really knew his stuff. He should get the commission."

"He doesn't work here anymore," the salesman said dismissively.

"You know where I can find him," I asked.

"Not here," he said. "Excuse me, but I'm with a customer," referring to Lewis.

"We're together." Lewis looked at me strangely. "Not like that," I clarified. "But I really wanted to talk to Fred. He had some suggestions about products. And stuff." Lewis' look told me that I was sounding like I was full of shit. He wasn't the only person who caught it.

"He doesn't work here, so he can't help you. And, honestly, if you're just looking for him, I can't help you either. We're closing now, so if you don't mind." He indicated the door.

"You know where he works?"

"No. But if you do find him, tell him to make sure he never sets foot in here again."

"That went well," Zee said when we were back outside walking towards the car. It was colder than the night before. The kind of cold where you can't even feel the toes in your shoes.

"Maybe we should just go home," Lewis said.

"Let's hit a hotel bar," I said. "Kick back by a fire with a nice brandy, check out the women. Regroup."

"No, I mean maybe we should just go back home. To Toronto."

"I knew it," I said. "You're backing out. I knew it."

Lewis looked over at Zee, then back at me. "It's not that. It's you. We were all wasted last night, Fisch, but you were partying at a whole other gear. I mean, the way you were drinking."

"Like you were trying to drown yourself," Zee said.

"Don't be so dramatic," I scoffed.

"Dave," Zee said. He spoke softly. "I had this dream a couple of weeks ago. I didn't tell you: You were sitting in the corner of my house, in a big chair. And you had a drink in each hand. Except it wasn't you, it was just the skeleton of you. And when you drank, I could see the liquid pour down the insides of your body."

"So what? You ever watch yourself smoke?" I asked Zee. "You're not exactly a poster boy for Men's Health magazine."

"Would you listen to what we're saying," Lewis pleaded. "We just think that this girl has really messed you up inside. Whatever it is that you think you can fix by killing this guy, we don't think you can fix it. Not this way."

"I'm cold," I said. "Give me the keys," I told Zee.

TV white noise and marijuana smoke wafted into the main bedroom. I lay on the bed thinking about how I was going to put it all together when Zee entered. "We have to talk," he said. Zee wasn't much of a talker. He chose his moments. He lowered himself into a hammock-like chair in the corner of the room. "I haven't been a good friend to you. The thing with Kris, I mean.... Part of me wanted to see if she'd let me go through with it... to see if she was good enough for you. And I realized, because she let me in, that she wasn't." He clasped his hands together, like he was pleading, or praying. "But, you're talking about killing a guy for her. And this guy looks like he'd kill you in a second."

"What would you do?" I asked. "If your girlfriend was raped! Or your sister!"

"Leave my sister out of it. My sister has not been raped! And *Kris* is not your *sister*! It's not the same!"

"Sorry."

"Dave – this has nothing to do with whether or not Kris was raped. This is all about getting her to love you. She's told you – she's shown you – she doesn't. Let it go, Fisch. She's not worth risking your life."

Zee stopped there. I heard what he wanted me to hear. I probably couldn't have heard it from anyone else.

"You know what it's like… to not know if… if there's anyone that will love you the way you want to be loved…? I mean, I hardly speak to my parents and when I do, it's like I'm the one trying to be kind so *they* won't feel bad. It's supposed to be the other way around."

"Dave. You're seventeen. You don't have to get married yet. You just need to have fun."

"But… what makes you so certain she would lie to me?"

"She was ready to let me sleep with her. Yes. The answer to your question? Yes. I would have and she would have let me."

Tears ran into my mouth. "You think she made the whole thing up?" Zee couldn't answer that, which, in a way, was worse. I wanted to let go of her, but something in me needed to hang on.

Since Zee couldn't speak for Kris' motives, I couldn't find the evidence to give up. If Kris was seeking attention with the story about rape then I was just as needy with my story of vengeance.

"So," Zee asked, "You want to get this guy, I'll come along to make sure you don't get killed. Or you drop this bullshit and we have a good time. Like we planned to."

"You heard what he said," I reminded Zee.

"It's bullshit, Fisch. He's just a little man with a Napoleonic complex trying to scare you. Ignore him, he'll go away."

"What if he doesn't go away?"

"Dave, you have to stop worrying so much. You need to move on."

"Fuckin' A! Let's get laid!" Lewis yelled from the living room. Zee and I laughed. He pulled me into him and we hugged. Lewis poked his head in and raised a dubious eyebrow.

"What're you faggots doing?" I reached for Lewis and pulled him into the group hug.

"Yeah, who's the faggot now?" I joked with him.

"Tonight, we get fucked up and go sledding down the ski hills!" Zee yelled.

"Face first!" I added.

Zee looked at Lewis. "You in? Or is that too homo for you?"

"Hey, I'll smoke a joint out of a polar bears ass if it'll get me into some pussy soon! My balls are gonna explode!"

"You'll get your action," I said. I had no way of knowing how true that would be.

When I had a little privacy, I picked up the phone. It was time to do the dutiful thing.

"Hello, Mom? I'm at the cottage."

"Thanks for telling me. I've only been worried sick. I've called every one of your friends and made an ass out of myself asking where you are. Now the whole world thinks I can't control my own children. So, you're up there doing god knows what with who?"

"I just wanted to let you know where I was. I'm okay."

"When are you coming home?"

"I… I don't know," I said.

"Someone called for you."

"Who?" I asked.

"A girl."

"What was her name?"

"I don't remember. Come home. I need to know you're okay," she said. Her voice was quivering. The tension between us had been so awful I knew my Mom was taking a huge risk getting honest with me. If I had been a good son, I would have followed her lead, I would have had the guts to tell her the truth, let her know what was going on with me.

I wasn't ready to go there yet.

"Was her name Kris?"

"Just… come home, David. In one piece. Please. I only have one son."

"Mom… I'm fine. I'll call you later."

"David? I love you."

"I'm okay, Mom."

I just couldn't do it.

The next call I made was to Kris. I got her answering machine and hung up. Then I realized what a lame move that was and dialed again. This time I told her answering machine where I was and what I was doing. I told the machine I was going to make things right. I told the machine I was sorry, but her machine was merciless in its silence. All it did was record. So I told it I would try to control my drinking. I told it my friends were saying things also and maybe it was something I should look into. I had to straighten out. But I had to straighten things out with Fred first. I told Kris' machine that I couldn't live with myself unless I tried to make it right. When I hung up I realized that I couldn't erase what I had said.

I was trapped in her machine.

CHAPTER TWENTY FIVE

Lewis threw down the paper in disgust. "Nothing but skank whores!" He'd been looking through the back pages for an escort ad.

"What're you talking about? They got photo's of them," I said. The girls they advertised in their ads were perfect. "Look!"

"Yeah. You think they're gonna send a girl they cut from a playboy magazine? They send toothless chicks forty pounds overweight. Bad breath. Bad hair. Out of Kazakhstan or some hellish place."

"So wait 'till we're back in the city," I said.

"You wait. My whole nervous system's out of whack," Lewis said.

"I am really getting sick of your whining crap," Zee said.

"Like I care. I get laid more than the two of you combined."

"I don't have to pay for it," Zee said.

"Hey, at least I get more than Fischer, but that's putting the bar pretty low."

"Didn't know you could measure," Zee said. "I mean, that's a pretty fucked up thing to say considering –."

"Considering what?" Lewis said.

"The only reason you're friends with Fischer is because he makes you feel superior. He looks up to you. He seeks your advice and in return you...."

"That's all right," I said, trying to calm Zee.

"No, Fisch. It's not all right. This asshole –"

"So, he's an asshole. So what?" And with that I turned on Lewis. "It's common knowledge amongst psychologists that the guy who has to brag about sex is compensating for something else. Maybe a small penis. Maybe the fact that you have no life of your own – because its already been planned out by your parents: You're going to law school whether you like it or not; you're going to pass the bar whether you want to or not; you're going into your Dad's well-respected firm no matter how badly you screw up in law school; you're going to marry a trophy wife - that your father approves of - who lets you cheat on her; you're going to move into an obnoxiously ostentatious house that your dad buys for you just down the street from your parents, and you're going to let your parents dictate the rest of your unimaginative life for you, because it's easier than working for it." I paused to check how this was being received. Lewis stayed tight-lipped, trying to be above it, hiding behind the cigarette he was smoking down to the filter. "Yeah, that's what I thought."

Lewis scoffed. "It's pathetic to me how jealous you are."

"Maybe you're right. I have looked up to you for advice with women. But ever since I met Kris you started acting like a total jerk. When my heart is breaking and I need your help, you act like I'm an intrusion in your pampered, effortless life. You might be able to get laid whenever you want – by tutors your Dad provides for you. But you've never made a decision for yourself."

Lewis chain smoked. His hand shook a little. He did not handle being spoken to very well.

"Well, well, well. How the tables have turned." Zee exclaimed.

"What about you?" Lewis retaliated, looking at me. "You don't exactly come from the poster-family. "

I could only laugh. "Why? 'Cause my family's so busy trying to save their own lost lives they don't give a shit about mine? My Dad's basically a lap dog for his new wife and my Mom's totally obsessed about her career and her social status. And my sister – I don't know where to start with her. She's probably going to invent a new eating disorder. But, hey, at least I can admit it! I don't have to belittle you to feel better about myself."

"Yeah," Zee said. "You can just belittle yourself!"

"That's right," I added. "When you're as pathetic as me, who needs friends like you?"

"Look, that's not how I meant it…" Lewis was trying to find the words. Not his strong suit.

"Here we go again," Zee said, egging Lewis on. There was something ugly stirring between them.

"Let's hear your story," Lewis said to Zee. "What makes you so high and mighty?"

"Well," Zee said, inhaling off a freshly lit joint, "this is what makes me high. Mighty high." Zee chuckled.

"What do the psychologists say about someone who constantly needs to be getting high and doesn't take anything seriously?"

"Fear of responsibility," Zee admitted. "My parents have a business. If I want in, I've got a life laid out for me. Just like you – they've already made the plans, just a matter of watching the dominoes fall. But that's not the life I want."

"What do you want?" I asked.

"I don't know," Zee said. "I'm supposed to know everything about my life now? At seventeen? Maybe I'll move to Israel and join the IDF. Serve my two years like any Israeli, maybe stay? Who knows?"

"That's just it," Lewis said. "My parents are always telling me I have to make choices about my life. When did I stop being allowed to be a kid?"

"I sometimes still play with G.I. Joe's," I confessed. "You think I can still be with a woman like Kris?"

"Why does being a man suddenly have to come with a job, a mortgage and car payments?" Lewis said.

"I'm buying my car. Cash. No payments," Zee said.

"What – for that piece of shit out there?" Lewis said, laughing.

"Fuck you," Zee added. And that was it. We were all friends again.

"Look, I've been an idiot about this whole thing," I said. "I don't know how I got so messed up over this girl. It's not just Kris. I've been screwed up for years. I take everything I have for granted. Kris even said so. I need to grow up."

"Man, do you listen to everything that chick tells you? You're seventeen, Dude," Lewis said. "Give yourself a break."

"Sure, we all need to grow up, Fisch," Zee observed," But what for? My parents... they're not happy. They run their business, they have a nice house, they take ski vacations – but they're not *enjoying* their life. They're just moving through it. I see way too many so called grown-ups going through the motions of life. Very few of them are any proof that growing up is worth it."

"My parents are miserable trying hard to pretend they're not. But that has nothing to do with me. This is my life," I said. "I've got to start getting serious."

"Why?" Zee pleaded.

"I should just forget the whole Kris thing. There'll be other girls, right?" Lewis nodded unconvincingly.

"What about this Fred character?" Lewis asked.

"Maybe I'm making a bigger deal out of it."

"He raped your girlfriend," Lewis said. Zee shot him a look to kill.

"I... can't know that... for sure," I said. I glanced at Zee. He was impressed. "Kris... could have said anything." I paused, choking back tears. I felt like I was betraying Kris' trust.

Zee placed an encouraging hand on my shoulder. "I'm proud of you, kid." I laughed. "This…? This is growing up right here."

"So, what's the plan?" Lewis asked.

"Whatever you want," I said.

Lewis' face lit up. "Let's go to a strip club!"

"Maybe we should just go home," I said.

"You sure?" Zee asked.

I had sucked my friends deep into something they had no business being deep into. It was selfish of me, dangerous for them, and an entirely stupid plan.

"What're you going to do back home?" Zee asked me.

"I don't know. Work out. Hang out. Maybe I'll even look at some of the stuff from class. Finals in January." Zee nodded, only to indicate that he had heard of final exams. In no way was he going to study for them. He just showed up and aced them.

"Maybe you should return the gun."

I shrugged. But I knew exactly what I would do. Kris filled the black empty and colored it in. She was all wrong for me. And I needed her.

I was addicted to her.

We packed to leave that night. We put food away agreeing that we would take another trip up to hang out soon. We all felt good about the decision. We closed the lights and said goodbye to the cottage.

I opened the door to leave and suddenly realized I wasn't going anywhere.

She didn't have to say 'hello' or anything. All she had to do was smile.

Which is all Kris did, sitting on a step of the front landing, outside the front door, like she'd been waiting.

"Hi," Kris said. "Miss me?"

CHAPTER TWENTY SIX

"Oh, that's just fucking great," Lewis said. "Just when he was making some progress."

Zee dropped his bags. "Seriously?" he exclaimed, and retreated to the living room.

"I'm going to make coffee," I said. "You want coffee, Kris? Jesus, how'd you even get here?"

"Look, he's not into you anymore," Lewis barked. "You messed with his head. He was thinking of hunting down this other guy - ."

"Lewis!" I yelled, glaring at him. "Do you want coffee or not?!"

"He was getting his head straight! We were going home. And now you show up out of the blue...?!?" He plopped himself in a chair, crossed his arms and pouted.

"Can I speak to you in private?" Kris asked me. I saw her glance towards a corner of the living room. I followed her look and found Zee. Zee was staring at her hard – examining Kris. Jealousy rose up. Zee raised an eyebrow at me. It was a warning.

"Can we have a word...?" Zee asked.

I turned to Kris. "Just a sec - ," I was cut short by her.

"I just need to borrow him for a second, boys. You've had him to yourselves for several days now. Time to share."

"David - ," Zee implored. But Kris was moving me into the master bedroom and I wasn't fighting it. She closed the door most of the way. I longed for this moment so badly, missed her so badly, and yet the question had to be asked:

"Why did you come – ?" Before I could finish she had her arms around me and her lips pressed against mine. If my life depended on it, I couldn't do justice describing how good her kiss felt. I was home again.

"I...," she licked my lips, "...felt bad...," more kissing, her soft lips, "...about what happened at my apartment...." She was my drug. I was lost in her. "With your friend out there. The tall one."

"I remember," I said. "I just didn't think you'd take me through it again." Her smile said touché. "So. You drove all the way up here? To apologize?"

"I got your message. I was on a bus an hour later. That guy – Fred – he's crazy, David. You can't beat him. He's a lunatic." Her tone threw me off, like she knew the whole scenario too well. "I came up here because I'm scared for you. You don't have to do this. *I don't need* you to do this."

"You came up here to tell me that?"

"She's lying," Zee said. He was standing in the doorway. He placed himself there.

"I'm not," Kris said. "I wasn't fair to you back in the city when you tried to make up. I should never have let him into my apartment. I used him. It was cruel. And childish. And all it did was create a rift between you and your friend and that's not fair."

"Ohh, she's good," Zee observed. "You've got real polish on that bullshit act, my dear."

"I know how this looks," Kris said, staring down Zee. "But then again, I'm not the one who tried to get close and private with my best friends girl. So just how good is your word?"

"Don't trust her, Fisch," Zee said.

"You are apologizing for a lot of things all of a sudden," I said.

Kris reached for my hand. "Listen to me. I grew up around here. I... I know... this place and... and you need to leave."

"She's hiding something, David! This is way too coincidental!"

"He called me! I came here!" she insisted.

She shook her head at me, and I started to shake mine like I was about to hear something I wasn't prepared for. She pushed off of me and threw open the closet. Hangers screeched across the pole as she rejected one garment after another. She plucked a thick cable-knit wool turtleneck sweater off a hanger and threw it at me. "You have a coat?"

"Upstairs," I nodded. Kris stepped close, kissed me again and whispered in my ear. "Out the back."

"Why do we have to leave? This is a private home."

She looked at Zee and back to me, even glanced at Lewis. "We have to get out of here. Now."

Suddenly the front door crashed open against a metal baseboard heater. Lewis yelled "Oh, shit!" Kris started tearing the blinds off the sliding glass doors that led from the bedroom to the deck.

"Lew?!" Zee shouted. "What's going on?!"

Lewis shouted something. There was a punch and a groan. Zee grabbed Kris by the arm. "You fucking ambushed us?!"

"Get out!" she yelled, shoving a hat she pulled off the shelf into my hands; then clawing at the lock on the door.

"You go. I got this."

"You're crazy," I yelled.

"Three summers in Israel. Kibbutz and army training. I got this!"

"Zee! This isn't some fucking Camp Ramah exercise. Let's go!"

"You go!"

He reached over Kris' shoulder and threw the slide bolt. Zee pushed us out onto the deck. We ran, turned and slid down the snow-covered stairs to the hill that led towards the lake.

The snow was deep behind the house. No one's step had broken its surface in months. Kris and I were stepping knee deep, struggling to make inches. Behind me, the cottage glowed with light.

Faces appeared in the windows overlooking the back. Zee's then Gord's. Zee's body was jerking back and forth, like he was being shaken by the neck. Someone yelled. Banging sounds. Then someone was on the deck, shouting and pointing. A sleight build and pit-bull stance, pointing in our direction.

"There!" Fred yelled. "They're down there!"

"Run!" Kris yelled at me.

My thoughts were firing a hundred per second: *What are they doing?! Where are you taking me? What are you really doing here?!*

"RUN!" was all Kris said. I stopped.

"My friends!" Kris pulled at my arm but my feet were planted. "My friends are back there! I can't leave them!"

"Listen to me carefully," Kris said, grabbing me by the sweater, bunching it in her fist. "He's not playing around. He intends to really hurt someone. They don't want your friends. They want me."

"Why?" I asked.

"It's complicated," she said.

"So *uncomplicate* it," I said.

"Not now!" Kris said.

"Now!"

"He's coming!"

"Let him," I said.

"He'll only use your friends as collateral. But if he doesn't get what he wants, he could really do some damage."

"How do you know this guy, Kris?!!"

"I'M TRYING TO HELP YOU!!" she yelled, and pushed me hard. The snow felt good when I hit it, then it stung with cold. "Get up. GET UP!" Kris yelled.

"This needs to happen," I said. "Finally. Once and for all."

"Yeah, that's what's going to happen, David. Once and for all." My breath was puffing cold smoke. "You don't get what this is, David! Goddam it, David – I thought you were smart!" I was about to make another grand statement about loyalty when I heard the unmistakable crunching of footsteps into deep snow. Then I felt the pressure of cold metal against my neck

"You really don't like to stand much, do you?" Fred said, looking down at me, again. I wadded up some spit, ready to spray it in Fred's face. Fred pressed a crow bar into my shoulder and on a nerve. The crow bar already had blood stains on it.

"Don't be stupid," he said.

Zee and Lewis had their mouths duct taped shut and their hands duct taped behind their backs. They were taped to each other, back to back. Gord walked them to the end of the dock and forced them to sit down at the edge, one small push away from falling onto the ice and probably through it into the freezing cold water. Gord stood over them. The roll of duct tape was in one hand. A hunting rifle was resting against his leg like a post.

Fred walked me and Kris up towards the dock. Zee's eyes narrowed. They were cold and steely with thoughts of revenge. Even behind the tape covering a third of his face I could see he was furious with me. Lewis looked scared. The front of his pants was dark where he had soiled them. Lewis' eyes looked wildly around seeking out an escape.

"Walk," Fred pressed the metal against my shoulder. Kris stepped forward to walk next to me.

"Just do what he says," she whispered. Fred grabbed Kris' arm and pulled her back beside him. There was an odd familiarity to the way he grabbed her and the way she reacted to it.

Why would he come back? Why would he come back for her? And who did she come back for, exactly?

As I walked the length of the dock, like a pirate's gang plank, it occurred to me that my friends were probably right: Kris had lied. The rape was probably not a rape, exactly. And I had just gotten us all into a level of trouble we'd never even imagined before – one that we might not get out of alive.

"Tie him up with his buddies," Fred said, pushing me towards Gord. Gord forced my wrists behind my back in a fast Nelson and duct taped them together, spinning the roll around the wrists in a matter of seconds, the tape tugging at my skin and hair and cutting into my flesh. I felt my blood ooze out and meet the cold air.

Fred held Kris close to him, gripping her by the arm. She didn't look like she was in any pain. Gord kicked a steel-toed work boot into the back of my leg. That got me down on my knees. Next thing I knew I was tied up with Zee and Lewis.

"There. You guys are all together again. The three little pigs," Fred said. "I guess that makes me the big bad wolf," he laughed. "So what's that make you, Blondie?" Looking at Kris. "You Goldilocks or Red Riding Hood?"

"Goldilocks was with the three bears, you moron," I said.

"I know *that*," Fred said. "I'm just checking with my little friend here to see how it's going to turn out for her? She gonna get eaten by the Wolf? Or is she gonna get pawed in bed by the bears? Whattaya think, Gord? Lone wolf or a team of bears?"

"That's your call," Gord said, avoiding the question.

"I'm offering you the opportunity, Gordo. You want in?"

"Hey, she's your sister," Gord said.

A sonic boom exploded in my brain. Thunder rolled across my eyeballs. I glanced at Zee and Lew to see if they heard what I thought I heard. I couldn't see their faces with my back to them, but a sudden and simultaneous tension ran through all of us like lightning, like we all just got punched in the gut, and I heard Lewis mumble '*I knew it!!*' under his duct tape.

"For Pete's sakes, Gord! Can't you shut up?! You're disturbing our guests!" Fred said.

"I'm just sayin'. I don't really feel comfortable getting involved in anything of a sexual nature with your sister."

"Jeezuz!" Fred balked. "You are a fucking moron, you know that, Gord? A fucking moron."

Tears streamed down Kris' face. She stared down at the ice like she wanted to disappear into it.

"Well," Fred said to me, "*Surprise!* "All this time, you thought there was something unique and special between you and my little sister here. Yeah, I can tell, you got a thing for her. That's sweet, isn't that sweet, Kris?"

"Stop it, Freddy," Kris managed through her crying. Lewis was doing his best to elbow me, trying to let me know that he figured out how Fred and Kris knew each other.

"Kris," I managed, "please… tell me this isn't true." Kris opened her mouth to say something then looked away.

"Tell the boy," Fred said, shaking her. "He deserves to know."

"Why couldn't you just keep running?" Kris said to me. Then, revealing her defeat and complete surrender, she said, "Let's just get this over with."

Fred pulled out a coin. "Wolf or Bears?" Fred asked.

"Please, Freddy," she said.

"Wolf or Bears?"

"Wolf," Kris whispered. It was all the energy she had left.

"Sorry, Gordie." Fred grinned his sick, hungry grin.

"Catch." Fred tossed Gord the crow bar. "If they try to get away use the crow bar first. Don't use the rifle unless you have to," he said with boyish glee. In that moment, I saw that Fred was, in his true nature, an animal. He acted out of a primal drive. Kris was his prey. We were next.

Fred jerked Kris to him with a snap of his arm. Her head bobbed submissively on top of her neck like a rag doll as Fred yanked her off the dock, onto shore and up the hill towards the cottage. My cottage.

"Kris! *KRI-I-I-S!!*" I yelled. I screamed. Until Gord wrapped my mouth with duct tape. Fred pulled Kris up the stairs, behind some trees and finally disappeared into the cottage. I kept yelling through the thick metallic grey tape; muffled, impotent yells that weren't heard by anyone who could do anything to help.

Zee shook his head, trying to tell me to give it up. I'd never seen his eyes so full of fear. His face was lacerated with cuts and bruised. Gord had beat him up badly. Lewis was in a bad way to start off and now he was nodding off. Out here, in the dead of winter, you don't know you're dying. Frostbite takes the fingers and toes while you fade out.

I kicked at Lewis to keep him awake.

I glanced at Zee for guidance. Zee shook his head. Then he looked down. Directly below us and spread out, the frozen lake lay like an empty, inviting tomb. Its black icy surface barely reflected any moonlight.

Ice you can see. It's white or clear; it hangs from roof edges like bangs. It glazes across surfaces. Ice is beautiful and alluring, part of the mesmerizing spectacle of winter wonder; and yet one must proceed with caution.

Black ice is different.

Black Ice camouflages itself on roads and other dark surfaces. It's indistinguishable from its surface host. You don't see it. Until you're on it. Spinning out of control.

My life had hit black ice.

My heart had driven recklessly over it: Kris. She looked safe enough. I never saw it coming.

All of a sudden, Kris was at my door, my heart was in her hand and my life was out of my control.

Kris. And Fred.

Sister and brother.

A brother who rapes his sister. Regularly. Like a wolf.

The thought alone beat the shit out of my brain.

CHAPTER TWENTY SEVEN

I was done.

Spent.

My emotions lay in a puddle of frozen tears around me.

I was duct-taped to my best friends and guarded but I felt utterly alone.

Neither Zee nor Lewis made any attempt to squash my crying. Nor did they join me. They were silent and still. We sat in the snow at the wintry edge of life, a frozen lake below us, while the fading tip of the northern lights reached across the night's sky.

Lewis kicked me. It was a small kick, meant to not attract attention, only mine. I shifted my position so I could see him. Lewis nodded his head towards the lake. Below us, at the end of the dock, there was a noticeable crack in the ice.

I elbowed Zee and we showed him the crack. Zee glanced towards Gord, sitting on a log he had pulled up, biding his time by taking sips from a metal flask and watching us. We weren't giving him much to watch over. And Gord didn't seem the type to incite us into a reaction he could justify quelling with a swing of the crow bar. The boredom of the situation seemed to be making him quite content. Comfortable enough to nap.

Zee nudged his elbow into me. With the duct tape over our mouths and our hands tied, we were limited to physical gestures to communicate. Left this way we would eventually diminish into

Neanderthal men, gesturing and signaling without the use of words.

We would de-evolve; we would become primal.

Which, perhaps, is what we needed to become if we were ever going to survive this.

Zee's shivering, however, was not an attempt to communicate. Left here, exposed to the elements, we would freeze.

Then we would die.

I thought about my ancestors, my grandfather and great grandfather, who killed in order to survive. My father would never hurt a fly. Maybe this ancestral trait, the ability to kill, skipped a generation.

I sure as shit needed it to.

Zee pointed towards his front pants pocket. He was reaching the length of his long fingers towards the opening of his right front pocket and a flat-sided, square-shaped object: his Zippo. Gesturing his neck forward, pushing at the tape, he was telling me what he wanted. I reached two fingers towards the bottom outline of the lighter, pushing it closer to the opening of the pocket and Zee's fingertips.

Lewis noticed what we were doing and immediately looked away to not attract attention. Smart move.

Gord was busy watching the stars attempt to push their light through the clouds. He seemed to be rooting for the starlight.

Soon the stainless steel lighter appeared at the opening of Zee's leather pants pocket. As I pushed it up another millimeter, Zee reached two fingers in clamp-like formation to retrieve it. With our fingers as frigid as they were, Zee's grip slipped several times. I kept pushing the bottom of the lighter up and out of Zee's pocket while pressing my palm against his pants in case I had to catch the lighter. Carefully, Zee pulled the weighted lighter out of his pocket, and closed his hand around it.

Zee and I had overcome many challenges for lighting joints in blizzard winds, torrential rains, and outsmarting smoke alarms; we lit up while balanced on the precipices of various bridges over Toronto ravines with winter storms blowing forty mile an hour warning gusts. Now we had to light Zee's Zippo without dropping it through the cracks in the dock's planks, we had to hold the flame close to our skin without burning it. We had to do it all with our hands tied behind our backs where we couldn't see shit.

And we had to hide the light from Gord's view.

Simple.

Zee slowly flicked open the Zippo and placed his thumb on the flint wheel. I had a hand cupped underneath. Lewis had to be our eyes. Zee spun the flint wheel slowly, to be as quiet as possible. But it was too slow for the flint to catch flame. Gord was nodding off. I patted Zee's hand to signal him to wait. He did. We held still, Zippo in hand, as Gord dozed off.

I tapped Zee's hand. He lit the Zippo. The light of the flame glowed between our united backs. We pressed as close to each other as possible to block the flame's glow from view. Lewis cocked his head to the left as an indicator. Zee tilted the Zippo's flame in that direction. My skin went red hot and I could smell burning hair. I bit my lip to stop myself from screaming. Lewis shook his head violently at Zee. Zee backed the flame off, then tilted it again, more gradually. Soon I smelled a different smell – the glue smell of burning duct tape.

Lewis kept his eyes trained on Gord while the chemical smell of burning rubber and glue wafted into the air. I forced my wrists against the melting tape until they ripped free. I reached behind me and tore at Zee's, and then Lewis' tape. My fingers felt like pieces of metal against the tape. We moved as silently as we could but the night was more silent. Every shift we made on the dock pressed against the dark ice of the lake.

CRAAAAAK! Roaring into Gord's ears.

Gord opened his eyes. He stood up and reached down in one motion, grabbing the crowbar. He approached, and it was obvious by the furl of his brow and the slight cocking of his head that he was confused, since we all still sat huddled with our hands behind our backs and the tape over our mouths. "What's that smell," Gord said. We did not respond or move. Our silence brought Gord closer. Gord bent closer to sniff the source of the hot glue smell. Lewis suddenly kicked out his booted legs hard at Gord's shins. Gord's legs went back and he fell forward onto his chest. I scrambled for the crowbar while Zee went for Gord's rifle. The second Gord landed, Zee rammed his heel into his lower back. There was an audible crack and Gord cried out. Lewis wrapped duct tape around Gord's wrists, then his mouth and then around his eyes. He kept wrapping and wrapping around Gord's face.

Zee kicked again at Gord's head. Gord struggled against the tape. His hands broke free. Lewis leapt back with a yelp. Gord stood up and waved his hands around swinging at what he couldn't see. I got low and swung the crow bar into Gord's stomach. Gord dropped onto one knee. Snot bubbled out of his nostrils, his only ventilation. I rested the cold iron bar against the back of his head.

"Next swing, I'm gonna smash the back of your head in!" Gord got still.

"Lie down." Gord used his one bent leg to launch himself to standing. I swung and smacked his arm, knocking him back. But Gord kept coming.

"Jesus," Zee exclaimed, "he's a monster!"

Gord went for the sound of Zee's voice.

"Dave!" Zee yelled. I knew what he meant. I tossed him the crow bar. He caught it without a sound.

"Come on!" Zee taunted.

Gord lunged, raised his arms, and Zee swatted the iron crowbar into Gord's ribs, cracking several on impact. Gord moaned, dropped down, struggled to breathe. He rolled over. I had the crow bar back. I swung again, this time at his knee, smashing it so he couldn't walk.

It felt good, hitting him. Gord screamed a muffled scream. It scared me, how good it felt to be this brutal, this cruel to another human being. I felt no mercy for Gord. He was willing to kill us, follow Fred's commands blindly, like a dog. He was prepared to kill us without hesitation or remorse.

We were just killing him first.

I swung the crowbar up high. Zee said 'don't do it' behind me but I didn't listen. I turned the crowbar around in my hands so the s-shaped prying edge protruded forward and the blunt end took a back seat.

I suddenly saw Gord as a large block of wood that needed to be chopped.

"Dave!" Zee yelled. "Don't!"

I smashed the crowbar down. It plunged into the back of Gord's shoulder, close to the neck. Blood spurted through his shirt, his sweater and coat and began to saturate his clothes.

"Jesus! Christ!" Lewis yelled.

"No!" Zee said. "We are not killers."

"He axed his neck!" Lewis exclaimed. "He's gonna bleed to death!"

"No, he won't. But he won't be chasing us anymore." Lewis looked nauseas. "Look – don't you get it?! It's him or us," I said.

Lewis blew his breath on his cupped hands. "I can't feel my fingers," he whimpered.

Zee opened the rifle's bullet chamber and emptied the gun of all ammunition.

"What're you doing that for?" I asked.

"When Israel is at their best, they wait for the right moment to attack. Then, under cover, they sneak in. Stealth. Precise. Deadly. They know their target. They eliminate, they rescue and they leave. In and out. Done and gone. That's the way of the Sayerot."

"The who?"

"Israeli Special forces. I didn't come here to kill just anybody," Zee said. "We came to accomplish a mission. Stick to the game plan."

"The game plan was and still is Fred. Gord is Fred's goon. So Gord gets eliminated, too. We're just being pro-active here."

"When did you get so cold?" Zee said.

Lewis bent over, puking bile. "This isn't fucking happening," he coughed.

Gord was bleeding profusely. Blood was spreading out onto the dock, freezing in place mid-stream.

"He's not going to bleed to death. The freezing temp's will save him," I said.

"How's that?" Zee asked.

"In freezing temperature, your heart rate slows down, so the blood flow slows down. Resting heart rate drops dramatically.

He's passed out so he's definitely resting. His blood's flowing so slowly it has time to freeze. He won't die out here."

Zee nodded, impressed. "Where'd you learn that? Boy scouts?"

"Chemistry."

"You took chem?"

"One semester."

"Hellooo! Guy dying at our feet…!" Lewis chimed in.

"How much duct tape do we have?" I asked.

"Why?" Lewis asked.

I nodded towards the thick maple that stood at the edge of the shore. "We make sure he doesn't get anywhere."

"Where the fuck's he going?" Zee said.

As if on cue, Gord groaned. That was all the proof we needed to go ahead.

We tied Gord up to the maple with what remained of the duct tape. We wrapped him up so tightly, he barely leaned away from the tree.

"He's not going anywhere, but I doubt he'll survive," Zee said.

"He's sheltered from the wind," I said.

"By a tree," Zee said.

"You seriously care about whether this scumbag lives or dies?" I demanded.

"If he dies then it's a murder, David. That we committed. Or were accessories to. That's years in prison." Zee was emphatic. "Not days, not months. Years. Years, David!"

"He was going to kill us!" I said. "With a crowbar and a rifle!"

"It's self defense," Lewis said. "My Dad's defended this kind of case before."

"And so we do nothing to try and save him?"

"Like what?"

"Call an ambulance!"

"With what? The phone in the cottage? Where Fred is?" I asked.

"I told you to call the police a long time ago," Lewis said.

Zee nodded. "We do that, we can get out of this and look good. We take this any further... we're going to hell, I swear to god."

I looked up at the light in the cottage, imagining what Fred was doing up there with Kris.

"We're going to hell anyway," I said.

So we waited and watched Gord.

We watched....

We waited....

For a sign of whether Gord was still alive or dead.

Lewis finally pulled a small mirror out of his wallet. Lewis wiped some cocaine residue off the mirror. Zee reacted, wishing he had had the chance to inhale it. "Place it under his nose, see if he's breathing," Lewis said.

"Go ahead," I said.

"No way," Lewis said. He handed it towards Zee. "You do it."

Zee reached out and grabbed the mirror. "Pussies, both of you!"

Zee walked up to Gord. Then he went around the back of the tree and reached around with his long arm. He got the mirror under Gord's slumped head, where his nostrils poked through the duct tape. Tiny bubbles of blood opened, expanded and contracted like lungs. Gord's weak breath cast a shadow of steam across the small mirror, faded away with his inhale, then spread out again as he exhaled.

"We're not going to hell yet," Zee said.

Part of me was relieved. Another part was disappointed. I could have killed Gord with one blow but I chickened out. I was sick and tired of being pushed around, beaten up, ridiculed, belittled, underestimated and condescended to. My parents did it to me, my friend's did it to me, and now these guys, Fred and Gord – I couldn't take it anymore.

"Bring the rifle," I said.

I took the rifle, aimed it at Gord's temple, pressed it against his skull there. It felt good. It felt possible.

"All right, let's go," and I handed the rifle back to Zee.

Zee strapped the weapon over his shoulder. We left Gord tied to the tree and we marched up to the cottage. It was time to finish what was started.

CHAPTER TWENTY EIGHT

The cottage loomed sinister above us now, on the hill. Fred was in there, with Kris as his hostage.

Brother and sister.

The thought made me sick.

The only lights on in the place glowed yellow from the living room windows, jaundice eyes peering down at us. We trudged as silently as possible through the snow towards the lower foundation of the house

Built on a hill, the first floor of the house was the basement. The top floor was at road level. There were two floors in between. 3000 square feet of danger.

I reached the foundation wall first and crouched down. Lewis and Zee stood, breathing fast. "Get down," I yelled in a whisper. We crouched below the basement window panes. "There's no way to know where he is, or even if he's still in there. Right now, all I want to do is get Kris out."

"Really, Fisch?" Zee asked. "You're still willing to help a girl who could have just pulled you into this mess?"

"She needs help."

"No shit," Zee said.

"This is way out of our league," Lewis said. "These guys are twisted. We need to go to the police now. We haven't killed anyone, the guy's inside your house; we have them on breaking and entering, home invasion, assault, kidnapping. It's an easy open and shut and throw away the key."

"Lewis is right," Zee said. "This is as far as we go."

"I can't leave Kris here."

"Yes you can!" Zee snapped. "This is a sick psychopathic white trash love story. The fact that you're even still thinking about it is entirely twisted."

Zee watched me, waiting for a sign of acceptance that was not coming.

"Dave – typically speaking – when you find out that your girlfriend is being brutally raped by her own brother on a regular basis, that's the point in the relationship when you have the talk about dating other people."

Lewis was nodding. "Come on. Let's get out of here while we still can." Lewis headed around the side of the house and started heading up towards the road, his footsteps crunching the autumn leaves left frozen under the snow.

"Wait up…," Zee whispered after him. But Lewis was only too eager to get out of there. I could hear his footsteps all the way up the side of the house. "Come on," Zee said to me. "We can't do anything here." I shook my head 'no'. "Come on, Dave. Please."

"He's in my family's house. This is my mess. My girlfriend in there."

"She's not your…!"

"Fine! But *I* brought her here. I started this. I've let too many people clean up my messes for me. And Kris needs my help!"

"Dave," Zee said, "I get it. But this is not the mess to turn over a new leaf with. Trust me."

"It's time for me to change. It's time for a new Dave."

"Not now. Right now I want the old Dave, the one who walks away. Walk away, Dave. Please. Walk away."

I shook my head. "I have to do the right thing."

Zee stood at the edge of the foundation, one leg already inching its way up the hill towards the road and the car, the other planted on my level, foot pointed towards me. He craned his neck to look up towards where Lewis had disappeared to. Then he bowed his head towards me.

"You can't ask me to do this."

"I'm not asking," I said.

Zee gazed up the hill towards the road.

"What would the Sayerot do?" he asked, smiling his wickedly charming smile. He headed up the hill.

"Hey," I whispered. "The rifle." Zee peered his head around the corner, his eyebrows raised in a 'what?' gesture.

"Then what am I gonna use?" Now my eyebrows went up. "You're not doing this alone, man," he said.

"Zee. You don't have to."

"You're damn right, I don't. But, since we're going to hell anyway…." Zee paused. We let that thought hang there, both of us wondering whether or not it was true. "Where's your gun?" he asked.

"It's in my bag," I said.

"And… where's your bag?" Zee asked.

"Inside," I admitted.

Zee shook his head. "Fucking amateur," he said.

"We were chased out, remember? I didn't exactly have time to say 'hey, let me grab my gun first, okay?'"

"And so what am I supposed to do while you get your gun?"

"We get in through the storage room. There's a bevy of artillery hanging from the walls."

"A bevy?"

"Yeah, a bevy. Like axes and hammers and fishing knives and a chainsaw. A fucking bevy. Can we just go?"

"And what do we do about her?" Zee added.

"Her?" I asked.

"My question – if the choice comes down to us or her psychotic brother, who is she going to help?" The thought made me nauseous. "We have no idea how messed up this girl is. What if she's actually in love with her brother? What if it's redneck Stockholm syndrome? We don't know how deep this incest shit goes." We were crouching underneath the windows. They weren't open but they weren't thick. Someone could hear us if they listened close enough.

"Shh. If we need weapons we have them, all right? We're going to enter from different access points."

"Whoa. Listen to you: 'Access points' Where did you learn to talk the talk?"

"You're going up the side of the house to the front, all the way up to the driveway. If his truck's there, let the air out of his tires, then wait by the front door."

"For what?"

"I'm going in through there," I said pointing to the utility room door. "Once I have weapons, I'll make my way into the bedroom for my gun. Wait for my signal."

"You have a signal?"

"You'll know when you hear it." Zee waited. "O kay, the signal is… Okay! Okay?"

"The signal is 'Okay'?"

"Yes. 'Okay'."

Zee placed a hand on my shoulder and turned me towards him. "David. This guy is really dangerous. We should stick together, go in as a united front and overpower him."

I shook my head. "You said yourself, IDF strategy is surprise. Deflate his tires, wait out front, listen for the signal."

"I wish Lewis stayed," Zee said.

"We got this," I said.

Zee held me in his gaze as a man adrift at sea claws at the hope of any floating object. He gripped the rifle tight, reminding himself of the power he held in his hands. He squeezed my shoulder, hanging on a moment longer than usual. Zee wasn't the type to admit fear. Israeli Defense Force did not admit fear, so neither would he.

With two quick, deep breaths, Zee scuttled along the foundation, hugging the walls of the house, moving with a silent, agile grace. He held the rifle as naturally as any seasoned hunter. We had become the hunters now; we were no longer the hunted. At the edge of the house, Zee peered around, then, giving a thumbs up back to me, turned the corner and was gone.

I was alone.

The wooden utility room door creaked when it opened past a certain angle due to seasonal swelling, and the handle needed a good shot of WD-40. Spider webs had been spun thick in the jamb over time. The trick was to lift up on the door handle while turning it, at the same time buffering the noise of the door with your body pressed against it. The door cracked across the threshold with an audible hiss of air. But the rewards were behind it – a vast variety of sharp, heavy metal objects that could brain a man good. One crow bar wouldn't be enough. The only problem was, the room was pitch black. I waited in the doorway for any sign that my entrance was detected. The house was eerily quiet and yet, I was certain Fred and Kris were upstairs. Maybe my movement alerted them, and now they were listening for me. The open utility room door was allowing moonlight in, as well as some freezing cold air. I was able to glimpse the weaponry before closing the door. The draft would draw their attention. I couldn't wait in this entranceway forever.

I took advantage of the moonlight to get a quick look at where various tools hung on the wall or leaned against it. Then, as silently as I could, I closed the door; back in pitch darkness. Even the silence was exaggerated. Listening as hard as I could I heard soft creaking but in the same spot. Someone was adjusting their position on a chair or the couch.

I felt the wall of hooks by memory: where the axe and hammers were hung, where the band saw and ropes, and knives, and gardening tools were. Reaching to my left I lifted the axe off the wall hook. Suddenly I was wishing like hell that Lewis stuck around so I could hand it to him and arm myself with more weaponry.

I understood that Lewis had to go – I pulled him in way too deep. And he'd been warning against it the whole time. He did what he had to do. Still, part of me couldn't help but wish he was with me now. At the same time, I felt a confidence that I had sorely lacked. This was my problem to face. I had to do it alone.

My hands next found garden shears: foot long blades and a strong wooden handle. But as my eyes adjusted to the darkness, more choices revealed their availability: Baseball bat, metal spikes, a rock chisel, and a tackle box with knives inside it. On the floor was a gas-powered chainsaw, my personal favorite as a weapon for terror, but far from ideal in a clandestine ambush operation.

I quietly gathered some knives and stuck them inside my pants and inside my boot. The axe was good but heavy. There was a smaller one somewhere.

Stepping softly and carefully so as not to bump or scrape anything, my feet found their way as if by muscle memory, from years of walking through this same space without a care in the world; so many irresponsible, joyous days spent here – a lifetime of carefree bliss.

Now I walked through this same life in terror, thinking every step could be my last – an audible minefield. Silence was my best weapon now. Perhaps my only one.

I reached for a small axe – or so I thought. My hands found a machete. A machete? And suddenly a memory washed over me,:

Zee and I dressed in military fatigues, our faces covered in shoe polish, armed with a machete and a sickle, laying siege to the nearby Holiday Inn. In our fantasy special ops objective, the unit we were seeking housed a meeting of top *Third Reich* leaders. Our mission: eliminate the enemy. Our supplies consisted of a bottle of Jameson's and two well rolled joints. We dug in and prepared for attack, drinking and smoking our supplies as we waited for the imaginary go-ahead signal. Ultimately, we passed out on the lawn. The next morning, our faces still camouflaged, we woke to four elderly women in bathing suits and visors examining us and telling someone to call an ambulance.

How many times did I drink myself into stupid situations?

I let Kris make me feel too much, want too much, need too much, hope for too much. I built a tower of expectation and then drank myself off it; and I dragged Zee and Lewis with me.

I gripped the machete. I was going to make it useful.

The utility room opened onto a foyer off of which were a bathroom, a laundry room and a small bedroom. A set of stairs led up to the living room level, which annexed the kitchen, the master bedroom, and my gun. The floor above creaked with the shifting of someone's weight. The television was playing. Sounded like news. Fred's watching the news. What's he watching for?

A weatherman announces that tonight's storm would bring high winds and severely low temperatures. Is Fred even wondering about Gord out by the lake? Does he even care?

I listened for voices. There was another brief shifting of weight above. It was hard to tell exactly where it was coming from.

I scuttled in and out of each basement room, checking for signs of anyone. Once satisfied, I wormed my way up the stairs, my machete in one hand. The pounding in my chest was so loud I was sure that Fred would hear me approach.

Crawling further up the stairs I was able to get an angle on the sliding glass doors of the living room, the one's that opened onto the deck – a deck that I once lounged on with morning margaritas; the deck that Kris and I ran out to; the deck where Gord nearly killed Zee.

The sliding glass door to the deck reflected the living room. In the reflection was Fred, standing back by the kitchen stove. He was far enough away that I could make my way from the top of the stairs to the bedroom, a distance of about four feet – four feet that were totally exposed to the living room, but hidden by a wooden-walled banister from the kitchen. Fred had his back to the glass, which meant he was facing the kitchen. I could see a cloud behind him – steam. He was boiling water.

I lay low along the wooden staircase and crawled up each step, one at a time. Watching Fred's reflection, I snaked my way up the stairs, along the four feet of carpeted landing, and into the bedroom.

A room can emanate misery. Thick terror and doom you can place a hand on. Kris was lying fetal on the bed, a blanket pulled over her. Her hair lay like a blond curtain drawn across her face, protectively. She seemed to be asleep. Then I heard her whimpering. What had Fred done to her this time?

I wanted to carry her off wrapped in that blanket to the safety of somewhere, far way from here. My brain was screaming to keep my impulsive emotions in check: *stick to the plan: get the gun, get the gun, get the gun*!

Silently as possible, I slid the folding closet door back and crouched to reach inside, looking for my blue travel duffel. The sliding doors knocked slightly. My heart jumped. The bag was there where I left it. I opened it and felt inside.

Kris' movements stole my attention. Her eyes were open now, looking at me. I placed a finger to my mouth. A smile crossed her lips. Or so I thought. She was stretching her lips in the efforts of a smile, as if she was trying to remember what the muscle motion was, but her mind had forgotten.

The luster that had once inhabited her sea-blue eyes had faded. What remained was an arid canyon dug out by incestuous abuse: Her own black empty.

But while my black empty hungered insatiably for love, hers was just empty. There was no welling of tears, no emotion at all. It was the look she had after the first rape, only this time it was flattened. Not only had she complied, this time her secret was out. Everything that was mysterious about Kris was laid out like a cadaver on a slab for examination. She was vulnerable. She was defenseless. She was defeated.

I felt so incredibly sad for her.

I understood now that by taking her for himself, Fred took from her the possibility of freedom. Kris was his prisoner. And he was her jailer. Her beauty was marbled by her inner pain, from having to freeze up inside. She was not being cold, she had never been cold to me; she was surviving. And now I understood why she didn't want to get to know anyone at school, and why she transferred with no history. And why she would have to transfer again. Because now that I knew, and Zee and Lewis as well, she could never be free in that school, ever. As long as anyone knew the truth about her past, Kris would be imprisoned by the rigid bars of their knowing. Eventually, every place becomes a small town after a while, and people get to know you. For Kris, comfort was the enemy.

So here, with Fred, in Laketon – the town she had once called home – Kris was as close to whatever freedom she probably thought was left to her.

Which was nothing.

Unless she escaped. Again.

With me.

There was no gun in the bag.

I searched the contents frantically. There were clothes and the towel that I wrapped it in. No gun! *Shit*! *My coat! It must be in my coat*!

In the mudroom, upstairs.

I pressed my body against the wall of the bedroom and shushed Kris with a finger. But when I got to the door of the bedroom, Fred was pointing my Sig Sauer at me.

"Looking for this?" he sneered. "Come out of there, and drop the knife," he said, waving me out of the bedroom with the gun. "You, too, Krissy." I never heard her called Krissy. She had said she hated the name. Now I knew why. "Get your friends out, too," Fred said.

"I don't know what you're talking about," I said.

"Yeah. I think you do. Call them out."

"Gord's watching them," I bluffed.

"No, he's not."

"They're tied to each other by the dock. I escaped by myself," I found myself trying to sell my story to him, like an excuse to my teachers for why I didn't have an essay done on time.

"Gord is an expert hunter and marksman. If you tried to escape, he would have shot you down like a deer. Easy. So, quit stalling me, get your friends out, and tell me what you did with Gord." He was surprisingly calm. Like he did this kind of thing all the time.

"I'm alone!" I insisted. Saying it loud enough maybe Zee would hear and figure out how to react.

"David," Kris said, "just do what he says."

Kris had given up. She was trying to get me to accept defeat as well. But I couldn't.

"You're testing my patience, kid. You don't call them out, and I find them, I'm not going to wait to see if they want to give up. I'm just gonna kill 'em. I'm gonna kill tem with your gun!" He laughed.

"Look, you got what you want, right?" I indicated Kris. "What else do you want?" Fred started to snicker. "We can give you money. We have some jewelry here, too, I think. Somewhere. Lots of good scotch. Single Malt. Take it. It's yours." Fred laughed.

"You don't get it, kid. I'm not the one who's leaving. You are." I glanced at Kris who seemed hopeful that I might finally get the drift. Leave my family's cottage? My party castle? My home away from home?

"What?" I said.

Fred cocked the gun. "I'm not asking," he said.

I never put bullets in the gun. I had them, but they weren't in my coat. They were somewhere else in the bag. Did Fred find them or not? Was the gun loaded or not? As if in answer, Fred pointed the gun at the wall and pulled the trigger. The shot blasted a hole through the wooden wall. I heard something leaking. Asshole probably hit a pipe. I made a mental note to fix it later.

"Okay!" I yelled, and immediately realized my mistake. Zee popped in from the front door, the rifle aimed at Fred.

As quickly as Zee showed up, Fred reacted. He hoofed me against a wall. Then he grabbed Kris. He pressed the gun – my gun – to Kris' temple.

"Drop it," Fred said, calm as can be.

Zee didn't budge; he kept a steady bead on Fred.

"I'll blow her brains out, kid, I swear to god."

"Zee…," I called, looking at Kris. Before she looked defeated, now she'd found a new level of fear to engage in. "Zee…?!"

"He's bluffing," Zee said. Zee laid flat on the higher level, his rifle leveled at Fred, sniper style.

Fred pressed the gun harder against Kris. "You think I'm not capable of putting a bullet through my own sister's head? You think she's that precious to me? This whore?!"

"Please," Kris whimpered to me, like a whisper. *Please what?* Her fight was gone. She wanted it to end. Or did she really want to die?

"You have any idea how many guys I've watched her fuck? It's a game. She seduces them. I watch her do it. I watch as she goes through the motions. Then, ultimately, I'm overcome with the need to kill them. I have to. It's a sickness, I admit. But if I'm sick, then so is she." Fred said. "So, maybe it's time I just end her pain and mine. What do you think, kid?"

"So what?" I said. Fred's eyes popped.

"What?" and Kris' expression said the same thing.

"You kill her and Zee will blow a hole through you so big they'll be putting the parts back together for weeks." *Where did I get the balls to talk like this?*

"You've got balls, kid, I'll give you that." Fred smiled.

"You play pool. It's a game of angles. You kill her, she drops and Zee takes you out. You're both dead and Zee and I clean up the mess. Or. You shoot Zee and I shove a machete through your heart," I said, as I calmly reached down for the machete and picked it up.

"Or...," Fred aimed the gun at me, while keeping Kris in a headlock, "I just kill you!"

"Well, then Zee...." I barely said his name when Fred quickly shot at Zee. Zee groaned. He crawled away from view.

Shit! Fred shot Zee. Fred shot Zee!

"What the fuck?!" I yelled. All badass was out the window. "Zee…?!" I yelled. No answer.

"What's the angle now?" Fred asked. He aimed the gun at me. "The way I see it, it's a clean shot."

Kris started to struggle in Fred's grip. He squeezed tighter. Her eyes went wide. He was choking her.

"You're going to kill her," I said.

"So what?" he shot back.

"Why… why are you doing this?"

Fred's eyes went very cold. Hollow. Inhumanly hollow. "Somebody needs to be the bad guy," he said. "I just happen to like it."

At that moment I realized that I was about to die. I suddenly felt regret for everything wrong that I ever did to anyone and everyone in my life. If this was it I wanted a chance to make it right. At least the chance to apologize.

Everyone deserves that, don't they?

I'm sorry, I said to myself. *Sorry for everything I did, and everyone I ever hurt.* It swept through me like a flash flood:

Mom, Dad, I'm sorry I never made anything of my life. I'm sorry I'm such a screw up. I'm sorry for ever hurting you.

Sorry, Zee, for dragging you into this.

Sorry, Lewis, for blaming you.

Sorry, Marcy, for being such a loser boyfriend.

Sorry, Kris… for not listening…

Sorry…

BLAM!!

Fred's shoulder exploded. Blood splattered the wall behind him. Kris jumped away and dove behind the couch. Zee had found his aim again.

"*Otzma Enoshit*!!" Zee shouted.

Fred tried to raise his gun but couldn't. His arm hung limp. I jumped him. I started swinging, but he managed to swing the Sig Sauer to his other hand and slam it against the side of my head. I went down. In that moment Fred grabbed Kris with the hand of the arm that had just been wounded. His grip was still clamp-like. *How did he possibly have the strength?* I struggled to get up and shake off the dizziness; I couldn't see straight. Feet rushed past me and down the stairs. I heard a door drag open over a concrete floor; howling blizzard winds swept through the house, its freezing bite nipping at me from the basement. I could see the blizzard kicking up outside. Fred must have left through the utility room.

This was going to end out there, in the freezing cold.

Zee was moaning from the upper landing. The cottage was suddenly quiet, except for the wind howling its threats from below; threats… or warnings?

Zee was lying on his back, holding his shoulder. "An eye for an eye," I said, meaning he and Fred had exchanged shoulder injuries.

"Get him!" Zee said. His voice was weak.

"What?"

"He's a fucking terrorist! He's attacked and invaded. Get that fucker! Kill him, David! Kill him!" Zee pushed the rifle into my grip.

I thought I heard the faint sound of a siren in the distance. I took it as a sign: we were definitely going to need an ambulance.

"Call 911," I said. "You're bleeding badly."

Zee nodded and pushed me away.

"Kill him."

CHAPTER TWENTY NINE

With Fred's blood leaving a trail it was easy to track him even with the winds whipping up snow over everything. A few giant steps brought me down the back of the house quickly.

Fred knew the territory well. Heading down to the lake offered multiple escape routes along the shoreline. He could round the peninsula to the west and be out of sight in seconds.

I gripped the rifle tighter. Fred's blood speckled the trail. He was taking the route of least resistance, already broken for him by our previous march. A cry pierced through the wind's screeching. It was a guttural howl of regret and anger.

When I got closer I could see Fred struggling to release Gord from all the duct tape. Gord didn't look like he was moving. Maybe he was dead. Maybe frozen. *"Going to hell."* Maybe we were.

Kris stood off to the side, watching Fred wrestle his friend off the tree, clutching herself close to stay warm. Every muscle in me wanted to grab her and take her away. But it wasn't the right moment. I needed to get closer. I needed a sure shot.

"I'm cold," Kris said to Fred. "Let's go."

Why was she even staying with him? He was hurt. She could run. She could get away from him. Why not get away? And then it hit me: *maybe she didn't want to.*

"I ain't leavin' Gord here like this!" Fred barked. He yanked at the duct tape, cursing it out at the same time. The sirens I had heard before came again. They were coming around the hills of the valley. Somebody must have heard the gunshots and called.

"Cops!!" Kris shouted at Fred, as if she was the fugitive. Fred swung his head up towards the cottage, looking for signs of squad cars.

He saw me. His expression darkened beyond the blackness that filled it. "YOU!!"

Kris followed Fred's look and her eyes landed on me. They weren't dead anymore. Now she was energized with the life force of the survivor. Maybe it was fear. Whatever was behind that look, I distinctly saw a smile spread across her beautiful face.

Fred reached for his gun.

"No!" Kris yelled.

I brought the rifle to my shoulder. Last time I shot a rifle was at summer camp, shooting twenty two's at targets. I was ten.

Fred aimed.

I aimed, too.

The sirens wailed. Blue and red cherry tops pierced the night sky.

Not now, I thought. *This is my game to end!*

Fred fired. Snow exploded near my face. *Too close!*

"NO!" Kris yelled. Fred fired again. "NO! NO!" Another near miss.

Fred moved closer, firing again and again. Four shots now. Snow popped around me. I raised the rifle and aimed. Kris yelled something. She ran towards Fred, reaching out, trying to stop him.

"Kris! Stop!" I yelled, but she kept running towards us. "Stop!" I rose to my feet, urging her to get down. I must have given Fred enough of a target just as Kris outran him and tried to get between us.

That's when Fred fired.

Kris arched backward, then she went down in the snow.

I aimed, fired. Fred fell backwards. *Did I hit him?*

"Kris!" I yelled, racing toward her. "Kris!!" A patch of red was spreading into the snow beneath her.

"Krissy...?" I heard Fred say faintly. He dragged himself towards her body.

The sirens were loud. Doors slammed. Shouts:

Down there!

By the lake!

Shots fired! Shots fired!

I just shot a man. Panic rose up; wild fear that this would all end way beyond my control and, once again, I would end up being a bystander victim in my own life.

This was my life. The only thing that mattered was that I step up, take responsibility, that I do something.

Fred shot Kris. Fred shot Zee.

I became what I needed to be.

I raced down towards where Fred and Kris lay. Fred was struggling to his feet. I swung the rifle like a bat and smashed Fred in the back of the neck. He went down flat. I jumped him and started swinging. I landed a few hard ones before he started to fight back. Where he got the strength from I don't know. It was like he could not be stopped. He swung and caught me in the chin. I rolled off him and we rolled down the hill towards the frozen shore. I came up first, punching, punching, punching. My hands connecting with his flesh again and again and again. My fingers cracked on impact with Fred's bones. I felt no pain, driven by fury. I pounded and pounded and pounded.

Fred found my ribs with his good fist. Even with one good arm he was still dangerous. He kicked. He swung his elbows into my side. I felt my rib crack. He sent his knee up into my thighs.

"There they are!!" Cops were closing in.

Fred's face was bloody and swollen from my punches. If I was going to lose the fight I was going to make him remember.

No – I couldn't lose again.

I got on top of him again and slammed my fist into his face just as his boot caught me square in the groin. The world went momentarily black and star-spotted. The next thing I felt was a hard blow to my jaw. My head snapped right and I went over, falling onto hard-packed icy snow beneath. I got clear enough to see Fred standing above me, saw him raise his boot above my head, ready to smash me like a bug.

BLAM!!

The bullet caught Fred in the back and spun him. I rolled away and saw Kris holding my Sig Sauer, smoke wafting from the barrel.

I scampered out of the way. My hands throbbed. My ribs were fire. "You stop, Freddie, or I swear to god I will kill you. I swear to GOD! ENOUGH!" Kris screamed.

"Freeze!" the cops shouted.

"Drop your weapons!"

"Krissy," Fred pleaded, ignoring the presence of the police. Kris held the gun steady on Fred.

"No… more." Kris said weakly.

Lewis appeared at the top of the stairs by the cottage. Red and blue police lights flashed behind him. He looked like the white night, leading the cavalry to the rescue.

Fred and Kris were in a standoff and I was in the middle and they did not seem to care who else was there.

"Drop your weapon!" The police yelled. Kris held the gun on Fred. Fred held his arms out as if to say 'Come on, Honey', but Kris did not back down. She moved towards him steadily.

"Sweetie," Fred said. The words stuck in my ear and made me nauseous again. This time I coughed blood. "Krissy…," Fred pleaded. "Please…."

"Go to hell," Kris said.

"You're my everything," Fred said. "I love you."

"No. No." Kris squeezed the trigger but she lowered the gun and fired into the snow. Then she dropped to her knees in tears.

"You're out of bullets!" he gloated.

"I'm sorry," she whispered to Fred.

Fred crawled towards Kris. He reached out and pulled her into him. Brother and sister embraced in the middle of the snow, the cops closing in.

"I'm sorry," Fred said. "I never meant to hurt you."

"Freddie," Kris wept.

The police were carefully closing in. They told them to put their weapons down. They warned them not to move. They told us all to get on our knees, hands behind our heads.

Suddenly Fred jumped up and ran straight for the lake, right out onto the ice.

The cops yelled their warnings but Fred just kept running out towards the peninsula. If he rounded it he would be gone – if he got that far. One of the cops went to chase after him but his partner stopped him.

"Not safe," the officer said to his friend.

They fired warning shots but Fred kept running, stumbling, holding his side. Kris was standing now and I moved towards her but another officer held me in place. Kris was dripping blood into the snow. She stood transfixed watching her brother run off into the frozen black distance.

"He's getting away!" I yelled.

Fred was halfway across the bay and heading towards a peninsula. Once he got around it, he could take off anywhere. There would be no way to know where he went. Kris and I watched him run. He was agile, small and light on his feet. But heavy enough.

"STOP!" The cop yelled. Fred kept running. HALT OR I"LL SHOOT!" Fred did not halt. The cop took aim.

A loud *CRACK* pierced the air as the cop's gun fired. Then the cracking sound came again. Fred stopped. He was looking down at the ice below him. The ice was cracking. He took a step towards the shore, which brought another, louder *CRACK.* Fred looked over at us. I heard the cop yell "*FREEZE!*" Fred looked back... at Kris. A weird expression came over him. Kris leaned towards him. She broke free of the cop's grip who was too fascinated now with Fred's attempted escape.

"Freddie!" she yelled. Fred turned. Kris raised the gun. Aimed.

"You're out!" Fred yelled.

The cops just watched what seemed like a futile attempt to stop Fred.

Kris fired. There was a slight delay due to distance but a half second later, Fred went down, grabbing his stomach.

"One in the chamber," Kris said.

Fred fell hard onto the ice. The ice broke and he went through. Chunks of ice flew up off the surface as Fred plunged into the frozen waters of the lake. I rushed to grab Kris who looked like she might go after him. Fred thrashed at the freezing water. Steel-toed boots pulled him down. Kris thrashed in my arms, trying to get away. I held on.

Fred's hands disappeared below the surface.

The cop yelled "shit!". He turned to the other two cops and said "Get a hockey stick, an oar, a paddle, something! Now!"

"Can't," the second cop said. "We have to wait for the EMT." My job was to hold onto Kris, and that's all I did.

"We have to get him!" the first officer yelled.

"The hell we do! Risking our lives for the safety of others is one thing. But everyone's safe," the second cop said and the third, the youngest of the three, agreed.

"He's drowning!" the first officer said.

"If a guy jumps off a building, we don't jump after him. Same difference here."

"Hell if it is!"

None of the cops wanted to go through that ice. They stood at the shore and waited for someone with a job title that included fishing people out of icy waters to show up. The second cop lit up a cigarette.

Kris was shaking from the cold.

"Help him!" Kris cried weakly, as if she, too, knew that it was too late.

"McNeil!" the older cop yelled. The youngest cop stepped forward. The older cop pressured the young officer to venture out onto the ice. McNeil shook his head nervously. His partner stood up for him saying how he didn't have to put his life in danger to save a dead body. The older cop argued that they couldn't be sure he was dead and the second cop argued that oh, yes, they could.

All the while Fred's body was somewhere below the surface of the ice. From what I knew of Fred, I could not discount the possibility that he had managed to swim below the ice to shore undetected. He might be on a road right now, hitching a ride back to warmth where he'd recoup and prepare to come back for us.

Kris finally went limp in my arms, weeping softly. I held on. The police stood around pointing and shouting, but none of them were going.

Lewis came up beside me. "Holy shit," he said. "You look awful."

"How's Zee?" I asked.

"Not good. They rushed him to the hospital already."

"Is he going to be okay?"

"I'm no doctor. He looked pretty bad, though. How many times did he get shot?"

"How many times? Once."

"Oh," Lewis said and glanced out over the lake. My heart sank. Zee couldn't die. He couldn't!

"Help me get her upstairs," I said. Lewis and I walked Kris back up to the cottage. She was practically lifeless; drained. She was a woman in mourning with a bullet wound.

"Call an ambulance," I said.

"Already here," Lewis said.

Kris and I rode in the ambulance together. They laid her down for her wound and I sat next to her, with my broken bones and cuts and bruises and frost-bite I didn't even know I had. They brought another ambulance for Gord and for Fred. The cops knew Gord already. None of them were surprised to see him involved in something like this. None of them were surprised by the fact that he survived.

"He's alive?" I said, shocked.

"Guy's part wolf," the second cop said. "He'll live through anything the winter throws at him. Why – you thought you guys killed him?" The cop laughed. I chuckled out of embarrassment, and relief. That was one murder charge we avoided.

It took them almost two more hours to fish Fred's body out of the frozen water. They had to search under the ice to find where his body drifted to. When they pulled Fred out, he was blue. Even his eyes were blue, like a fishes eyes. He passed close by on a stretcher and I got a good look at death up close. There was no expression, there was no danger. There was nothing, just a blank blue emptiness.

I had seen my grandfather in his coffin all prepped, hair combed, and made up for viewing. But real death – cold, blue death – I had never seen. It seemed unreal, and at the same time, so close; like it was waiting around the corner for all of us. Today it was everywhere.

It was Fred, and maybe Zee.

Oh god.

No.

Not Zee.

CHAPTER THIRTY

The cottage became a crime scene. The yellow tape was pulled and the police went through everything. Even the bags in the car. They found Zee's dope and all his paraphernalia. They found Lewis' leftover cocaine. They confiscated a blood-stained crow-bar, a hunting rifle, a machete; they confiscated one illegally acquired Sig Sauer P230 semi-automatic handgun.

In the hospital I was treated for a broken hand and some broken ribs. My various cuts required a total of thirty stitches. Kris needed more attention. The bullet had penetrated her shoulder, above the chest. She wasn't in any danger, but she would have to remain for observation for a couple of days, to see how the wound healed.

The police asked a lot of questions. They took statements. They didn't care that we were tired or hungry or hurt. They wanted answers. They needed to call it something.

Fred was no stranger to the Huntsville police, but he was dead, and Kris was suspected of firing the shot that killed him. They needed to explain it all to the chief and the news people somehow. Kris could expect to be questioned.

The only blessing was that the cop saw Fred run out onto the ice and fall in. Fred was shot. There were two bullets in him, but there was no guarantee, he said, that it came from her gun. The cops fired some shots, too. Still, we would have to wait for the official coroner's report to determine cause of death. I could tell by the way officer McNeil was explaining it all to me that they all just wanted to put the thing to bed. Nobody seemed to care very much about the actual outcome. It was routine police procedure and we would all just have to endure.

I offered to stay at a motel nearby, to keep Kris company while she was staying in the hospital. I wasn't in any hurry to get home. The police and the hospital had to make calls to my parents. I was facing charges of illegal possession of a handgun. Zee was facing charges, too, if he survived. They found enough pot and hash to convict him of trafficking, which, in fact, he did; it brought a severe penalty even under the juvenile code.

Lewis' coke mysteriously disappeared from evidence. Mr. Cohen was pulling strings on behalf of his son.

Zee was in a different hospital in Toronto. His parents had him rushed there to the best doctors they could find. No one was telling me anything. I figured they just didn't want me around him anymore, which I could understand. I wouldn't want me influencing my kid, either.

Kris was lying in her bed, looking off out a window. The window overlooked a parking lot and a mini-strip mall under development. So far they had a Tim Horton's, a Shoppers Drug Mart and a Bait and Tackle shop.

"Typical incongruity," I said, moving by the window, looking out of it with her.

"What?"

"Three things that couldn't belong together less."

She rolled away from me.

"What's wrong," I asked, stupidly.

"I have a bullet hole in my shoulder. My brother is dead. Other than that, things are peachy."

"I'm sorry," I said. "I meant…."

"Stop apologizing." She paused. "How's your friend, doing? Zee?"

I shrugged. "Nobody's telling me anything."

"I'm sorry," she said.

"Stop apologizing," I said. Kris smiled. "I can get a room in the motel and stick around so you won't be alone."

"Go home, David. Go back to your life."

"My life is stupid and meaningless."

"Then find some meaning in it. 'Cause you won't find it with me. And I'd really like you to stop trying."

"I might have to face charges," I said. "The gun and some other things."

"I'm sure someone will get you off. That's the way it usually works for you guys, isn't it? Mommy and Daddy to the rescue, right? Calling lawyers, calling favors, making deals. You'll be fine, David. You've got no worries. All the worries you have you invent. Not like people with real problems."

"Kris…. I never knew…."

"You weren't supposed to." She turned to face me now. "It never included you!"

"Who else do you have?" She looked away. "I mean, is there someone you can call…? Someone who will take you home?"

"I'm fine," she said to the window.

I slunk out of her room feeling so incredibly sad.

I walked out of Kris' room and right into the outstretched arms of my mother and father.

"Oh, god," my mother exclaimed, "David, are you all right?" I said yes. She looked me up and down and hugged me close. "When the police called and then the hospital – I didn't know what to think and I… and I…." My mother started to cry. "I'm sorry. I'm just so glad you're okay."

My father was equally emotional. He pulled me close with my mother still hanging on and the three of us hugged. "You realize, you have some explaining to do," my father said. "But we can help you. Whatever you need, Son. We can help you." Then my father broke down. I backed up enough to be able to look back inside Kris' room. She was sitting up, looking at me with a knowing eyebrow raised up. '*Mommy and Daddy to the rescue*' is what it said.

My father and mother hadn't spent two minutes in the same room since they divorced and now they were stuck in the same car with me because my mom claimed to be too distraught to drive. So my dad had picked her up and now he was driving us all home.

"Where's Beth?" I asked. "Is she okay?"

"She's at your cousin's. She's fine. She thinks you got into a car accident. That's all she's going to know, understand?"

"Yes sir."

"David admitted to being in possession of a handgun," my mother said to my father. "He told the police straight out. Didn't even plead not guilty."

"Why would you admit that?" my dad asked. "And how the hell did you get your hands on a handgun?!"

"And why the hell would he need one?" My mother continued to direct to my father. She could barely look at me now. "It's not like I ever showed him one."

"And you think I did?!" My father snapped.

"Did I say that?" my mother.

"You implied it."

"Oh great, here we go with the implication accusations."

There was a long pause, then, "At least nobody was killed," my father said.

"One person's dead. He froze in the lake. Horrible," she shuddered. "Zion was rushed to surgery for a bullet wound! A bullet wound!" I didn't tell her about Gord. She didn't need to know.

"Christ – sounds like the morning news. Who's Zion?"

"Zee," I said. They ignored me, continued their conversation like I wasn't even there.

"Don't you remember Zee?" my mother harangued my father.

"Of course I do! I just don't know him as Zion."

"He was shot by the boy who froze to death. Oh, god! It's so awful. How the hell did you get yourself involved in all of this?" my mother asked me without turning around.

"This is in no way over, David. And there will be no shutting us out. This is serious."

"Maybe it's our own fault," my mother said. "Maybe we just weren't paying attention."

"Wait, are you suggesting that our divorce caused him to buy a gun and plan to kill someone? Is that what you're saying?"

"We've been too involved in our own lives."

"You wanted this more than I did. You just remember that!"

"Oh, so this is my fault?" my mother yelled.

"If your career wasn't more important than your family!"

"Like you were the perfect father!"

"I was here! I was present!"

"Not emotionally!"

It went on like that. Worst car ride ever.

"Only an idiot would avail themselves emotionally just to have their feelings disregarded over and over and over...."

"Is that you or your psychologist wife talking?"

"Catherine doesn't take me for granted."

"So you finally found a woman to stroke your ego twenty four seven; another mother to take care of you and tell you how you're the second coming of the Jewish people."

"Fuck you, Heather!"

"Finally, the real Michael Fischer speaks."

"Jesus Christ. Is that it – you just want an argument?"

"I want you to fight back, yes!"

"What's the point?!"

"I want to know that you're there!"

"I was. I was, I was, I was, I was there! I was always there!"

"No. No, you acted the part. You did the right things, you supported the family and the household and took the kids to swimming and skiing and all that but you weren't *there* there."

There was a long pause. I wanted to say something. To fill it. We sat in it, the three of us, we sat in the fat, murky silence of our family muck. Until I broke it.

"Did you guys ever love each other?"

My parents didn't speak. My dad drove silently forward. My mother peered out the window as if searching for a passing rock face with the right answer etched into it.

"I thought I loved this girl. I wanted her to love me back but she wouldn't. So I tried to make her and then I got into this mess. This guy raped her and then he turns out to be her own brother!"

My mother spun around on that one. If expressions could speak hers would have invented a new version of shocked profanity.

"So I tried to make it right. 'Cause that's what a guy's supposed to do, right Dad?"

My dad looked sad and deflated as he listened.

"I tried to show her how much I really loved her. So we went looking for him. And we found him. And... and he nearly killed us. I might have gotten my best friends killed and now I'm going to jail for maybe years and..."

"We're fighting that. We're getting a lawyer!"

"...and she still doesn't love me. She never did."

My Dad slowed the car down. He pulled off the highway onto the shoulder then further onto the grass field patched with snow. A barren thicket of trees stood naked and weak behind us, wiggling their arms at bursts of wind.

We sat there, stewing in it.

"We have to get a lawyer. We have to plan his defense," my mother said. "Is Larry Greenglass available? I'm not paying his lawyer's fees, though. David will have to. He needs to learn some responsibility. Why are we stopped?"

"Right. Greenglass is like five hundred bucks an hour. David can't pay that."

"He'll give us a friends rate. He owes me one."

"For what?!"

My Dad turned around to face me. His eyes were red from crying. "Did you really love this girl?" I nodded. Tears streamed down my cheeks like I was four years old.

"This stuff... between your mother and I... it's not your fault. Or Beth's."

"I know."

"No, I mean... it was here, brewing long before you." That made my mother stare down my Dad, like he'd just exposed an ugly secret. "It's true, Heather. You know it." My mother softened, her shoulders conceded defeat.

"Your father and I... we married for love. Something just.... People change, David."

"But we are here for you," my dad said. "Both of us."

"Both of us," my mother agreed.

Once we got inside the house I asked to see my parents alone in the kitchen. Naturally, they took seats at the kitchen table, the same seats they sat in years ago when they announced their separation. I stood in the foyer, where I had before. Only this time I had the announcement to make.

"I have a problem," I said. "I get this need to get out of my head and... so I drink. A lot. I do a lot of drugs."

"I told you, son, anything you want to try I would try with you just so we could know and be safe."

"What are kids into these days," my mother inquired? "Cocaine? Pills? I hear heroine's on a comeback. Are you shooting heroine? David?! Are you a junkie?!"

"No! I'm not a junkie! Just listen! Please! I... I need help." They looked at each other skeptically. "Look, I'm only seventeen. I'm still under juvenile jurisdiction. If this thing goes to court it'll look good that I went to rehab or something."

"Conviction?! I thought you didn't -- !"

"No. I didn't! It was an accident. He ran across the -- ."

"This boy... was he...," my mother hesitated, "I mean...was it anyone we know?"

"No. He's from Laketon."

"Thank god," my mother exclaimed. "Can you imagine?"

"Look, I am going to take full responsibility for this. But I need you to do something for me."

I asked my parents to stand in the kitchen foyer, side by side, where Beth and I had stood to receive their news several years earlier.

"Why?" my mother asked.

"Just... please. It's important."

My parents remained dubious and managed to avoid looking at each other. My father moved first. He took a spot in the foyer, turned and faced the table. My mother found her own spot, standing in front of my father and about four feet away.

"Would you mind standing next to each other?" I asked.

"Just what is this about, Son," my father asked, annoyed, shifting his weight to one leg, hands in his pockets fiddling with his change.

"Could you stop that, please?" asked my mother.

"Please. A little closer together."

My mother backed up slightly and took a step to her right, closing the gap between them, but remaining a step in front of my father. "Well…?" she said to my father, expecting him to move the rest of the way.

"There's plenty of room," he said, gesturing next to him. She crossed her arms.

"Look," I said. "I'm not asking for a miracle. I just… I need you to work together to help me out. Okay? I've never asked for your help before. Can you, please, for once?"

"For once?" My mother exclaimed. "How about for seventeen years!"

"Oh, don't start," my father said. "You could have left anytime. But you liked the house and the cars and the trips to Europe and summer camp for the kids."

"And I would have liked it all a whole lot more if I could have shared it with someone who was emotionally available!"

"Available for what – your ingratitude? Your abuse? Your – ?"

"STOP IT!" I yelled. But it was useless. They'd built up seventeen years of animosity over unresolved differences. This is where their marriage ended. Brought together, it seemed they would always return to this spot in their timeline until they moved on.

"Look," my mother said, "I understand what you're trying to do here, but...."

"We'll get you help. We'll make sure this stays quiet, too. Anybody asks, you just went on a vacation to..."

"Family in Florida," my mother added.

"Yes. Florida. But after that, you're on your own. You've got to get hold of this thing." On this my mother agreed, nodding. Now they were working together, to cover up my failure; not for me, but because it was a blemish on their own reputations.

"Maybe he really should go to Florida," my mother said. "Get him away from all this for a while."

"I'm sure there are more local solutions, Heather. He needs family around him now. We can't just ship him off to tech support and hope he comes back fixed."

"Oh, don't be such an asshole, Michael!"

CHAPTER THIRTY ONE

"Possession," Zee said. "With intent to sell. You know what kind of shit storm that is?" We were in our smoking spot, where we hid from the realities of the world and escaped into our own adventures. Only now the real world had snuck in and was staring us in the face: Drug charges, rehab and jail time.

Our childhood was over.

Zee's arm was in a sling. "Does it hurt?" I asked.

"Fuck yeah, it hurts, you idiot! I got fucking shot! If it were one inch closer to my heart I'd be fucking dead right now."

"That's...."

"Don't tell me it's unbelievable or incredible or a miracle or any of that bullshit. I got shot. I got lucky. Another guy would have gotten killed. I didn't. Plain and simple." Zee let out a long stream of smoke. "And you know what? I'd do it again in a second. I swear to god."

"You're insane!"

"Don't misunderstand me, Fischer. I'm seriously pissed off at you. You got me into this shit. I had a good little business going with steady clientele and now nobody will touch me. The police want names. They want my sources, my suppliers, my client list. I can't touch anything for months. Maybe years." Another long pause. "I don't know the next time you and I will actually be able to hang out together. I mean, they're coming down heavy. I shot a guy, Dave!"

"Me, too!" I said.

Zee nodded. "Fuckin' right we did. Did what we had to." I slapped him on the back and held on. "But… shit. I was working my way towards total independence from the 'rents and now it's all screwed up!"

"You really think you're going to go to prison?"

"The way these cops are talking to me, man, they paint a bleak fuckin' picture."

"They're supposed to."

"I got a plan, though. The Zee-man's always got something up his sleeve."

"What?" I asked. He smiled to himself, flicked his cigarette into the grass and stepped on it.

"Have fun at rehab. Just keep it to the drinking, though. 'Cause when all this blows over, we're going to toast up a major fatty!"

When I got home there was a message on voice mail. "Twenty eight days and no chicks?! Good luck, Asshole."

My sendoff from Lewis.

CHAPTER THIRTY TWO

Rehab was not a good time. They gave me a full physical and determined that I had the liver and lungs of a guy twice my age. I wasn't allowed a radio or a newspaper, which meant I couldn't get any news. I never really paid attention to the news normally but part of me was curious to see if there was any story about what happened up in Laketon.

Also, the whole place was segregated, guys from the girls. Not that I was interested in any of the girls I saw in there. Most were pretty beat up from their addictions; none of them were Kris.

There was a lot of healing talk about responsibility, about the choices we made and why we made them. I was forced to talk about my family and my parent's divorce.

When I was alone, I worked out and drank tea. Being without a buzz of some kind was harder than I expected. I wasn't ready for it. Maybe I wasn't ready for the whole change, but then I remembered what Kris had said – *find meaning in your life.*

I had to start somewhere.

I was allowed one visit each week. My mother came up once. Beth didn't want to. She didn't get why I was there really and that was fine by me. Another week it was my Dad and his wife.

Lewis and Zee came up once. I was psyched to see they were hanging out together. "You know, you go through something like that with somebody…," Lewis explained. "It's like we're bonded together now."

"I thought you needed to stay away from me," I said to Zee.

"Until the whole thing blew over." Zee smiled at Lewis. "Well, it blew over."

"Your Dad?" I asked. Lewis just shrugged.

"Word on the street is the Fashion Show is shaping up to be a total disaster. The main reason…? You!" Lewis announced.

"I'm not even in it."

"No. You're here."

"So? Wait – nobody is supposed to know that!" I protested.

"Yeah. Well. You know how things go," Lewis said. "One person talks and next thing you know, everyone in school knows we were involved in a crime scene with a dead body and it's all anybody can talk about!"

"How did they find out, Lewis?!" I knew the answer, but I needed to hear Lewis admit it.

"I had to tell my father. He got Zee off. Had the thing thrown out on an improper search technicality."

"They had no just cause to remove our luggage from the car and search it," Zee said with a degree of self-righteousness.

"Dude," Lewis said, "You're like a celebrity now. I am bagging so much ass off of this it's unreal. I am so proud of you, Dude."

I go to rehab and Lewis uses it to have sex.

Lewis went on to say how much Sharla was asking about me now, like she was really sorry about how things turned out and how she wanted to make it up to me. Zee was loving it. It confirmed everything he had always claimed was superficial and ridiculous about high school anyway. Now he was vindicated.

"You guys hear from Kris at all? See her in school? Anything?" Lewis and Zee shared a glance – the same look I had seen them share before. It was that 'are you going to tell him or am I?' look.

Zee leaned in. "Look, Fisch, since you're here, maybe you should speak with someone about her...."

"Whattaya mean?"

"I mean, it's like you're *addicted* to this girl and you just won't face it. She doesn't love you."

"I just want to know if she's okay." Zee leaned back. He was waiting for me to get it. Lewis was shaking his head with disappointment. "All those girls out there," he repeated. I couldn't get my mind off Kris.

Before they left, I asked Lewis for one favor. I needed to meet with his father. Lewis said he'd pass the message along.

"Fourteen more days," I said.

I took Zee's advice: I talked about Kris with my counselor. The counselor said I was trying to fix feelings of unhappiness with anything that would take me out of myself. I wasn't addicted to Kris as much as I was addicted to the idea of a perfect love:

Panacea in a bottle, rolled in a joint, or in a girl's love. It was all an escape. I told him I called that escape place the black empty. He said it was a good name for it. He also said that I wasn't the first person to describe it like that, and that I wasn't the only person who had it. He said the black empty won't just go away. I'll learn to live with it, just like everybody else. The only thing I had to face was my fears. He gave me a journal and a pen and told me to write down my thoughts when I felt the black empty coming on. He said it would help. And anything was better than drinking over it – that wasn't helping anything anymore.

That night I tried to write some things down. It was hard, but it did make me feel a little better.

Two weeks later, I paid a visit to Lewis' house. Lewis answered the door and invited me in.

"He's in there," Lewis said, nodding his head towards his Dad's office.

For the first time I walked into that wood-paneled room with a sober head. Mr. Cohen was a tall, intimidating man, but he greeted me warmly, despite the recent events. We shook hands and sat down to talk. I didn't feel like a boy talking to my friend's dad. This time I felt like a man, speaking up for himself.

Mr. Cohen listened.

CHAPTER THIRTY THREE

"Wow, that's deep," Nancy said, pouring both of us some more coffee. I had been back a week from rehab and in my favorite booth at the diner, next to the bus stop, St. Clair Avenue and all the people going where they go – work, school, home, a first date, a new life.

"Don't bullshit me, Nancy."

"No, I'm serious. Never would have expected it from you, I have to admit."

"Expected what?"

"You're not the first person I know who went in to rehab. Most people don't get it, though. They go in, they clean up, go to the group sessions, then come out preaching *the message.* Then they get back with their friends doing the same stuff they were doing and before you know it, they're back right where they left off. And it's always the same, Fischer: 'Oh, I can handle it. I got tools now.' But, you seem different. You actually have a bit of humility." Coming from Nancy, it made me feel good. Nancy was good people. "So, you coming back to Spanish anytime soon?"

"Nah. I think I have to chalk up last semester as a total bust. Accept my failures. Salvage whatever credits I can, like gym and English, and get a fresh start. So, maybe I won't graduate this June. That's okay. I think I need to take it slow for once."

"If you slow that school career down any more than it already is you'll end up back in middle school." The restaurant manager stepped out from behind the register and peered in our direction. "I'm getting the evil eye. Gotta go check on my tables," Nancy said. "Keep my coffee warm, I'll be back. I'm really proud of you, David." It was the first time she called me David.

"Wait," I said, looking over at the manager. "You think you could get me an application? I need a job." Nancy stared at me for a moment longer than seemed natural. "Nancy? You okay?"

"Yeah," she said. "I just thought you said you wanted a job here."

"An application, yeah."

"O-kay," she said slowly. "Sure. That would be cool working with you." She went off with a bit of a bounce to service her tables. I sipped my coffee and took a bite out of the apple pie in front of me. It tasted bland. I was feeling lonely, so I did what I was told to do. I took out my journal and started to write.

I wrote about Marcy. About how I didn't treat her right. She deserved better. I wrote about Sharla and the fashion show. I had no business being there – I was there for all the wrong reasons. I wrote about Lewis and Zee and my parents and all the partying and the wasted nights. I wrote about Kris: about the way she looked at me, the way her hands touched my skin. The way she made me feel – like I wanted to be a man for her, not just a boy. I wrote about the pain of her terrible secret; I wrote about the loneliness she kept deep inside her – what I thought was a shield against me was really her protection from a world that had done terrible things to her. I wrote about Fred – his sociopathic terror. And I wrote about Kris some more – the Kris I wanted to remember forever: The beautiful survivor; and my heroine.

I didn't notice the flow of people outside the window. I didn't notice the buses pull up, the passengers who stepped off, the other regulars who stared out at the world. I didn't notice people walking past my table, stopping to look, or linger or move on. I was lost in my writing and thinking about Kris: *where is she? What is she doing? Is she okay?*

Someone sat down across from me.

"Anything good?" they asked. I kept writing. Zee reached for my neglected pie and dug in. "What's in the envelope?" he asked.

"What envelope?" On the table was a plain white envelope with my name written on it. "An application," I said.

"What – you're gonna work somewhere?" Zee laughed.

"Thinking about it. I might take a year off. Find a new school. Make some changes." Zee studied me.

"Seriously? This is David Fischer talking?"

"The old way isn't working, Zee. Gotta try something new."

"But the old way made the rest of us feel so much better by comparison. No matter how badly I screwed up, I could always look to you and say – *at least I'm not that bad.*"

"You'll have to look elsewhere. I'm done with that."

"Good," he said. He was quiet a second. Looking out the window, then looking back at me, then back out the window at the passing world of people.

"I'm gonna do it. I signed up."

"For what?"

"The Israeli army."

I nearly choked on my coffee. "You're kidding me!"

"I'm eighteen years old in five months. I speak fluent Hebrew. And... and you know what? It felt good firing a rifle at that putz. I enjoyed it."

"You know I looked up that thing you said – Otzma enosheet, right?"

"Yes."

"I don't think you're right about that – I don't think anyone in the Israeli army says that."

"Ask someone from the Israeli army. They do."

"I met a guy in rehab. Ari. He never heard of this phrase."

"Was he in the 931st division?! 'Cause that's who says it! Ask *them*!"

"So, in other words, it's not exactly a commonly used expression for Israeli soldiers."

"So what? I should stay here, instead? I can't deal, can't smoke anything, gotta stay clean for a year, take a piss test. It's too much. I'm going crazy. I swear I'm gonna go straight home after this and shave my fucking head. Right off. Then I'm going to find a cheap one way ticket to Israel."

I could only shake my head.

Zee grabbed the application off the table. "Maybe I'll apply for a job here, too," he said.

"Good idea." He opened the envelope. I went back to my writing. "Dave...." I watched the street. Wondering... was she out there...? "Dave... this isn't an application."

The way he said it, I snatched the envelope from his hand. Inside was a folded piece of blank paper. Somebody had hand-written a mailing address on the outside of it: a general post-office box, but I recognized the handwriting. I had seen it once before in a photo scrap book in a small, carpeted apartment the night I lost my virginity. I slowly unfolded the paper to reveal the words she had written:

Dearest David,

I'm proud of you that you went to rehab. I needed to let go of some things, too. My brother was my prison. I couldn't escape him. Until you helped set me free. I can't deny the pain; his death haunts me. The cops were on top of me for shooting him. They were coming down hard. Then they stopped. A lawyer named Cohen got the whole investigation dropped. Any idea how he knew about it? Thanks for that, David. I will always be grateful to you. You did more for me than you can possibly know. I'm on a new journey now. Time to find out who I am and who I can be. Write if you want. Can't promise I'll write back. Hope you understand.

Kris.

And then, below that, she added *If I could love anyone, I would love you. Maybe. Some day.*

I raced out of the diner and into the busy sidewalk. People pushed past me in both directions. I looked up and down the street, but there was no sign of Kris.

She was here.

She was still here.

I could feel it.

"Dave...!" Zee called, running after me.

I scanned the intersection. There, across the street, passing behind two delivery vans, was a blonde woman in a black turtleneck, walking with a rare confidence. She turned to look behind her. Her shoulder length hair swung across her face, nearly veiling a stolen glance in my direction by her pale blue eyes; the same look I fell for in that first fashion show audition in a high school classroom; the same look that conveyed both her boldness and her terror – accompanied by that knowing smile.

If I could love anyone I would love you.

Oh, Kris, I thought, *just give me the chance.*

Trucks drove by, paused at the light, turned. And just like that, she was gone.

"Dave...!" Zee called, catching up. "What're you doing?"

What was I doing? I was chasing something all over again. Maybe it was a dream. Maybe a fantasy. But I realized then, that if I let someone else lead me through life, I would never be true to myself.

"Can I get a light?" Zee offered his Zippo and a cigarette.

"By the way," Zee said, "Lewis is having a thing at his house this Saturday. He told me to tell you. It's kind of in your honor."

I let the invitation hang out in the breeze while I flicked open the Zippo and got the flame up in one smooth motion. The flame licked the corner of Kris' letter, cooked it brown, then caught the rest of the page in a fury. The flame chewed at the paper. It ate through the address. It devoured the words. Black ash danced up into the air, against the afternoon sun, then swirled off on the breeze. With every grey flake that floated away, I felt my grip on Kris – on the idea of her – release and dance with the ashes up, up, up, then get carried off on the breeze, away, away. Kris' note burned down to flakes and when it had all floated away in its new direction, I flipped the Zippo closed. And the flame went out.